THEIR DOUBLE LIVES

THEIR DOUBLE LIVES

JAIME LYNN HENDRICKS

SCARLET
NEW YORK

To Tara Feehan, Jennifer Higgins,
and Lauren Mikucki for trying to save my life.

1

KIM
NOW

It's just a dog.

Whenever Kim heard that phrase, it made her want to physically harm someone. Not that she ever would, at least not in an up close and personal way. A week ago, Kim never would've considered herself capable of killing, but things changed. When she said she'd do anything to keep her dog alive, she meant it.

It was the beginning of Kim's shift. The country club's décor was Instagram page ready, as expected in that zip code. Rich maroon walls with gold accents, trickling fountains with plastic Japanese cherry blossoms floating in them, and people dressed in couture with shoes and bags that cost more than Kim made in a year.

Well, up until then. Her new nest egg would be doubled by tomorrow, as long as she completed her deadly task tonight.

She showed up to work in her required uniform—a black button-down and black slacks, even in the stifling June heat. New Jersey was having a hot flash like it was going through menopause. She entered through the kitchen and went downstairs into the employee locker room. It was a small, dank space with a rickety table and four plastic chairs in the center. Piss-colored walls. There were no locks on the wall of lockers because most of the staff had nothing worth stealing. It was just a place to store their Canal Street luxury knockoffs while coveting the real thing.

She stuffed her Michael Kors bag—not a Chanel like she wanted—into a locker and closed the door, then pulled her dark hair into a ponytail. God forbid a runaway strand fell onto a tray. The rich assholes she served would have the health department there in five minutes to shut the place down after calling in a favor from a senator friend.

They all had senator friends.

When Kim got upstairs, she approached Dana at the podium. Dana was the food and beverages manager-slash-hostess-slash-Jacqueline of all trades. People in her position always seemed to carry the attitude of *this place would shut down if it weren't for me!* But in her case, it was true. Kim didn't know how Dana handled everything with a smile while dealing with those bitter, wretched housewives.

"Are we busy tonight?" Kim asked, sticking her head over Dana's shoulder to scan the books. It was all she could do to steady herself, knowing what she was about to do. *Act normal.*

Dana blew out a breath. "I'm still trying to move a few things around. You know the Boswells like that table"—she pointed to the back corner of the bar, the table next to the floor-to-ceiling windows overlooking the island green at the eighteenth hole—"and they're dining with their regular crew *and* two new members tonight. So, I'm trying to fit it all in. I have Glen moving tables around already."

Two new members. It gave Kim pause. The new members would be there tonight, clinking glasses and breaking bread, not knowing that only one of them would make it home. The person she'd been in touch with the last week, who only called themselves The Stranger, knew everything. They were pulling all the strings behind the scenes to mastermind tonight's eventual chaos.

"Hey, how's Murphy doing?" Dana asked.

Murphy, the reason for everything that was about to go down. He was Kim's five-year-old Goldendoodle that she'd adopted as a puppy right after she moved back to the East Coast. He was her favorite thing in the world, and he had saved her life.

He was two, still a big puppy, when she met Nicholas, who had moved in with Kim six months later. It was a year after that when Kim was confronted by a pregnant woman in the grocery store—one of Nicholas's coworkers—saying she was carrying his baby.

Wallowing in her loneliness after kicking him out and unable to come to terms with Nicholas's deception, she could barely get out of bed, but she had to take care of Murphy. He became her sole reason for living. When she was home, he rarely left her side. Last month, he'd had a seizure, and a trip to the vet showed a small tumor that he needed to have removed. It was over ten thousand dollars—money

Kim certainly didn't have—and without the surgery and the follow-up treatment costing thousands more, he only had months to live.

Kim pressed her lips together, thankful everyone cared so much about Murphy's well-being, but she also held back tears at the thought of having to put him down. She'd never let that happen. "I'll figure something out soon."

She did figure something out, and she was being paid handsomely. But she needed everyone to think she was still struggling. She'd never be able to explain her windfall.

She pictured Murphy now, alone in her apartment, hopefully not in pain. Maybe he was rolling on his back with one of his squeaky babies in his mouth. Maybe he was sleeping. Maybe he was staring at the door, waiting to wiggle his tail and pounce the second he heard the key in the lock.

"Do we like the new members?" Kim asked, trying to push Murphy's pain out of her mind. Secretly, she hoped the new members were horrible. At least the guy. It would make her task easier.

Dana scoffed. "Yes and no. You'll see. It's all very . . . typical. Ron Boswell said he works with the guy."

"Ah. Gotcha."

It was all Kim was able to say, letting Dana know that yes, she understood—it was a sugar daddy situation. Most couples in the club were. It was probably why the self-appointed club queen, Carla Boswell, so often had her tail feathers in a huff. Her core table was age appropriate. She wouldn't convey that a wife half your age was acceptable.

Memorizing everyone's first and last names after meeting them once was a job requirement. Kim gave them nicknames to keep them all straight. The ringleader was the well-deserved *Cunty Carla*. Kim gave her the nickname after running into her at a nail salon. Carla was paying at the register and gingerly lifted a stuffed wallet out of her expensive bag like she was holding an atom bomb. She peeled a crisp bill from the new-and-stuck-together-fresh-from-the-ATM pile and paid with a hundred-dollar bill. Had the nerve to say "keep the change" with a wink when the technician handed her a Lincoln. Five dollars? Cheap bitch.

As Kim helped set up behind the bar, she sang "Piano Man" in her head as the regular crowd shuffled in. Because there *was* an old man sitting at the bar, making love to his tonic and gin. Mr. Larson. He'd lost his wife the year before and still came to where they had dinner every week. No one ever sat in the empty seat beside him.

Five p.m. turned into six p.m. as the early birds got drinks, and Kim eyed the empty corner table assigned to her. The elite table for six was now set for eight.

They should've set the table for seven. One wouldn't survive the night.

It was the table reserved for Carla Boswell and her husband Ron, Mayor Hector Alvarez and his wife Wendy, and Ben and Emiko Xiang. And now, the new members. The mayor was half Puerto Rican, allowing this ridiculous conservative town to congratulate themselves for being oh-so-progressive for electing a Hispanic mayor.

Kim had heard Carla make contrasting comments around the other wives, who weren't nearly as . . . judgmental . . . but they'd always nodded in agreement. No one challenged

Queen C, and she'd needed everyone to believe she was progressive as well, hence the other two guests.

Ben and Emiko were the only Asian members of the club, and as far as Kim was concerned, the nicest. Ben always tipped extra—in cash—and Emiko even slipped Kim her phone number after they got to talking one afternoon. Emiko had asked her to lay out some ideas on remodeling their sunroom since Kim had an "artistic eye." She was a freelance graphic designer by day, but she hadn't called Emiko yet and made excuses about being busy. Truth was, she was intimidated. She didn't belong on that side of town and decided to stay in her lane.

Minutes later, a fake cackle cracked through the sound of the forks and knives clanking on dinnerware. The first ones to turn the corner into the bar area were Carla and Ron Boswell. He was in his fifties, and she was in her early forties, but well-preserved. She could easily pass as a decade younger, even though it was all fake. A Real Housewife to her core.

Ron was balding and stood five foot ten with his shirt buttons stretching out around his belly. Back in the day, he was probably a catch, but now, he had money and didn't need to work as hard. Always in a sport coat with suede elbows, he'd been one of the first members to sign up when the club opened ten years ago. Or so Kim had heard. Of course, Carla was expertly dressed in a silky white tank and navy linen pants with nude open-toed heels to show off her new French pedicure. Red bottoms on the shoes, naturally.

Carla approached the bar where Kim stood, tray in hand, wearing a smile as fake as the hair extensions Carla had just removed. Her thin, overprocessed hair was now shaped into an angled bob, "a new cut" as Kim overheard Carla telling dinner guests last week. There was no doubt in her mind that Carla had her Kardashian-like extensions taken out, but she couldn't let anyone else think she grew anything other than shiny, luscious locks, even at forty-plus, when hair naturally starts to thin, because she was the queen.

"The iPad," Carla demanded. Her voice was shrill and raspy, still a smoker even though she only snuck them in her Expedition from the parking lot; smoking was crass in her circle. She put her hand out. No hello; just demands for the iPad that housed the list of bottles members stored in their fifteen-hundred-dollar per season wine locker.

A memory rattled in Kim's brain.

"Go find me another bottle of red, and make it a good one. For seventy-five thousand a year for membership, I'd assume you have something back there better than a 2005 Penfolds Grange Shiraz?"

It was the first time she'd met Carla, and okay, maybe that was the moment she'd come up with her nickname. The scene at the nail salon just solidified it. God, how she wished Carla would be the one to drop dead under mysterious circumstances tonight. No such luck.

Kim handed her the iPad. "Yes, of course, Mrs. Boswell." To call her by her first name would be like calling the King of England "Chuck."

Carla looked Kim up and down, as usual, disapproving of everyone who wasn't in her circle. And of course, Kim was just the lowly waitstaff. She took the job to supplement her now-freelance graphic design contract work. She'd lost her steady job a couple of years ago when everyone started working from home. The country club was close to where she lived, and it paid twenty bucks an hour, plus whatever cash most members slipped to servers in a goodbye handshake at the end of the evening. Never Carla, though. The one time Ron was caught doing it, Carla chewed him out in front of everyone.

It was okay. Kim didn't plan on staying much longer after tonight. She wouldn't need to. Only long enough to dodge suspicion. She could say the episode scarred her and she needed to quit. Everyone would believe it. In fact, she'd be surprised if anyone showed up for work tomorrow.

Carla chose two bottles of red from her wine locker that Kim knew cost more than she made in a week. "Bring them to the table. We have new guests tonight. Anthony Fuller works with Ron, and he'll be with his fiancée, Poppy Jade."

Kim could hear the crack of Carla's whip snapping on her heels, but the anxiety of what she was about to do was getting the best of her, because now he had a name. *Anthony Fuller.* It made what she was about to do too real.

"As a matter of fact, there they are." Carla pointed a mani-cured finger to the entry. "Anthony and Poppy Jade." She gave Kim the side-eye. "Mr. Fuller and Ms. Walsh to you."

Kim swiveled her head but her heart stopped when she saw the new members. Her, young and blonde and college aged. Him, dark haired and tall and clean cut, but that wasn't what made her almost drop her tray. How did she not put it together at the mention of the name?

His *new* name. His *clean-cut* name.

She suddenly regretted everything about the last week. *Everything.* How the hell was she supposed to pull this off now?

She wanted to shrink, to hide in the kitchen, to quit . . . anything but have Tony Fiore—*Anthony Fuller*, God that was going to be hard to get used to—see her like this, being ordered around by rich assholes. She wondered if they all knew about the heavy tattoos under his sleeves. His prison record. She wondered if they knew he didn't belong.

She was a thirty-three-year-old waitress. He was the love of her life for her first three years of high school. The five stages of grief started. *Denial.* It's just someone who resembles him! *Anger.* He's engaged? To that fucking teenager? *Bargaining.* You haven't seen him in a decade and a half, maybe if he sees you again . . . ? *Depression.* It's been over for a long time, and you're the one who ended it, remember? *Acceptance.* Tony Fiore was back.

And someone wanted him dead. Tonight.

And it was Kim who was supposed to kill him.

2
KIM
NOW

They were from the same neighborhood in Brooklyn—at the time, Kim was a hood rat with big hair and a thick accent, with dreams of marrying Tony, her boyfriend of three years. Tony, to put it simply, was a fucking criminal back then. He got into fist fights, sold drugs, took bets, and then there was that little armed robbery with his best friend, Jose Sanchez, that ended in murder.

That was when she begged her parents to ship her to California to finish her senior year three thousand miles away, nowhere near bad boy Tony Fiore. She needed to get away from him and planned to live with her maternal grandparents, get straight, go to college, and "make something of herself" since Tony was headed nowhere but prison. She was afraid she'd end up there by extension. The entire relationship was toxic, and she disappeared in a puff of smoke like a magician's parlor trick.

The last time she'd seen Tony in person, his dark hair was slicked back, and he wore an extra-medium T-shirt over his tattooed arms. A cigarette hung from his lip, and the purple bruise on his left eye had yellowed in its healing process. Now, Tony was dressed cool-casual in what appeared to be a tailored button-down shirt, off-white with thin blue checkboxes. His navy slacks were pressed and his brown shoes polished. His gold watch shone under his cuff, and he had sunglasses tucked above the top button on his shirt. Ray-Bans, she thought. Polarized lenses.

He cleaned up well. Money could do that.

It also made enemies, apparently.

Before he could notice her, Kim turned her attention to Poppy Jade. She was *so young*. She wore a too-short-and-too-tight black dress. Hervé Léger, naturally, but Jesus Christ this was just dinner at a country club, not dancing at a nightclub in New York City. Her long blond hair caressed her back in waves. Her perfect skin seemed makeup free except for eyelash extensions and a puffy, glossy-red pout. Big, blue doe eyes, like a character from a Disney movie.

Tony's fingers were interlaced with hers when Ron Boswell tapped him on the shoulder and curled a finger. Tony kissed Poppy on the head and whispered something in her ear. She smiled and nodded, and he took off to a secluded corner with Ron, surely talking business.

Tony. Talking business. It was so weird to Kim.

"Well? Introduce yourself, my goodness," Carla spat with venom when Kim didn't beeline to her shiny new toys.

Kim almost took her tray and laid it across Carla's head, WWE style, but instead bit back the fear and fingered the capsule full of deadly powder for his drink, and the backup—a vial full of sweet-tasting liquid for his dessert—in her pocket. She'd already taken more than half the money. How the hell was she going to do this?

It had been a long time—fifteen years—but she used to love Tony. Now she loved Murphy, and she swore she'd do this to keep him alive.

Still, it hit too close to home, and she couldn't kill Tony.

Nervous as hell, her tell-tale heart sure to raise red flags, she plastered on a fake smile before she strode to offer Poppy a drink. She cleared her throat in front of her. "Hello, you must be Ms. Walsh. I'm Kim. I'll be taking care of you this evening. Can I start you off with a drink?"

"So formal!" Poppy peppily said like her poppy peppy self. "You know, you can call me PJ. I'll have a glass of Merlot." She looked over in Tony's direction. Thank God his back was to her. "He'll have a bourbon. Something small batch."

Small batch bourbon. This man used to drink Mad Dog and forties in a paper bag on his stoop. Tony still hadn't spotted her, as Ron Boswell had his ear.

"Sure thing, Ms. Walsh." No, she couldn't call her PJ.

As she turned to the bar to have the bartender, Lucy, fix the drinks, PJ followed her. "Hey, can I ask you something?" she whispered.

"Sure." What was she about to ask? *Hey, are you planning to murder my fiancé tonight?*

"How long have you worked here?"

Kim shifted from one weight-bearing leg to the other, unsteady. "A little over two years."

"What am I in for tonight? With these women? My fiancé Anthony works with Ron Boswell, but I haven't met this group of wives yet." She paused. "Only Carla a few times." She had a long, thick swallow before her next words. "She seems nice."

Kim read it all over her face, because that comment had more gas than a Mack truck. Poppy likely knew all about Cunty Carla but was too proper to say it. Kim wanted to laugh out loud and tell her that she was a baby lamb being thrown into the Colosseum, but she stayed professional, for more reasons than one. She couldn't give any of it away. She was in big trouble. "Everyone here is wonderful."

"They're so much older. I'm not sure what we'll have in common."

As Lucy poured PJ's wine and searched for the bourbon, for no reason, PJ started talking about herself, loudly. She probably felt more comfortable talking with someone like Kim rather than Carla, due to their closer age, even though the decade between them felt like a hundred years at that moment.

Her peachy, natural collagen-filled cheeks rounded as she excitedly spoke about graduating from NYU with a business degree the year before. But, for now, she was a yoga instructor—of course—and spent her time volunteering at an animal shelter and a homeless shelter, and she oversaw a website dedicating herself to running errands for little old ladies who didn't want to leave their houses. She drove them to doctor appointments, did their grocery shopping, their laundry—for free.

Fine. If any of that was true, then she was a saint, and Kim felt bad for hating her simply because she was with Tony. Only a little though.

After one sip of wine, PJ caught eyes with Tony. She nodded her head toward Kim and he started to walk over, and *oh no*—

"This is my fiancé, Anthony," PJ said, wrapping an arm around his waist.

Tony stopped like a deer in headlights—in complete and utter shock and about to get run over—when he squinted. "Is that really you?" His expression said it all in one look. He was afraid Kim was about to take it all away with one mention of his real name—Tony Fiore.

Instead, she did him a favor. "Oh, wow, Anthony Fuller. It's been a long time." She widened her eyes at him. *Your secret is safe with me.* She did it because that seventeen-year-old she used to be was still scared of him. They were always able to communicate through silence, through facial expressions. It had kept them both out of jail when they were younger and getting questioned about stolen cars and drugs. With just a few quirks of the lip, a raised brow, a smirk—they played off each other well. That was young love for you. Young love was always easy until reality set in.

She had so much to say to him, but she couldn't. Not here. Not in this company. Somebody there wanted him dead, and she didn't know who.

"You guys know each other?" PJ asked. Her smile was curious, amusing, and genuine, and again Kim hated herself for hating her.

"We grew up in the same neighborhood," Kim said as Tony's shoulders relaxed and his jaw unclenched. He knew he had an ally. He was going to owe her for that. For so, so much more than that. "His sister Maria was my best friend back then, but we all lost touch a long time ago. I moved out west to California to finish high school. It's been what, fifteen years?"

"Something like that. You sound different," he said.

Kim had taken dialect classes to lose her accent when she was in college. Back then, she waitressed with a bunch of wannabe actors and actresses who got her a good contact, but being an actress was never Kim's thing. She wasn't starry-eyed off a bus from Des Moines, trying to land parts on a casting couch. She just wanted to sound intelligent.

Tony sounded different too.

"And you look different," Tony said. Kim noticed the way his lip quirked at her, like it had done before, and just for that split second, he spoke to her in their secret silent language. Old habits die hard. Then he quickly turned his attention to Poppy. "We should sit, Peej. Good to see you, Kimmy."

Kimmy. It stabbed her right in her heart. *You're my little Kimmy Kat*, he always said. Now he had a *Peej*.

With a literal snap of her fingers, Carla called them all to the table. She certainly didn't like that PJ was fraternizing with the help.

"You better go," Kim said, nodding in Carla's direction. "Mrs. Boswell doesn't like to be left waiting."

"Got it," PJ said with a wink. "Thanks."

Throughout dinner, Ron, Hector, and even good-guy Ben couldn't stop staring at PJ. Ron became somewhat shameless after his third bourbon. He sat to PJ's left and touched her arm every time she talked. Carla kept side-eyeing her and looked like the skinless Terminator—mean, rigid, and red eyed.

Tony noticed for sure, the way his eyebrows raised quickly, the rubbing of the back of his neck, the yawn. Still, he remained patient, with his arm around the back of her chair, sneaking kisses whenever they could while Carla scoffed in their direction.

If he only knew about the trouble he was in. That he *could've* been in. He was lucky that Kim had the job, not some other random person. Did The Stranger know about her past with Tony? This couldn't be a coincidence. She felt like such a fool. A played, stupid fool, and she'd make sure things were set right. Somehow.

Everyone at the table talked, laughed, and shared stories. Ron was a little smashed, and as he shared his expensive bottle with his guests, he knocked over a glass of wine, the stem cracking as the wine pooled on a plate. The incident came and went, and they were all back to their loud, obnoxious, masters-of-the-universe actions. They didn't all know it, but they were swimming in shark-infested waters in the dark.

Who was going to bite first? And *who* were they going to bite?

It didn't matter. Kim never put that pill into Tony's bourbon. She never poured the liquid onto his dessert. No one was going to die tonight.

As usual, they were the last table at closing time. The club closed at ten, but Carla reveled in keeping the staff later than they had to be there. *Peasants.* After every dinner, Ron would grab an expensive bourbon from his private locker, and the guys would all have a glass at the bar before they left.

Kim had just dropped the individual checks at Tony's table, the poisons still in her pocket. She'd failed at her task, and she didn't know what the fallout for that would be. She didn't even know who she'd been dealing with the past week—The Stranger was just that—but there was going to be hell to pay. She was sure of it. She was going to have to return the money, and Murphy's precious life was going to be the price.

Waiting for them to sign their respective checks, Kim noticed PJ's face go red. PJ swallowed very quickly, then her big blue eyes strained, bugged out, frightened. She screwed up her face and clutched her throat, then hit the table twice with her right hand. Hard.

"PJ?" Tony turned toward her, his brows dented. "Peej? Are you okay?"

She hit the table again. She couldn't talk.

"Is she choking?" Ron asked, then took it upon himself to lift her and attempt the Heimlich. Kim thought it was a cheap way to cop a feel. Carla's horrified face said the same.

"She can't be choking. There's no food left on the table!" Tony screamed to Ron, ripped PJ from his arms, and lightly shook her. "PJ!"

Holy shit. Her eyes were open, but she was frozen. She looked like she wanted to talk but couldn't. Her body started to contort, like she was doing a backbend; it stayed that way as she rolled out of Tony's grip. What was happening to her?

She couldn't have been poisoned. PJ wasn't the target tonight. Tony was.

"Does she have an allergy?" Emiko asked, panicked.

"No. No allergies. Someone, help! Call 9-1-1!" Tony said to no one. He pushed everything off the table. Carla skidded back in her chair, but not before some of that billion-dollar wine spilled and dripped on her couture. She made a disapproving noise—to hell with the dying woman—as Tony ripped the tablecloth off and placed it on the floor. He laid PJ down gently, stroking her head while demanding everyone give her room. He dipped the cloth napkins in the leftover water and patted her forehead. "Come on, Peej. Hang on, baby. Hang on."

There were real tears in his eyes. They were in everyone's eyes. PJ looked like a monster, her body twisted in a way no body ever should. Horrific didn't begin to describe it. She looked like she just crawled out of a well and then through the television to kill everyone around her.

Except she was frozen into that shape. No crawling. No movement at all.

Everyone at that table stood and stared in shock. Dana screamed that the ambulance was on its way.

"Come on, Peej. Come on, baby," Tony said, her limp head in his lap.

Her eyes were still open, as was her mouth, her tongue hanging out. Her head leaned to the right like dead weight. Her back still didn't touch the ground. She was an arc. Tony's face was close to hers as he whispered in her ear. Tears fell from his eyes, dripping down onto her face.

"Come on, Peej. Please. Someone help her, please!" He was desperate. Pounded the ground next to her. "Peej, please, baby." Tony placed his fingers on her wrist. "She still has a pulse, but it's weak."

Ron approached. "Listen to her heart." He bent down like he was going to put his face near her tits, and Tony shoved him away with his left arm and did it himself.

"Where's the goddamn ambulance?" Tony shouted, tears staining his cheeks. "Come on, Peej."

She made a guttural, vibrating noise. Kim recognized it; everyone in their old Italian neighborhood called it the death rattle.

By the time the ambulance arrived, there was nothing that could be done. Although she was still breathing, barely, they couldn't even move her, like rigor mortis had already set in. She gasped for that last breath, memorializing her body into that awful shape while she was still alive.

Ten seconds later, there were no more breaths. No gasps. It was official: PJ was dead.

And if Kim had done her job, Tony would be dead too.

Someone there wanted them *both* dead. But who? And why?

3
POPPY JADE
THEN

Well, at least he's nice to look at.

I play my part of the infatuated schoolgirl very well. When I heard that Anthony Fuller was giving a talk as part of the Stern Business School program, I jumped at it. Certainly, it saved me time. I've had my eye on him for the better part of a year. It's been hard trying to nail down a chance meeting, one that would make him think it was his idea. I tried it one time when he was having dinner at STK, but there were too many business associates around, even if I did notice him look my way more than once. Then, there was that time he was on some cable show to talk about his big score, but I heard later he was whisked away in some millionaire's helicopter from the roof. So much for a run-in in the lobby.

But this was kismet. If he's like any regular white finance guy a few years shy of hitting forty, this should be easy. He doesn't have a girlfriend right now—my Google search on him yielded nada—but even if he does, so what? He'd love to have me on his arm. And as my ex-boyfriend turned BFF Matt always says, I'll have him wrapped around my finger in no time.

Gotta love Matt. We dated for a little bit in high school, until he realized he liked men. I'd always suspected, but my love for him was because of who he was in general. That hasn't changed; in fact, my love for him is stronger. Matt helped me come up with the plan. The plan to find this guy, marry him, emotionally destroy him like he's done to so many others, take his money, and fucking kill him. I cared less about the beginning stages, only the last one.

Kill him.

If it goes as planned, I'll be the grieving widow with all his money. Not that it's a sufficient punishment for him, but it'll have to do. I'll give Matt a cut, of course. He deserves it. A budding photographer, he moved from Texas to New York with me a year ago, just to be by my side when this all goes down. He's been helping me with every aspect of research. In fact, while taking some candid shots near campus, he was the one who found the flyer that Anthony would be a guest speaker at the school this week for their summer program, talking about leveraging capital.

I don't even go to NYU. I graduated from Texas Tech in Lubbock, near some other shit-kicking town where I'm from. But I'll make this guy believe anything.

So, I sit in the front row, my chin on my palm, my elbow resting on the surface of the desk, and stare dreamily at him like he's a goddamn Disney prince. My cleavage is out, also resting on the surface of the desk. Every time he glances my way, I give him the come-hither eyes, the slow, seductive blink, the pursed lips, and I pretend I'm hanging on every word he's saying. Starry-fucking-eyed. Men like him, they love all that shit. God, the ego. The *audacity*. They just want to be worshipped.

I can do that. Just enough that he feels seen, but never enough that I'll smother him, which will make me the perfect woman. Because I don't care about him, and I won't ever care about him. Kissing and touching and sex will make me cringe, but my body, my choice. And this plan is my choice. My body is just a supporting character in the scheme.

When the talk concludes, most people file out, and a few hover in a line to ask questions. I keep my sculpted ass planted in my seat, head in hand, dreamy look. Staring. Making him feel seen.

The last person leaves, and he turns to me. "Do you have something you'd like to know?"

Yes, asshole, I have a ton of questions for you.

"Hi, Mr. Fuller," I say, my head cocked to the side. "My name is Poppy Jade, but you can call me PJ. I'd like to know if you'll come with me to have a drink?"

Right to the point. Make him feel adored.

He smiles. "Well, that would be awkward, unless you agree to call me Anthony and not Mr. Fuller."

I stand and strap my purse over my shoulder in such a way that my chest sticks out and my hair whips like I'm in a music video. "What's your favorite drink, Anthony?"

He smirks. "That accent is dangerous."

No, you son of a bitch, the accent is fucking adorable and I'm the one that's dangerous. "I grew up in Texas. I just graduated from here a couple months ago. I'm interested in how to invest my savings. I came into some money when—when my grandfather died." Easy, cowgirl. Stick to the script.

"Ah, I've never been to Texas. You'll have to tell me all about it." He glances at his watch, one that looks shiny and expensive, and I'll own that one day too. "I've got an hour to kill. Did you have a place in mind?"

Yes, I researched the area. There are a lot of dark, sticky college bars full of teenagers playing darts, but I need him to think I'm classy. Wifely.

I make what my father, God rest his soul, used to call a *scutch face* and always told me that God would make it stay that way if I didn't stop. Daddy was fantastic. "I don't like the places around here. They cater to the kids. I don't drink beer from a keg. There's a great steakhouse a few blocks away if you like that sort of thing."

He does. And the place two blocks away has his favorite bourbon. The expensive stuff.

"It's like you already know me." He says it with a smile, not realizing that yes, I know you. All too fucking well.

We make small talk on the walk, mostly me asking him questions about himself. Men with egos like his, they love to talk about themselves. They want fans, and I transform myself into one, hanging on his every word. He opens the door for me, and when we're seated at the dark, cushy bar, my eyes drift to the top shelf.

"Oooh, they have Pappy Van Winkle here," I say. Of course they do. I researched everything.

His eyebrows raise. "You know your bourbon, then?"

I shrug, then squint. "I prefer the eighteen, and that's only the twelve year, but it'll have to do. Don't worry, I can pay for it myself. I'm not here for free drinks."

He's not going to let me pay. No way. He's rich and I'm hot. Plus, he wants to impress me, the young gorgeous girl who knows the difference between which bourbons are good and which are bad. What years are good and bad. I'm a keeper.

"Very nice," he says, and orders two. "So, tell me a little about yourself."

You will never know the real me.

"Oh, you know. You've probably heard the same story a hundred times. I grew up in a small town in Texas, had the itch to get out, so I moved to New York to attend NYU. I graduated with a marketing degree, but the job market is a little tight, so right now, I'm a private yoga instructor. I have a contract with Elite too. It's recent. Hopefully you'll see my face start to pop up on ads soon."

No, I do not have a modeling contract, but now this asshole thinks he's having drinks with a model. He thinks I'm yoga-bendy. He probably just got a hard-on.

"Wow, that's great, congratulations. Beauty and brains." He lifts his glass. "Cheers."

"Cheers." Clink. Seed planted. I sip the drink and it burns my throat and I try not to let my eyes tear—I hate bourbon. Back to him. Because I *adore* him. "Did you grow up around here?" I know every single thing about this motherfucker.

He clears his throat. "Yeah, I'm a New York boy through and through. Brooklyn originally, but I've been in the city for about fifteen years. Now that I've made my money, I feel like getting out of the rat race. I'm thinking about selling the penthouse, moving to the beach, settling down." Ugh, I hope this doesn't mess with my timeline. "Where do you live?" he asks.

I sip my bourbon and give him the story that will have him dying to rescue me. "Well, right now I live with a gay guy, Matt, in a one bedroom over on the Lower East Side. I met him through Craigslist. The neighborhood is safe. The place is a decent size, so Matt has the bedroom, and I had the maintenance guy put up a temporary wall in the living room. I just sack out there. I have a little privacy, so it's not that bad. He's not home much."

"Wow. Sounds tight."

"Nah, it's not so bad. I'm pretty simple. I don't need a shoe wall. I'm not that kind of girl."

I'm not that kind of girl. What every man wants to hear, but honey, we're all that girl. I'm just planning to play him like a fucking fiddle.

I do very well for the next half hour, laughing at Anthony's idiotic jokes, asking him all the right questions, and always keeping eye contact. I even spilled a tiny bit of bourbon on my chest on purpose, just so he could stare as I blotted, likely wondering what it's going to be like for him when he gets his hands on my body. I playfully wrestle with the check—I would've paid for both expensive drinks—but I let him win. Because men never want to be perceived as weak. I need him to think he's the Alpha.

He asks for my number, but I play coy. He gives me his card and tells me to email him my phone number so he can call me up and ask me out properly. He really thinks he's impressing the Gen Z with his old-school charm. Okay Boomer.

Phase one, complete. I hooked him like a fucking minnow.

It's going to be so much fun to kill him.

4
KIM
NOW

Kim had just come from the bathroom. She was nauseated after seeing PJ's dead body, contorted like a Gumby doll she used to play with when she was little. Yes, Kim threw up, but that wasn't the real reason she went. She had to flush the pill. The liquid. Then she wiped down the small vial, wrapped it in toilet paper, and stored it behind a vent, one she unscrewed with her hoop earring. She'd have to get rid of it later, but she assumed cops were about to swarm the place. They'd check the garbage, but no one would look in that dusty old vent.

Zero evidence left that she'd been tasked to murder someone. Zero chance it was her who did that to PJ.

Once there, the police wouldn't let anyone leave. Not the employees and not the diners. They'd uttered the words *crime scene.* They wanted a statement from everyone. Kim wondered how much extra time she'd have to spend there, since Murphy had to be let out. He had trouble holding it in with the anti-seizure medication he was on, and she didn't want him to feel abandoned if she came home too late. She'd read that dogs didn't have a visceral sense of time like humans did, but he had to know that it went from light to dark. She assumed dogs knew more than *experts* let on.

Dana had gathered everyone into the main dining room and closed the doorway that connected it to the bar room where PJ collapsed. Where she *died.* The only ones still in the bar room were Tony, a couple of cops, and of course, dead PJ. Tony wouldn't leave her side. Love really was blind, because Kim couldn't look at that mess for more than a couple of seconds without feeling nauseated again.

"What do you think happened?" Lucy, the bartender, whispered to Kim.

Kim shook her head. She couldn't answer, even though she had an idea. That was some hardcore poison, and she wondered if Tony was supposed to die the same way—she had no idea what she was supposed to feed him. "This is nuts. We're all going to be on the news."

Carla sat in a corner, clutching her Chanel bag on her lap and fanning herself dramatically. "Can I get some water? Or at least grab another bottle of wine out of my locker. It's right there," she said as she waved her hand toward the storage locker area before the kitchen.

"I don't know if we're allowed to go in the kitchen, Mrs. Boswell," Kim said. "I mean, it's a crime scene. She could've eaten something tainted."

Carla slapped the table. "This is unacceptable. I refuse to be a prisoner. *I* pay *you* with my membership dues. How dare you."

"Don't worry," Emiko Xiang said soothingly, taking a seat beside Carla. "You don't want to take a chance on anything right now. What if something really is wrong in the kitchen, or there's something on the glasses?" Her brow furrowed, looking toward the bar, probably thinking she could be next.

Lucy giggled, a nervous tic. Someone was dead, this was hardly funny. "This isn't a movie. She probably ate some shellfish or something."

Kim didn't serve shellfish of any kind to anyone at that table. She knew it wasn't an accident.

Finally, through the glass, Kim was able to see the rest of the medics come in, along with the coroner. She had to look away when the gurney was pushed in. What struck her even harder was Tony—he was all alone. He didn't appear to have called anyone. He came to the club that night to have dinner with his fiancée and coworker and friends, and now . . . what? Was he supposed to just leave, go to his car, and go home alone?

Someone could've been waiting to finish the job. Do what Kim couldn't.

"I should talk to him," Kim said. She had to speak to him in their silent language. She *had* to. He was in big trouble.

Carla's head snapped back. "You most certainly will not." She said it like it was the most obvious line anyone had ever muttered.

"I know T—Mr. Fuller. We're old friends. We grew up together."

Carla shot a distrusting look at Kim. "Is that so?" A chuckle escaped, and she said under her breath, "A waitress and a multimillionaire. Sure."

What looked like a forensic team came in to collect evidence and asked Tony to move away from the body. His wails were audible to everyone in the dining room. Hell, they were probably audible to the people having dinner in the next town over. Kim peered into the room, and she'd never seen Tony so . . . despondent.

He truly was a different man. She'd seen him getting arrested before with a huge smile on his face while the cops secured his hands behind his back. He was Teflon back then, superhuman, and always got himself out of whatever trouble he'd managed to get himself into. Being a smooth talker worked to his advantage. It was no wonder he was able to segue that into a successful career in finance.

Now, he was just human. Bent over, his head in his hand, sleeves rolled up to where Kim noticed he still had his sleeve of tattoos on his left arm. The outline of the cat—the one he'd gotten for her, his *Kimmy Kat*—was still there. He hadn't covered it up.

Kim didn't know what to feel. On the one hand, they shared history, and leaving him was one of the hardest things she'd ever had to do. On the other hand, that happened when she was a kid, a teenager with her first love—it wasn't *real* love, like she thought she'd had with Nicholas. A whole lot of good that did her. She was a grown-up now, even if she hadn't gotten to "that" place in her life. No real career, no mortgage, no fiancé. She felt like nearly every other millennial: stuck.

Now Tony was here, as Anthony Fuller, a true grown-up with all the bells and whistles she'd read adults enjoy, and his fiancée just dropped dead right in front of him.

That could change someone. That could even revert someone to who they used to be. Do people ever *really* change? No matter how it shook out in the press or the courtroom back then, she knew it in her bones that despite his friend Jose Sanchez taking the fall, Tony had killed that woman fifteen years ago, and maybe he deserved what was supposed to happen.

"Excuse me," Kim said as she exited the spot behind the bar and made her way over to the glass door.

Two policemen were still in the room, talking to a red-eyed Tony. They seemed sympathetic, even squatting down to him so they could be eye level and not asking him to get up off the floor. Tony's head nodded *yes* a few times and shook *no* a few times, and she couldn't make out anything anyone was saying.

She tapped on the glass, and all three heads looked her way. One of the cops put up a hand—stop—but Tony waved her in after uttering something to one of the cops. She opened the door and tiptoed inside, then closed the door behind her, noticing only Carla's wretched face, *how dare the help try to talk to a member* written in her scowl.

"Don't come in any farther," one cop said.

She stopped where she was and strained hard not to look at PJ's body. She'd see that shape in her nightmares for years to come.

"I—I'm so sorry." She didn't know what else to say. She looked at the cops. "We've known each other a long time."

One of the cops stood, now eye level with her, and looked her up and down as she shrunk into herself. She didn't want to be under a microscope again after all these years. The cop was probably in his fifties, tall and fit, balding with kind blue eyes. He flipped open a pad. "I'm Mahoney. Your name?"

She gulped. "Kimberly Valva. Call me Kim." Deafening silence. He was going to look up her record. All misdemeanors when she was a minor. They were probably sealed, but as Kim remembered, cops could do what they wanted.

"Did you know the deceased?"

Deceased. My God, this was so real. "No, I just met her tonight."

"You were the server for her table, correct?"

"Yes, sir." Sir. She wasn't a *sir* person. "She ordered the petite filet and drank red wine. Merlot. House Merlot. And she had the bread pudding for dessert." She was trying to be helpful. She was going to have to pull their entire check for the cops. They'd want to know about every single piece of food and drink on that table tonight.

"She had some of Ron and Carla's wine too," Tony said. "And she had a bite of my Chilean sea bass. As far as I know, she didn't have any allergies. We've been together a year. I would've known. We live together." He lifted his head to Mahoney. "She was getting over a sinus infection, but that was over a week ago. What happened?"

Mahoney shook his head. Took a quick, pained look over at PJ, then back to Tony. "We don't know, but that—position—doesn't look like an allergic reaction. It looks . . ." He stopped. "Was she taking medication?"

"Yeah, she was on an antibiotic. Two days left."

"Is it on her?"

Tony reached into his jacket pocket and retrieved a bottle. "Augmentin. She made me carry it. Those tiny designer purses only hold credit cards and a lipstick." He handed it to Mahoney, who placed it on the table beside him, waiting for forensics to bag and tag it.

"We're going to talk to everyone right now. We understand you work with one of the people you dined with tonight. Was anything going on behind closed doors that we need to be aware of?"

"Nope."

He shot Kim a quick look. Their silent language said he was lying.

5
PJ
THEN

P hase one complete. I feel like a million bucks when I walk
into my apartment. I texted Matt when I was on my way
home. He just finished up a Grindr meetup that turned out to
be a bust, so he said he'd pick up coffee for both of us on his
way back. Easy for him since he's a barista at the Starbucks a
block and a half away. Until he gets his shots in a gallery, we
all have to do what we have to do. I offered to pay his way,
but he's got too much pride. He's always felt like he needed
to be doing something, anything. Plus, he said it was a good
way to meet people.

I throw my beaded purse onto my futon and strip off my
tight clothing. It's not my style to walk around all made
up like a Barbie doll, but right now it's a means to an end.
I tie my hair up into a messy bun and throw on an NYU
sweatshirt purchased for my first sleepover with Anthony.

See, I was a student! In the bathroom, I wash all the makeup off and do my nighttime routine of clay mask and moisturizer, and then I get comfy and scroll through the Instagram account I recently made, one that's going to eventually make Anthony drool.

I've filtered a shit ton of pictures that Matt took of me in a bikini by Long Beach, and a bunch of me at various New York City locations, orange sunset in the background, my hair gently blowing in the breeze. In all of them, I have on tight dresses and high heels and red lipstick. Model shots. I've tagged Elite Management in all of them, but it's an account I made up—he'll never check to see if it's the real thing. I made the "L" in "Elite" a capital "I" so it looks the same. All my hashtags have the same spelling. I paid a company to set me up with over fifty thousand followers. I don't care that they're junk accounts. If Anthony sees it, he's going to think he really did score a model.

I never found him on any social media. He's probably one of those guys, the "I'm above it all" and "I don't need it to be relevant" types. Finance guys—so secretive. If only he knew my secrets. By the time he learns he's been deceived, it'll be too late.

The door squeaks open, and Matt comes into the small space, a cardboard carrier holding our Starbucks mocha lattes. He places it on the small table next to the bowl that holds our keys and drops his own in it with a clank.

"Hello, awesomesauce. That meetup certainly wasn't worth me scuffing my new kicks," he says.

It's a greeting we've been using on each other since middle school. I laugh. "Hello, awesomesauce. Was he bald?"

He shakes his head. "Spinach in his teeth. And I'm not even talking about a small piece. I wouldn't have needed dinner if I kissed him."

I make an exaggerated gagging face and stick out my tongue.

Matt is literally the greatest person I know. He moved to Texas in the fourth grade and we became instant friends. All the girls had crushes on him throughout middle school, and he dated the cheerleaders in high school. He was a star track and swimming athlete with a great physique and blue eyes that everyone got lost in. Including me, senior year. When we finally had sex, it was awkward and messy—I thought maybe our friendship had gotten in the way and we couldn't see each other as sexual creatures. Turns out, he never really saw me as one anyway. When he came out to me, it never even occurred to me that I "turned him gay." It was like everything had fallen into place, and I understood him even better.

"So, how did it go with the douchebag?" he asks, handing me my coffee.

I give him my wry smile. "Fucking perfection. Like you said, I'll have him eating out of my hand in no time."

He shakes out his man bun and lets his light brown hair fall over his face, then rubs the scruff. He loves the unshaven look, and I won't lie, it looks great on him. "Date number two?" He sips his coffee and makes his *holy fuck it's too hot* face.

I remove the lid and blow on the top of mine. He just took one for the team. "He gave me his card and told me to email him with my phone number so he can ask me out on a proper date."

"And?"

"And what? I'm waiting three days."

Matt leaps over to me and grabs my phone. "No, girl. You're doing this now."

"No!" We wrestle for a few seconds. Matt wins, waving the phone in my face, but this has to be handled delicately. "Remember the plan, Matt. We can't fuck this up."

"But it's coming together. You remember what that guy said when we came here to visit after graduation. It's been five years since then. We've lived here for a year now, and you're finally in the position to be able to pull it off. It's time to get the show on the road."

That guy. Jose Sanchez, the one who's been sitting in jail for a crime that Anthony committed. It riles me up. Matt is right.

I hold out my hand. "Give me the phone. I'll do it now."

He smiles, hands it over, and then positions himself behind me to look over my shoulder as I type.

I enter Anthony's email, and in the subject line I put *It's Poppy Jade*, like he can't tell from the name it'll come from. My fake email account. Poppy Jade isn't even my name.

"Girl, you're so vanilla. Be flirty. Did you take him to the place with the bourbon?"

I nod.

"And he told you he has a stash of it, right?"

I nod again. "Yeah, he has the eighteen year. We had the twelve tonight."

"Then use it." He tears the phone from my hand. "I promise I won't hit send."

I trust him. He smirks as he taps at the phone for a minute or so, then turns it in my direction. It's perfect.

> To: *Anthony Fuller*
> From: *Poppy Jade Walsh*
> Subject: *Refill?*
> Hi Anthony. *I think I'd like a taste of that eighteen*
> *sooner rather than later. Let me know when you want to*
> *fill me up. 917-555-5022*
> *PJ*

"Hit send," he demands.

Pressing my lips together and scrunching my eyes closed, I do what I'm told. It's so shameless. So out of my wheelhouse. Not my personality, no matter how fake I acted with Anthony the other night.

The phone rings. It's a New York number, and we both know it's Anthony.

"Answer it," Matt whispers, like the caller can already hear him. "And be sexy."

I stifle a laugh and answer in a low, breathy voice. "Hello?"

"Hi, Poppy. Or would you rather be called PJ? It's Anthony Fuller."

I point to the phone and then pump my fist in the air while smiling. "Oh, hi, Anthony. Everyone calls me PJ. That's what I answer to." Always have. Pause. "Glad you called. That was quick."

"Well, you said sooner rather than later. Are you busy tomorrow night? We can go to dinner. I know a place that has the eighteen."

My lips curl into a satisfied half-moon shape. "Text me an address and a time. I can't wait."

"I'll see you tomorrow, PJ."

"See you tomorrow, Anthony."

I hang up and drop the phone onto a chair. This has to go perfectly.

"See, girl. Get the show on the road." Matt smiles.

We finish our coffee over a chess game—I always beat him—and then I decide to turn in, and Matt gets dressed to meet some friends out to go clubbing. As I lie in bed, I stare at the ceiling, contemplating how the date is going to go. Do I want to hook him with sex immediately? Or hook him by not having sex immediately? I don't want him to lose interest, but I don't want to be a dime a dozen, dinner-will-get-you-laid girl either.

I pull my phone from the charger and look at the list of his interests I've gathered over the years. He likes to gamble. I'm a quick study. Before I know it, I'm watching YouTube and learning how to play blackjack and craps.

Anything can happen on a roll of the dice. That's what my daddy used to tell me all the time. And I'm doing this for him.

6
KIM
NOW

K im knew something else was up. Tony's eyes gave it away. "Ms. Valva, can you step out of the room so we can finish questioning Mr. Fuller?" Mahoney said.

Tony shot her another look. *It's okay.*

Kim saw so much more than just *it's okay*. She saw his palpable grief. She'd seen it before, even when he was just a messed-up kid at twenty. The first time he got arrested, before it all became a joke to him; the first time he lost a big bet, before he started taking them instead because let's face it, the house always won. And worst of all, when she told him that she was fleeing his bullshit and moving across the country.

When Kim moved back to the East Coast five years ago, she started off in Brooklyn again, but she was a different person. Educated. Had seen more than just the four-square blocks of their neighborhood. She had a passport, one that actually had stamps in it. The old neighborhood felt small, a coffin, and she refused to lie down in it and have her old friends close the lid. She got a job in graphic design that was located in Jersey City, so she started over, just over the bridges and through the tunnels. She moved to the beach. Fresh air. Sunshine. Salt life. She'd brave the winters again if it meant living at the beach the rest of the time.

And truth be told, she didn't feel like she belonged in her old stomping grounds without Tony. No one even knew where he'd gone—the people they used to hang out with weren't much for MSNBC or Market Watch, so as far as they knew, he dropped off the face of the earth. Everyone thought he'd gone on the run after the robbery had gone bad. Jose Sanchez got convicted for the murder—Kim had kept up with the story online. Tony testified in exchange for immunity.

He lied. She knew it. Then he was gone.

"Don't go anywhere, Ms. Valva. We'd like to speak to you next," Mahoney said to her as she headed toward the door, back to the dining room.

She nodded. Exchanged another look with Tony. She'd have to make sure they stared at each other one more time when he was finished talking. She didn't know how much he'd tell the police about their past or how much it mattered in what happened tonight.

7

KIM
ONE WEEK AGO

Kim walked to her ground-floor apartment with her house key between her index and middle finger, as usual. There was never a decent parking space on her street by the time she finished her shift, and she'd been relegated to parking four blocks away. Under the cloak of darkness, anything could happen. Better safe than sorry.

She stopped at the mailboxes outside of her complex and turned her key into the one for her unit and grabbed the envelopes. *Past due* was stamped on the outside of one of them. She wasn't irresponsible, but her income was unsteady. Her parents were just scraping by. Her mother was a cashier at Trader Joe's, and her father worked as a laborer for a tile company, but she didn't know how much more he had left in him. He was out of work for almost two years during the pandemic, and they were in no position to help her. New

Jersey was expensive, especially on the beach, and especially because she'd agreed to pay thirty percent more in rent from Memorial Day to Labor Day. Where she lived was a hotspot in the summer. Her landlord could've charged her double and gotten away with it.

Kim tucked the envelopes into her purse, and when she got to her door, there was a manila envelope on the ground waiting, with just "Kim" written in sharpie on the front. She grabbed it and opened the door, then quickly shut it behind her, chain locking and bolting it. Murphy waited obediently to be showered with affection. She got down to the floor, and he got as close to her as he could, a hug in his own way. She kissed his head.

"How are you feeling, good boy?"

He answered with a butt wiggle. He looked so normal on the outside, and she always tried to forget about what was growing in him on the inside.

She'd figure something out. Robbing a bank came to mind. She'd do it for him.

She tossed her keys into a bowl on a console table near the front door and went right into the kitchen for her nightly red wine before she took Murphy out. He'd already waited this long; he'd wait five more minutes for her.

The bottle of cabernet was opened from the night before, so she tossed her purse and the manila envelope on the counter and grabbed a wine glass from the yet-to-be-unloaded dishwasher. Holding it up to the light and inspecting it, she grabbed a towel and rubbed the outside and inside, making it shine like she did for every glass of wine she poured at work when Lucy was backed up. It was a habit she couldn't get rid of.

Once the glass was full—super full—she refilled Murphy's water bowl, grabbed the manila envelope, and sat on a stool at her kitchen counter. She ripped the top open and dumped out the contents.

It was a burner phone, with a Post-it on top. *Answer me when I ring.*

What the hell kind of *Scream*-slash-*Phone Booth*-slash-*Speed* bullshit was this?

Someone was playing a prank. Maybe it was her friend Maddy, who'd said she was going to set up a Tinder account for Kim with a different phone number. This was probably it. Maddy was right, and Kim needed to be more open to meeting a guy again, but she didn't want to put her real phone number on Tinder. *Very funny, Maddy.* She'd deal with her later, and she set the phone aside, still a little concerned about the cloak-and-dagger-ness of it all.

Scrolling through her real phone with one hand and petting Murphy on the head with the other, she absentmindedly looked at Instagram and Facebook, and eventually more websites to see about natural painkillers for dogs. She was Murphy's whole life, and she hated the thought of him thinking she didn't care and that she left him in pain.

No, he knew that wasn't the case. He had to know how much she loved him.

A half hour later, after Kim finished her wine and walked Murphy, the burner phone rang. She jumped. The ring was low and ominous, and she thought maybe it wasn't Maddy playing a joke on her, so she pushed it away. Stared at it like she could make it disappear by sheer will.

Curiosity killed the cat though, didn't it?

She answered the phone but didn't say anything. A voice boomed out from the other side.

"Kim Valva."

It was an electronic voice. Her heart beat so loud she was sure the person on the other end could hear it. They knew her first and last name. This wasn't a Tinder hookup.

"Who is this?" Kim asked.

"I'm a stranger. I need your help, and you could use twenty thousand dollars in cash."

Kim's heart was no longer beating loudly. She thought it had stopped altogether, and she took a few short breaths to keep it going. Her hands started to tingle. How did this person, this *stranger,* know she needed money? Or was it an assumption that everyone could use an extra twenty grand? "What are you talking about?"

"No questions, just listen," the voice garbled out. "New members are joining your country club. Once their payment is sorted and they join the regulars for dinner, I need you to slip a pill into the new male member's drink. He'll die. You'll be twenty—"

Kim hung up and skidded the phone across the counter. Looked around maniacally like there were hidden cameras trained on her, in her own apartment. Who the hell thought she was capable of murder?

She was being set up. She grabbed the phone to smash it when it beeped, and a light started flashing with a text message.

There's another envelope at your front door.

Kim's head swung toward the entry to confirm the door was locked and bolted. Whoever was fucking with her was close. Inside? It was a ground-floor apartment; easy to break into. Murphy might've looked like a twenty-five-pound stuffed animal, but he could be fiercely protective—one attempt to get in and he'd go medieval. Anyone who didn't know him would be terrified. He'd shown teeth to the man who brought her Chinese delivery once.

She grabbed a knife from her butcher block and stood in a corner of the kitchen, shaking, too scared to move. She closed her eyes and listened. Nothing. No breathing, no footsteps, nothing but Murphy's tail skidding across the floor, oblivious to Kim's terror. She strained her neck over to her windows beyond her couch to see if they were broken; they weren't.

Forcing herself out of the corner, she flipped on every light in her kitchen and living room. At the living room window, knife still in hand, she yanked the curtain closed. She tiptoed to her bedroom, hall light on, bathroom light on, and then bedroom light on. No broken glass on the floor. Those curtains were already closed—blackout shades enabled her and Murphy to sleep in. She checked under the bed and opened all the closets and pulled the shower curtain back.

She was alone.

Again, she tiptoed toward her front door and looked out the peephole. No one was there. With a quivering hand, she undid the chain and then pressed her ear against the door. Looked out the peephole again. Still nothing. She looked at Murphy with a *here goes nothing* face, like he understood what she was about to do. In under three seconds, she undid the bolt, opened the door, grabbed the envelope, closed the door, locked it, bolted it, and chained it. Murphy yelped with curiosity.

"It's okay, good boy."

Her heart was definitely working again, because now it was going a mile a minute. This was a smaller manila envelope, thin. She opened it and there was a typed note.

> Bank of Cayman, Account # 34-445-07781
> Password: TheStranger$20000
>> Go ahead. Access the account online and change the password. Half the money is already there, and it's yours.
>> Pick up the phone when I call you.

This wasn't real. It couldn't be.

That dead, curious cat had it coming.

She grabbed her laptop and logged in, then typed in the relevant information. The account popped up. It was in her name. Ten thousand dollars had been deposited that morning. She clicked on account information, looked up how to change the password, and it needed to be at least ten characters with capital and lowercase letters, numbers, and symbols. She changed it to something silly that no one would ever guess. A random string of words and numbers that had nothing to do with her.

> J0lly@ppleTr33
>> Jolly Apple Tree. She could remember that. She hit enter.
>> *Congratulations. Your new password was saved successfully.*

No one would be able to access this account except for her. Technically, she could grab her passport and take off with

Murphy, live in Panama or somewhere else obscure for a while until the dust settled, then camp out somewhere else for good. Somewhere cheap. Florida. Alabama. Somewhere she could disappear with Murphy after getting him the surgery he so desperately needed.

The ten grand that stared back at her was a hell of a start.

The phone rang, and this time Kim answered after one ring. It was the electronic voice again.

"You won't get caught. It's well thought out. There are two more steps I'll be in touch about later. You'll pick up twenty-five-hundred-dollar cash payments at a set spot after each step. Public. No one will know what you're doing, and you'll get the final payment on completion. Answer the phone when I call."

It disconnected.

She contemplated smashing the phone and heading to Panama, but something set off inside her.

Murphy. She could save him.

She could fix her life the way she needed to, and it was just feeding a pill to a random new member. But Kim wasn't a murderer.

Right?

8
ANTHONY
NOW

Anthony still couldn't stand up, the reality of his dead fiancée setting in.

What a mess.

"Mr. Fuller, you work with Ron Boswell, correct?" Mahoney asked.

He nodded. Mahoney raised an eyebrow.

"Yes," Anthony said. "For the past twelve years."

Mahoney wrote into a notepad. "And Poppy Jade . . . How long were you two together?"

Anthony gulped. Poppy Jade was gone, and it was going to be difficult to talk about their beginning. "We met a year ago when I gave a talk at NYU. Started chatting and went out. I guess you can say it's all history from there." A tear escaped and he wiped it away.

Mahoney paused. "I'm so very sorry for your loss, Mr. Fuller . . ." Anthony nodded in response. ". . . But you understand I have to keep asking questions while everything is fresh."

"Yes. I do."

Mahoney looked at his counterpart, a cop named Guiterrez. He was a nice-looking dude, with dark hair and dark eyes, and while he looked like he wanted to be any place else other than a crime scene, Mahoney seemed to revel in it. A born interrogator. Curious.

Great.

"When is . . . was . . . the wedding due to take place?"

You'd think Mahoney had just admitted to murdering PJ by the strained look on Anthony's face at the mention of their wouldn't-be wedding. "This fall, in Hawaii. We got engaged there a couple months ago. She wanted it to—" He paused to put his head in his hands to cover his face and stop the tears. "She wanted to repeat the entire feeling."

Mahoney pressed his lips together. "Has she met the group you dined with tonight?"

"Just Ron and Carla Boswell at a few work events over the last year. I only met Mayor Alvarez and Ben Xiang once before tonight. We all golfed together last week after I joined. I didn't meet their wives until tonight."

Mahoney jotted their names down and then underlined them. "Did PJ get along with the Boswells?"

Anthony dented his eyebrows together. "I'm not sure where you're going with this?"

"Well, healthy twenty-three-year-olds rarely drop dead at dinner. You mentioned when we first got here that she couldn't breathe, that she slapped the table and grabbed her throat before she passed out."

"Yes."

"Suspicious, no?" Was Mahoney accusing Anthony of something? Was he accusing Ron and Carla? "The server, Ms. Valva—she mentioned that you were old friends."

"Yes." Anthony learned long ago to keep answers short and sweet when dealing with cops, and never to give any additional information unless asked.

"Care to describe your relationship with her?"

Where to begin.

He was a senior, for the second time, and she was a freshman. They knew each other from the neighborhood, from hanging out on corners and at parties when one of their friends' parents were out of town. It was love at first sight, the kind you read about. Puppy love, of course. They were kids.

Against all odds, they stayed together after Anthony finally graduated. He didn't go to college and stayed directionless while Kim was in high school. Her parents excused the age difference because their parents were all neighborhood friends, and it wasn't like he was a child toucher—they grew up together and went to school together and stayed together after. Still, his road got more convoluted as he tried to find ways to make money without putting in the grind. Gambling. Drugs. Knocking off a bodega. He'd been arrested half a dozen times, but the last four, the charges were dropped.

It was when he was with purse-grabber Jose, a former friend, that things went sideways, and he knew that he needed to change.

"Kim and I were in a relationship for three years in high school," Anthony said.

"Oh?"

"Yes. She moved to California her senior year, and I never saw her again. Not until tonight."

In addition to her new zip code, her parents got her a new phone number. He was sure she'd asked them for it. She ran and never looked back after the incident. He never got into social media for various reasons. People who needed him knew how to get him.

Mahoney and Guiterrez exchanged a look, and Mahoney scratched the side of his head with his pencil. "A coincidence, for sure."

"Yes. We just joined the club—PJ and me. This is the first time we were having dinner here."

"Is there anything else pertinent that I need to know about your relationship with Ms. Valva?"

He closed his eyes for a few seconds, contemplating his past. "Back then, I was trouble. You're going to look it up anyway, so I might as well tell you." He was going to break his own rule of *don't say too much*. "I was a bad kid back then. Multiple arrests. But then I—"

He was going to have to tell them. They'd find out anyway.

"I was given an offer to be an informant to get some later charges dropped. I testified in a homicide. Then I gave it all up. Made some money during a great night in Atlantic City and learned how to invest it. When I made a killing in Apple stock, then Amazon, I cleaned up my act. Took my mother's last name, legally. I wanted to reinvent myself. Go straight."

They both looked at him questioningly, raised eyebrows and doubting eyes.

"Don't worry, everything that happened with the gambling money and the investing was legal. My brokerage account is legal. I pay my taxes and everything. I'm not that bad guy anymore."

That was all true, and Kim knew none of it. She didn't know he was ratting out their friends back then. Like the saying goes, snitches get stitches. After the homicide, he knew he had to get out. He was with Jose when Jose tried to rob a woman. In the struggle, a gun was turned on her, and she was shot dead. That lady was a fighter, but it didn't take long for Jose and Anthony to get caught. CCTV cameras caught them a block away, running from the scene with her purse.

"Do you think anything in your past may have caught up with you and Poppy Jade?"

Anthony shook his head. It was impossible. He didn't even have the same name. He'd left Brooklyn for an Upper East Side penthouse, and more recently, the beach house. "No one knew me anymore. It's been fifteen years since I got out of there. Fourteen since I've been investing. Ron's had that company for almost thirty years, and I've been there over twelve. Everything in my life was exactly where I wanted it to be. And now . . ." His voice trailed off.

And now . . . what? PJ was dead, and his life would never be the same.

Good. It wasn't all it was cracked up to be.

9
PJ
THEN

Matt makes me change outfits three times. *That's too long, that's too loose, that's too pink.* He wants me to be a vixen. I know he's right, which is why I don't fight him on it. We settle on a tight black dress with a square neckline and a light gray section in the middle to give the illusion of an hourglass shape. I mean, I have one already, but this dress really highlights it.

Matt pulls my hair half back and curls it while I do the whole smoky-eye thing and then he grabs a pair of silver pumps from the floor next to my futon. I sit on it, and he slides them on like I'm Cinderella.

When we're done, he takes a few steps back and motions with his index finger for me to turn around. I twirl, bopping my head from side to side. Then I catwalk with a hand on my hip from left to right.

"Girl, don't sleep with him. Look at you. Just play into his ego, and he'll be on you like me on Matt Bomer."

I nod.

"You have your whole backstory straight, I hope?" He raises an eyebrow.

"Don't worry about me. I've had it for years."

Matt air kisses me on both cheeks and smacks my ass to send me on my way.

I take a cab to a very expensive restaurant in Soho—of course, I looked it up. Anthony offered to pick me up, but I have to show him what an independent person I am. I can show him I need him *just enough* later.

After paying for the ride, I head to a walkway lined with a velvet rope where a tuxedo-clad man opens the door for me. I'm in a small vestibule, which I'm sure is the coat check in the winter. It's blocked off from the main restaurant by heavy velvet drapes—violet, with gold trim and gold tiebacks pulling each side to create a small opening. I slither through, and the maître d' stand is in front of me. It's not the tiny old man I expected, but instead someone younger than me, gorgeous, and possibly an actual Elite model.

"Bonjour, bienvenue a l'endroit ou il faut être." *The place to be.* Her speech is flawless, and she smiles. Veneers. Her teeth are too perfect. "Je m'appelle Nikole."

Nee-cole. "Hello, I'm meeting Anthony Fuller," I say.

Her manicured nail scrolls through an iPad, up and down. The faint glow from the screen looks like a spotlight due to the dim lighting around the hostess stand. She stops scrolling and her eyes light up. "Ah, oui, you can follow me, Mademoiselle Walsh. We have you at the chef's table in the back."

She's definitely a real Frenchie with that accent. I follow her past the bar, which looks like it serves champagne exclusively due to the encased water wall with floating bubbles. There's a crystal chandelier high above the bar, backlit with soft purple lighting and flutes hung upside down like little glass bats. The dining room is just as dimly lit, though I can make out the violet tablecloths and linen napkins. Soft French rock plays in the background, and there's a faint smell of steak and peppermint, an odd combination, but it works in this atmosphere. In the back, we go through more velvet drapes and through a French door to a room with a long table that can fit at least a dozen people, but there's only one sitting there: Anthony Fuller, at the head of the table, and one place setting caddy cornered beside him. He stands when we enter.

"Bonjour, Monsieur Fuller," Nikole says, and it sounds like *Full-ee-yay*. "Mademoiselle Walsh, s'il vous plaît." She gestures out a hand, welcoming me into the grand space, and as Anthony makes his way toward us, she leaves.

Smart woman.

Anthony puts his right hand over his heart. "Breathtaking." He takes my hand in his other and twirls me around, and I silently thank Matt for making me do it in the apartment. If I can pass his twirl test, I can pass anyone's. Anthony kisses my hand and holds it as he guides me to the table, then pulls out my chair.

There is already still and sparkling water on the table, next to a charcuterie spread, red wine, white wine, and champagne. He's really pulling out all the stops. *Sucker.*

"What, no Pappy Van Winkle appetizer?" I ask playfully.

He smirks. "That's for dessert."

That's all you're getting for dessert, buddy. I can't move too fast. "Sounds fabulous."

A young man, Pierre, comes in to tell us about the first of the eight courses we'll be served tonight. He explains that all of them are small and shareable, and they make a point not to fill us up before we've had a chance to enjoy them all. The first one coming out is *pieuvre,* and I inwardly gag like I was surprised during a routine blow job.

"Mmm, a delicacy," I say, picturing how I'm going to swallow the little octopus and have its disgusting brains spill into my throat. Talk about a blow job gone bad. "Can't wait." *You're not like other girls.*

During course three, after I Oscar-worthy acted my pure love of *pieuvre* and *huîtres* (oysters, more gag), we finally get a small soft-boiled egg over a piece of thick bacon, and I try not to gargle with it just to wash away the previous yuck. But I never falter and eat all my food with a billion-dollar smile.

I spend forty-five minutes *enthralled* over his job and his hobbies and his apartment and his designer and his bourbon collection and his blah blah *blah*—can this guy be any more rich-man basic? I keep pressing my gloss-covered lips together and give the sexy *Mmmmhmmm* sighs with the slow blinks. I let him be the king, and then he finally asks me about myself.

Showtime.

"My parents still live in Texas, and I miss them dearly, but I needed more culture. There's only so many libraries and museums in a small town like where I grew up. I'd often visit the bigger college campuses, and I even went to Austin once.

What a fun city. Lots of culture there, but it was like a drug to me, outside Texas, you know?"

I'm soooo naïve, Mr. Fuller. Please show me the world, I've never been anywhere but Austin!

He does all the right things. Tickles my wrist, refills my glass, offers me his jacket when the AC comes on full blast—Mr. Fucking Charming. I do all the right things as well. I act embarrassed when I purposely drop a fork onto my plate with a huge clank (I'm so relatable!) and use my napkin to wipe a nonexistent piece of spinach from his lip (I've got your back, baby!) and force myself to stop after two glasses of wine (I'm such a lady!). By Pappy time, I respectfully decline—I didn't want to drink that lighter fluid anyway—and thank him for dinner, telling him I need rest before I meet with a photographer tomorrow. That way, he doesn't expect me to sleep with him. Not tonight. Your *model* future girlfriend has things to do.

We walk outside, and he offers to have a car take me home, but I opt for the cab. We get to the corner, and before he hails one for me, he turns me to face him and places his hand under my chin, looking up at his eyes. How many girls have fallen for this shit?

"I had an amazing time, PJ," he says, then swipes some of my hair behind my ear, the piece that fell out of my crystal barrette.

Doe eyes. "Me too." I close my eyes, and his breath is hot, close to my lips. He kisses me, more than a peck but not a full-on make out session. I open my eyes and give him the come-hither stare, then pull the back of his neck closer to me and give him a *real* good night kiss. After about ten seconds,

I make a show of stopping it, with my dainty hand on his chest, then chuckle.

"Can I see you again?" he asks.

I never break eye contact. "I'd like that."

He kisses my forehead. "Good. I'll call you. Can you text me when you get home, so I know you're safe?"

Like a perfect gentleman, he opens the cab door, and the night whisks me away as he stands there, falling in love.

At least he's nice to look at. Decent kisser too.

I still can't wait to kill him.

10
KIM
NOW

Kim tried to control her breathing. She kept putting her hands into her empty pockets to make sure they were empty. Even though she knew they were. The pill was gone, into the bowels of the city, disintegrated by the water. Gone, gone, gone. She'd dispose of the empty vial she'd hid in the air shaft next week when she came to work and all this was over.

How close things almost came to completely falling apart. Not that ending her night in a crime scene was ideal, but things could've been worse.

Much worse.

Never religious, Kim said every silent prayer she could think of as she watched Tony talk to the cops through the glass door. He finally stood and raked his hand through his hair. His shirt was untucked now, wrinkled, and he looked like a completely different person than Kim saw two hours ago.

He shook both cops' hands and, with one hand on the back of his neck, walked into the dining room. He was immediately accosted by almost everyone who sat at their table—Hector and Wendy, Ben and Emiko, and Ron. Carla didn't move from her bar seat. Lucy had finally acquiesced and retrieved one of Carla's wine bottles from her locker. Carla demanded that Lucy wash the glass in front of her—soap and water, twice, and dried with a fresh paper towel, not a bar rag—to make sure that it wasn't tainted, then she poured her wine with flourish. A measly dead body wasn't about to stop her from enjoying her Friday night at the country club. Especially since she was trapped there against her will.

Kim knew she was up next to give a statement, though it would likely turn into a full-on interrogation because of her past with Tony. She needed to talk to him, but she couldn't. Not here. Not around these people. Not the day that his fiancée died.

Not that he'd believe what she wanted to tell him anyway—that *he* was the target tonight and someone beat her to it and killed PJ instead. Come to think of it, she should probably do what she used to do best and keep her mouth shut. What she had to tell him didn't exactly paint her in the most flattering light either. *Be careful, someone here wants you dead! I was paid to kill you tonight!* She wasn't an assassin; she was a waitress with bad luck.

Mahoney opened the glass door. "Ms. Valva?" he said. "Can we have a moment over there in the corner?" Guiterrez followed him out, and he shut the door to the bar behind him.

"Actually, I should go first." Dana hopped up from the barstool she'd camped at, saving the day. "Hi, I'm Dana O'Hare, I'm the bar manager. I handle the dining room on the weekends. I'll answer anything you want, take you to any part of the club you need to see before you start questioning the staff."

Mahoney looked at Guiterrez, who shrugged and then nodded. "Okay, Ms. O'Hare."

Dana looked nervous as she weaved her way through the rest of the diners to the Spanish Inquisition she was about to face. She had nothing to be nervous about, did she? From that moment on, Kim would question everyone and everything. Clearly, at least one other person wasn't who they seemed. Someone else here was probably neck deep in the same shit she'd gotten herself into. But who?

Dana and the two cops broke off into a far corner, and the chatter was still low. There were only thirteen people left in the club. Tony's table. Kim, who was the last of the waitstaff and scheduled to be the closer tonight. Lucy, the bartender. Dana, the manager. And Freddie, Quincy, and Hank—the chef, sous chef, and dishwasher.

Kim knew it would be smart to stay next to Lucy and the kitchen staff, but she wanted to hear what was going on around Tony. She strained her ears and heard the barrage of "I'm sorry" and "Oh my God, do you need anything?" and "What do you think happened?" but Tony was a ghost—he even looked like one. His skin was ashen, his lips were thin, and his cheeks tearstained. His eyes were vacant. He kept shaking his head. Disbelief. Numbness.

"Why did you go into that room with Mr. Fuller?" Lucy asked, interrupting her eavesdropping.

Kim snapped out of it, pissed that she couldn't hear the rest of their conversations.

"I—I know him. I haven't seen him in a long time. Fifteen years, probably."

"Oh, wow, that's crazy. Where did you guys meet?"

If there was a full-on investigation, things would come out. Life could get tricky for Kim, so she decided to be honest about everything, except the one thing she'd lie through her teeth about, all the way to a trial if need be.

"We dated in high school. He was a totally different person back then. So was I." Kim saw the quick accusatory glance. "I didn't know they belonged here. When Dana said we had new members, I had no idea it was him," Kim said, getting ahead of it. "I didn't even know he lived here in New Jersey. I moved from Brooklyn, where we dated, to California when I was seventeen and never saw him again. I've only been back on the East Coast for five years. I didn't even look him up when I came back here." That was true. "High school relationships, you know? It was forever ago."

She tried to laugh it off as Lucy nodded. Lucy was fifty with adult children and married half her life, and Kim was sure she equated high school boyfriends to past lives. Which it really was to Kim.

She also knew the past could sneak up on you. Someone in this room had to have killed PJ. Kim breathed a sigh of relief knowing that it wasn't her.

Even as she got a sneaking suspicion she was being set up.

11

KIM

NOW

While Kim waited for her turn to be grilled, she decided to do some research on PJ to see if there was any reason for someone to want her dead. She pulled her phone from her back pocket and went right to social media. Now that she knew how to research *Poppy Jade Walsh*, it was easy to find out about her. Young people, ones her age, grew up putting their entire lives online, and this one didn't disappoint.

Her public Instagram page was only a couple of years old though. Also typical for someone her age, it was childish and full of inspirational quotes. Tons of Pinterest design ideas. Bikini shots. Lots of city shots, her in sunglasses, looking out at the river. Sometimes she had a big hat on. Sometimes she was dressed to the nines, and sometimes she was in workout gear.

Kim scrolled until she got to a few shots that looked pro-
fessionally done. Not that PJ needed airbrushing, but these
pictures were a little *too* perfect. Kim read the captions. *Thank
you to @MattysPhotos for allowing me to live my dreams!* and
OMG I'm an @elite model!

She was signed with Elite?

Something didn't sit right. Kim clicked on the tagged page for
Elite, arguably the most famous modeling agency in the world.
The page's picture looked like a stock photo of supermodels
from the past, and it only had twenty-eight followers. This
wasn't the real modeling agency. Unless PJ tagged them
wrong? Kim scrolled back to the other photo and clicked on
@MattysPhotos. The profile picture there was an old-
fashioned-looking camera, and the only photos on the account
were pictures of PJ and random ones of New York City.

Toward the top of PJ's page, there were ridiculous pictures of
her and Tony, of course. The vomit-inducing *"I said yes!!!!!!!!!"*
with their foreheads touching. The engagement was rather
new. A couple months old at best, and it looked like it happened somewhere tropical, with palm trees and fiery sunsets.
Scroll, scroll, scroll. Ah. It was Hawaii. PJ posted pictures of
the Maui airport and both of them wearing leis.

All the pictures after that were scenery from hikes, helicopter tours, boat tours . . . and food. So much food. Where
did she put it? Then the money shot—one with her left hand
on his chest to show off the diamond. They both had tears
in their eyes. They both looked so happy.

Looks could be deceiving.

Kim's stomach roiled at the thought of what had gone on
in the past few days. She wondered if anything was on film.

There were no records of anything. Burner phones, cash payments, and impossible to prove pickups and drop-offs. Whoever set her up didn't want her to get caught.

They might need her again.

Murphy's surgery was scheduled for a week from Monday. She'd planned to tell everyone the age-old story—a rich uncle died, and now she had enough for Murphy's tumor removal. Easy peasy.

Still, once she walked out of the country club, she had no idea what waited for her at home. If she even made it there. The Stranger could be waiting in the parking lot to take her out and make it look like a mugging. They could have a red laser focused on the back of her head and blow her brains out, sharpshooter style.

Easier, as witnessed—anything she ate or drank in the future could be poisoned. The Stranger clearly knew poison and knew how to get others to do their bidding.

This was bigger than Kim wanted to think about, and she looked around. What made the most sense was the Boswells. Business dealings. Jealousies. Was Tony making too much money or not enough? Was he defrauding Ron? Did Ron and Carla plan this together? A bigger question, *why did The Stranger pick me?*

And who did The Stranger assign to murder PJ?

12

PJ

THEN

Three months into my relationship with Anthony, and he's eating out of my hand. It's Saturday morning, and I wake up to the smell of toast and the sound of bacon sizzling. I roll over to look at the clock, and it's ten minutes to nine. When I'm not with Anthony, I sleep till noon. I hate the mornings, but of course, the two or three days a week I stay with him, I fake it. I jump up out of bed and onto the floor, waiting for him to come in. When I hear him approaching from the hall, I contort into a mermaid position and close my eyes.

Namaste.

He slowly pushes the door open, his face lighting up when he sees me. "Hey. Breakfast is almost ready."

My eyes open and I make my surprised face—wide eyes, then lots of blinks, like I'm trying to figure out who he is. That

I'm *soooo* into my daily morning yoga that I'm transported somewhere else.

"Oh, wow, you scared me. I'm just finishing up."

My twenty-third birthday is in two weeks, and *I'm not like other twenty-three-year-olds*, right, Anthony? I *don't* get wasted all night and throw up on my shoes and sleep till noon, then wash it all away with Gatorade and bacon-egg-and-cheese sandwiches. The truth is I do, especially when I'm with Matt. When I'm with Anthony, all he sees is a responsible young woman, up early and ready to tackle the day.

"Come out when you're finished. I need to ask you something," he says.

I would've been worried that he figured me out, but he winks before he closes the door to let me finish what he thinks is my grueling daily forty-five-minute session. I don't do yoga, but this asshole is obsessed with me and believes anything I show him. He thinks I'm a private yoga instructor with high-end clients that I visit for individual sessions, and that's where I get my money. He doesn't know I had to sell Daddy's farm, the one I grew up on, to make all of this happen.

He loved that farm. I bite back the tears at Daddy's memory. I miss him.

When the door shuts, I relax and fall onto my side. I'd give anything to crawl back into that bed. With the money Anthony has, everything is top of the line. The first time I got into his bed, I felt so comfortable I would've fucked Charles Manson in there.

The comparison is close enough, in my opinion.

The mattress was so thick it needed special sheets, and they were top quality Egyptian cotton, with a down comforter and down pillows that made me feel like I had died and gone to heaven. He didn't suck at sex either—in fact, he was pretty goddamn good—so I was getting more out of my charade than I had planned. Orgasms good, Anthony bad. I'm lucky I can separate the two.

In the bathroom, I brush my teeth, then throw on a silk robe, cinch the waist, and put on my furry slippers. I pad down the hall to the gourmet kitchen. His decorator was worth every penny of the probable hundreds of thousands he spent on furnishing this stupid penthouse. The kitchen has stainless steel everything, sleek black marble counters, and shiny red backsplash with underlighting beneath the rich espresso-colored cabinets. His cappuccino machine and toaster and teapot are all red, bringing out the modern look. In the main living area, there's a fluffy, oversized red area rug (he mentioned he'd had it flown in from Italy) with two low-to-the-ground black couches, offset by black end tables and a black coffee table. His cleaning lady comes every Friday and brings two dozen red roses to fill out the middle of the table. An industrial-looking black chandelier hangs high over the room.

It would be unconventional if he wasn't so goddamn generic. Finance man decorates in sleek red and black. How original. The interior designer must've seen this doofus coming from a mile away and used stock inventory. The rug probably came from Target.

Still, he cooks for me and that's nice. My stomach grumbles. I walk to the cappuccino machine and pour a coffee (of course it's a high-tech combination cappuccino/espresso/ coffee thing that I looked up online—fifteen hundred bucks.

Moron). He's scraping the egg white omelets onto the red plates when I come behind him and wrap both of my arms around his torso, my head against his back, like I *really really really* love him *so so so* much.

Jackass.

I kiss the back of his T-shirt and make that morning comfy mumble sound that he loves. "How'd you sleep?" I duck underneath his arm, and he wraps it around me and kisses my head.

"Always great when it's with you," he says.

He puts the plates on the long black table, and we sit. There are already two glasses of freshly squeezed orange juice on the red placemats. I dig into my omelet and, of course, I act like he ripped the eggs right from the chicken's ass and grew the peppers and tomatoes himself.

"Mmmm, you did it again, baby. You're so good to me."

He smiles and takes a sip of OJ. "Hey, so I know you have plans tonight, but something came up and I'd like to know if you can accompany me somewhere."

Intriguing. He has my attention. I widen my eyes.

"My boss Ron is having a dinner party at their place tonight. I was planning on going alone because I know you like to hang out with your roommate on Saturday nights and I don't want to infringe on your independence. But considering what happened this week, I'd like it if you would come with me." He smiles.

What happened this week.

Yes, the brass ring before the diamond ring. He told me he loved me, and I said it right back with all the heat and passion and truth in the world. I deserve an Oscar for this acting. It really is my A-game.

His smile is goofy, and he's lucky he's hot. "Oh, wow, this is such short notice." Matt won't care in the least bit, and in fact, he would push me to become ingrained in Anthony's inner circle. It's all happening right on schedule.

He kisses my hand. "I love you. I want everyone else to love you too."

I lower my eyes. Second thoughts, of course, even though it's fake. "But the other wives . . . What are they going to think of me? I feel like I'd be a little out of my element. Aren't they all high-powered people?"

He chuckles. "They're married to high-powered people. If anything, maybe you can pick up a few clients. God knows private yoga lessons are something they're all into."

Fuck. I'll have to learn how to bird-dog really fast. "I can't stay late. I have a client at eight in the morning." It's a great excuse to leave in case I get uncomfortable, or in case they figure me out. Also, look at me all responsible. I'll go meet Matt at the bar after this stuffy dinner and then sleep all day tomorrow.

After breakfast, I go home and nap the rest of the day away. I wake up a little after five, since I have to be back at Anthony's by six forty-five. Matt just got home from his shift, and I hear the door slam, then things rattling around in the kitchen. I toss on a robe.

"Hey," he says when I walk out of my cave. He's eating a bowl of colorful cereal in front of the TV. "How does it feel to be *in luuurrrve*?"

I lightly kick his ankle. "Shut up. It's great. He's taking me to meet his boss tonight, so I'll meet you at the bar a little later than usual."

His hand goes up for a high five, which I slap. "All's on schedule, then?" he says before he shoves another spoonful of sugary something in his mouth.

I nod. "The time is coming. That son of a bitch will pay for killing my mother."

13

KIM
NOW

Kim kept looking at the time—Murphy needed to go out. He was a good boy and never went inside the apartment, but that was before he got sick. Now, he had a tumor and was in pain, and she wouldn't reprimand him if he had an accident inside. Because it *would've* been an accident. Murphy didn't want to disappoint his mama. One look at his sad eyes the first time he pooped inside when she first brought him home was all she needed to know that it was an apology and it wouldn't happen again. It didn't.

Still, the clock was ticking. And if The Stranger decided to punish Kim for not finishing the job by hurting Murphy, all hell would break loose. She'd show them just how fast she could kill someone.

Dana and the two cops headed toward the kitchen. Freddie, Quincy, and Hank all stood, wondering if they should follow. Dana curled a finger at them, answering their question. Kim tried to read their faces to see if one of them looked guilty as they walked the plank to the kitchen. Freddie and Quincy handled the food, and Hank handled the place settings. If one of them poisoned PJ, they were about to be found out.

Two forensic people, both women, were placing small, numbered cones next to everything in the bar room. Evidence. They bagged and tagged and logged all the remaining silverware and glasses on the table and dusted everything for prints. Kim wasn't sure what good that would do. It was very possible everyone left in the club had touched everything on that table. Even other members had stopped there to say hello to all of them and press palms like they always did when they saw each other. Their DNA had to be there too.

Kim wondered if they'd find different prints. Maybe someone who was there earlier slipped PJ something that wasn't fast acting. The possibilities of the killer could be endless. There had to be a hundred people at the club tonight, not including the staff that had already gone home.

Kim looked at Tony again, and this time his eyes met hers. Through their secret language, she deciphered his message. *I want to talk to you, I want to catch up, but I just can't right now. I can't believe this happened.*

She tilted her head slightly to the right and softened her face. *I know. I'm sorry. I'm here if you need anything.*

He said something to his friends, then excused himself and walked over to where Kim was huddled behind the bar with Lucy. He looked like a completely different man. He fifty percent resembled clean-cut Anthony in that outfit with that new hair and that gold watch, and he fifty percent resembled Brooklyn Tony, who was going to get revenge on the one who wronged him. The fiery eyes said it all.

Kim grabbed a glass, washed it, and filled it with club soda. Tony never drank regular Coke or Pepsi, but he liked the fizz of soda and she didn't think she should ply him with more bourbon. She pushed the glass to his side of the bar when he got there.

"Thanks," he said and took a long sip, then wiped his mouth on the back of his hand like Brooklyn Tony would've done. He had no interest in being clean-cut Anthony at that moment. "I can't believe this."

Kim didn't know what to say. Of course, she held the key to finding out who killed PJ. If anyone—the cops, Tony, anyone—knew what was going on behind the scenes, they'd have a much better idea of where to start looking. That someone else—*not Kim*—had a mission that night as well. She couldn't even use that in her own defense. She wasn't going to jail for this. Technically, she didn't do anything.

As learned, *what do you know and what can you prove?*

"I don't understand," Tony said in a low voice, lightly shaking his head. "I don't understand what happened. Did you see her? What the hell does that to a person? She was so beautiful. I can't even . . ."

He leaned onto the bar, and put a fist up to his forehead, his eyes closed tight. Deep breaths. He was going to lose it.

Kim knew the signs. That one, the fist and the closed eyes, was him trying to talk himself out of complete rage. It rarely worked, and she waited for the explosion.

Then he picked up the almost empty glass of club soda and threw it as hard as he could at the wall on the far side of the room. Everyone gasped as the glass shattered with a bang—well, Carla screamed in an overdramatic way—and Tony collapsed on the floor. Crying. It was the only sound now, as all the hushed talking came to a halt with the broken glass. Kim walked around to the other side of the bar, leaned down next to him, and wrapped her arms around him while he blubbered into her shoulder.

Even though it ended badly, she used to love this man, and he was in pain.

Maybe he would've been better off if she'd done her job and he didn't have to live through this.

"I'm sorry, Tony," Kim whispered.

She'd only seen him cry once. His cousin William, who lived in northern New Jersey, was visiting Tony in Brooklyn on a Saturday night to do typical guy stuff—cards, beers, shooting the shit. It had started to snow pretty hard on the drive back home, and William lost control of his car on some black ice. Spun around into oncoming traffic and was hit head on. Both drivers died in the crash. It was tragic and horrible, and Tony was inconsolable. Kim remembered him collapsing into her arms when they got back from the funeral, a mess of tears and guilt and grief.

"Is anyone going to clean up that mess?" Carla shouted. "My shoes are open-toed, and if I get a cut because of the incompetence of—"

"Carla, will you just shut the fuck up?" Ron interrupted. "Enough already."

Carla's hand flew to her open mouth in shock. Kim saw the sheen of sweat instantly on her face, and her eyes were daggers, and Kim was convinced there was about to be another murder tonight. Ron would have hell to pay when they got home for embarrassing her in front of everyone. Then she picked up her red wine, held it to her lips, and with a wicked smirk, threw it all over him.

"You crazy bitch!" Ron shouted.

"Shut up and drink your after-dinner bourbon, asshole."

"You think we're doing our regular bourbon tonight? What's wrong with you?" He grabbed a napkin and wiped his face and shirt. "My lawyer is going to have a field day with this. You just screwed yourself out of what little settlement you were going to get." He stared at her with the heat of a thousand suns, then looked at his audience. "Yeah, I filed for divorce. Surprise!" he said nastily, throwing his hands in the air.

Hector and Wendy, then Ben and Emiko took their turns being in shock. It was all over their faces. How could their friends' marriage have been in such trouble and they never knew?

Ron and Carla lived in New York City and only used their beach house in the summer. Hector and Wendy, as well as Ben and Emiko, lived on the beach year-round, so they were basically summer friends. Ron and Carla moved to the beach every summer to escape the city—too touristy—in favor of sun, sand, and surf and to have full use of the country club. Considering it was June, they probably hadn't hung out much yet this year. Maybe the cracks were there for their New York City friends to see, but these four wouldn't have known. Especially since the Boswells played the part so well.

Carla played the part *very* well. She knew how to act, and apparently, now she needed money. Kim wondered how far she'd go to get it.

14

PJ

THEN

I show up to Anthony's house at six forty-five on the dot. We have to be at this fancy-ass dinner party at seven, but it's only a few blocks away. The doorman already alerted Anthony that I've arrived, and the door is open when I get up to the top.

Wow. He looks great. His dark hair needs a cut, but I like it full. He's in a black suit with a red tie. He wanted to match me—ownership—and texted me asking what color I'd be in.

He puts his hand over his heart when I walk in. "Good Lord, you are gorgeous." He takes my left hand and twirls me around. "You're going to make everyone jealous tonight."

Yeah, I know. I'm wearing a skintight red dress with a square neckline and strappy gold heels. All my jewelry is yellow gold, from my large hoop earrings to the thick cuff on my wrist. The money shot is the V-shaped charm on a delicate gold chain, practically pointing toward my cleavage. I'll be smart—just not too smart—and make good conversation. He needs to think he's above me, and he can think that all he wants until he's six feet below me.

Anthony offers to get us a car, but of course *I'm not like other girls*, and I tell him I'm fine walking six blocks in heels. When we get to their building, the lobby is much like Anthony's. He gives our names to the doorman, who must have some knowledge of the dinner party because he doesn't call up, just presses a few buttons on an iPad and then gestures his hand out toward the elevators, telling us it's the last elevator bank on the left. Anthony hits the only button on the panel—P2. The doors close, and there's a fifteen-second pause before we start going up.

"They probably have staff check the cameras before they let anyone up," Anthony says.

Staff? Good Lord. And oh wow, this is going to be a super fancy place with the private elevator that opens directly into their apartment. When it does, we're greeted by a woman with a short brown pixie cut. Her waifish features make her look twelve years old, and she has a leather notebook in her hand. She smiles at Anthony, then at me.

"Mr. Fuller and Ms. Walsh, I presume?" she says.

"Yes, Anthony and PJ," Anthony says.

"I'm Amy, the planner for the event. Let me show you into the salon for the predinner cocktail."

Ooh la la, the *salon*.

We're still in the entryway, which has a shiny black floor and black painted walls. There's a door to the left in a shimmering gold, and the trim and wainscotting are the same color. There's a gold and crystal chandelier above the center table, which is adorned with at least two dozen fresh sunflowers. Opulence. It's oozing.

We follow Amy through a hall, where I notice another elevator door. Ah, this is one of *those* places—elevators to multiple levels. At the end of the hall, the space opens up, and even I have to allow myself a gasp. It's the most stunning place I've ever seen. It's all windows, twenty-five feet high, and it's decorated to perfection. All white and soft baby blues and grays. The backdrop of Central Park on one side and the skyscrapers on the other is remarkable.

We walk down three stairs into the sunken space and head to the left, through another hallway and then into another huge room. Same windows, but this one has low lighting and violet carpet and plush velvet chairs, and there's a bar that seats ten—taps and all—on the far end. Three couples are chatting, with wine glasses in hand, when Amy announces us.

"Anthony, you guys made it!" I assume this is the boss talking, and he grabs my hand. "And you must be Poppy Jade. I'm Ron Boswell."

His hand is sweaty, and his belly hangs over his belt, with those buttons on his shirt screaming for dear life so loudly I want to tell them to shut the fuck up. He's in his fifties and looks it. Losing his hair, hard lines on his face, and a ruddy complexion. He still has my hand, and I've already caught him looking everywhere he shouldn't, but that's okay. That's what I'm here for.

"Carla, come meet Poppy Jade," Ron says.

A woman with long blond hair stops talking to one of the other women and turns around. Her smile turns into a scowl as she looks me up and down. Relax, sweetheart, I don't want your dumpy man. I have a hottie, one I'm planning to kill in one of those honeymoon accidents. Not my fault he fell out of the boat.

She strides toward us as I pull my hand away from Ron and slip my arm around Anthony's waist. Up close, she looks good. She might be older, but she's more Real Housewife than Golden Girl. The long hair extensions, the eyelashes, the too plump lips, the too perky boobs, the so-smooth-this-has-to-be-fake skin—it all screams that she's trying too hard to be . . . well, me.

I smile. "Hi, I'm PJ. It's wonderful to meet you. Your home is lovely."

"Yes." That's all she says to me, then she turns her attention to Anthony. Her smile shows her veneers, her eyes sparkling. "Anthony, how good to see you again." She touches his forearm. Way too familiar, and I feel like I'm interrupting something with my very presence.

Ron rolls his eyes, then looks at me like a dog in heat. "Whatever, she's always had a little thing for him. Let me introduce you to everyone else."

It's a good thing I have zero feelings for Anthony. I can be a jealous type when I really love someone, and Carla is rubbing it in pretty thick. It almost wouldn't shock me if she tried to grab his ass.

Ron introduces me to the other guests, who he tells me are neighbors. They all seem to be in their forties. Teddy and Melissa Silverman are both lawyers. Jacob and Gayle McDougall are both doctors. The elite.

Carla comes back and eyes Ron. "Go talk to your friends." She clearly wants him away from me. When he scurries in the other direction, where the men have gathered, Carla turns her attention to Gayle. "So, as I was saying, the donation would give us the dedication on the wall, correct?"

Her back is to me, and I don't know what to do. She didn't even offer me a drink. That's when I notice a different woman in black pants and a white button-down with her hair in a low bun refilling champagne glasses and placing them on a tray. She comes over to us, and I take one and thank her.

"Yes, that's right," Gayle says. She looks over Carla's shoulder at me with a warm smile. "So, Poppy, what do you do?"

I swallow my sip of champagne. "Please, call me PJ. I'm a yoga instructor."

Carla chuckles. "Yoga. Mm-hmm." I swear she rolls her eyes and takes the attention back. "Not very lucrative. But I guess that's what Anthony is for."

My cheeks burn hot, but I kill her with kindness. "Actually, it's a lot better than you'd think. I don't teach at a studio; I have private clients and go to their houses for one-on-one sessions. It's very exclusive."

Carla shrugs. "I know everything exclusive in this city, and I've never even heard of you."

She says it to be cruel, to take me and my natural C cups down a notch. I wonder what Anthony's past girlfriends looked like. Carla is probably sick of the Barbie Doll parade.

"I haven't heard of you either," I say, and Melissa and Gayle widen their eyes. Shit. I said that to be cruel as well, to take her fake old ass down a notch, but can't be cast out. "I just started out though. I guess word of mouth hasn't made it to the Upper East Side yet. You can say you knew me when." I give her a smirk, then look out the windows. "This view is really stunning, Carla. I'll have to borrow your decorator one day. You have fantastic taste."

I'll be the bigger person. Well, the smaller one in her eyes but whatever. It's all just a means to an end. I look in Anthony's direction, and he winks at me as he takes a California roll from one of the cocktail trays being served. I blow him a kiss and grab a napkin and a fried shrimp off another tray. It's all I can do not to shoot him with my thumb and forefinger. Boom. Dead.

Cocktail hour ends with the sound of a bell coming from Amy at the head of the salon. A. Fucking. Bell. Melissa is talking to us about a case involving an NYPD shooting, and Carla abandons her without a word. She turns around, walks toward the dining room, and in front of one of the servers, drops her cocktail napkin on the floor before she exits the room, leaving it for the server to pick up. Good Lord, I hate this woman and decide right then and there that if I don't feel too much guilt after killing Anthony, she's next. The world doesn't need Carla Boswell in it.

Anthony waits at the entryway, and I bend down to pick up the napkin and place it on one of the trays and mutter a *sorry*, even though it wasn't me who dropped it. On purpose.

"Do you know where the bathroom is?" I ask.

"One of them is right down that hall," Anthony says, pointing a finger.

I nod and head that way, wanting to wash my hands and rinse out my mouth before dinner. I'm sure I'll be read the riot act by that insufferable bitch for not playing follow the leader, but I was raised with proper Texas manners, and I wash my hands before dinner. I also silently pray before I eat, but no one except Matt knows that. I've been sneaking in more prayers than usual, and yes, I do see the hypocrisy.

I'm in the hallway that Anthony pointed out and I open a door and—it's not the bathroom. It's an office. Ron and one of the young blonde servers jump away from each other far too quickly for me not to believe they were right about to have a predinner hump.

I pretend not to notice. I smile, even give a little wave. "Hi, I was just looking for the bathroom."

Ron eyes me up and down again as if I'm an appealing candidate for a postdinner hump. "The door across the hall."

"Excellent, thank you. And thanks again for inviting us tonight. Your place is grand." I give a little nod to him—I don't even look at the server—and close the door behind me.

Inside, I'm jumping for joy that Carla is being made a fool of under her own roof. I wonder what she'd do if she found out?

15

KIM
NOW

t came as zero shock to Kim that Ron Boswell had filed for divorce. Carla must've been impossible to deal with behind closed doors if her public actions were any indication. For him to scream it out like that showed everyone just how much shit he'd been taking.

Kim was still on the floor with Tony. "Did you know about that?" she whispered.

He lifted his head and didn't say a word. His eyes told her he knew everything.

Tony stood and brushed himself off, so Kim did the same. Ron was on one side of the room, covered in red wine, speaking animatedly with Hector and Ben, while Carla camped at the other side, shrugging off the attempts of niceties from Wendy and Emiko.

"I guess I'll go over there," Tony said. "By the way, I told the cops we dated. So don't worry, just tell them the truth when you talk to them. You're not going to be under suspicion for anything unless you lie."

Unless you lie. Kim's head spun with all the lies from the past few days. She nodded and was about to head back behind the bar when Dana came out of the kitchen with Mahoney and Guiterrez, and also Freddie, Quincy, and Hank. They all had their backpacks on their shoulders.

"We've got statements from the kitchen staff, so they're all free to leave," Mahoney said, then looked at Kim. "Have a minute?"

"Absolutely," Kim said, and they went to a private end of the dining room.

"How long have you worked here?" Mahoney asked.

Kim's eyes went up and to the left. "A little over two years. I'm only here Wednesday, Thursday, and Friday nights. It's my second job. I do freelance graphic design as my day job." She was speaking too fast and gave out too much information. When they were young, Tony had told her to only answer the questions you were asked.

"Did anyone at the table, or at the club in general, seem a little off to you tonight?"

"No." Kim shook her head. "Just like any other Friday night, except with new members." She shut her mouth, then decided to overspeak again, just so it didn't look like she was trying to hide it. "I was surprised it was my ex-boyfriend. I'd pretty much forgotten all about him. We dated in high school."

"It was a long relationship?"

"It was high school. We were kids. I moved to California when I was seventeen and we broke up. There really wasn't any drama." Just a wee murder investigation. Kim looked over her shoulder, then back at Mahoney. "While you were in the back with Dana and the kitchen crew, Ron and Carla Boswell had . . . an altercation. That was really the only thing that stood out to me tonight. They announced their divorce, and to be honest, it was shocking." No, it wasn't. Carla throwing the wine and the subsequent screamed confession, yes, but the actual realization they were divorcing, no. Kim gulped. "Well, of course, and PJ dying was unusual."

Kim ran through a list of what she served everyone, if anyone ordered anything strange, or if she saw anyone handle PJ's food or drinks. Finally satisfied, Mahoney looked at Guiterrez. "I guess we should get statements from the Boswells next." He reached into his shirt pocket and handed Kim a card. "If you think of anything else or see or hear something out of the ordinary with any members or crew in the next few days, let us know."

She tucked the card into her pocket. "Will do."

Thank God it wasn't an interrogation—they just wanted a statement. She was free to go. To go home to Murphy, to forget about the hell the night turned into, and to whatever hell was waiting for her at home. She ran downstairs to the locker room to grab her bag, and on the way back up said goodbye to Lucy. She gave Tony a look, and he said the same thing back to her. *I need you. I'm here if you need me.* ·

Kim couldn't wait to get out of there. She couldn't wait to *not* see this place for the next five days. She just wanted to do her regular job and play with Murphy and not have to be near poison or death or murder.

Still, before she left, she went behind the reception desk at the front lobby and keyed Tony's name into the search bar. As soon as she memorized his phone number, she clicked the page off and walked into the darkness, awaiting her fate.

16
PJ
THEN

Christmas is always hard. Daddy died two years ago, right before Christmas. Colon cancer. I knew it was coming—he was diagnosed with stage three when I was in high school. He cried when he told me and said he'd explore all available options. He did chemo and surgery, successfully, but it came back with a vengeance two years later.

Daddy dropped everything to raise me when Mama died, so I stayed close to home for college and took care of him. At the end, we had a hospice nurse daily. Those last three weeks were the worst, although Daddy said it was okay because he was going to be with Mama again. I failed that semester because I didn't go back to class after Thanksgiving, and I missed all my finals. I made it all up over the next summer to graduate on time. That would make Daddy proud.

At the time, Matt had been working as a barback at some honky-tonk dive bar in the sticks, and when they wouldn't give him the time off to take care of me and attend the funeral, he quit. He stayed with me for six weeks and helped me settle the farm, and by settle, I mean sell the land that my daddy had such pride in.

But I couldn't stay there.

Mama grew up in Connecticut and went to Texas Tech for college, where she met and fell in love with Daddy. They got engaged right after college and married shortly thereafter. From what I remember of Mama, she couldn't have been more different than Daddy. She didn't work the farm, because she always had nice shoes and fancy hair and nails. She bought and sold commercial real estate in Dallas, which was about an hour outside of where we lived.

Daddy woke up at 4:00 a.m. to tend to the crops and the livestock, both of which he sold locally. Daddy used to say during their busy seasons, they were ships passing in the night. A cliché for sure, but now I understand.

I never saw them fight. They were in love, and that's all I remember. It's funny how a feeling can outlast your memories.

Packing up Daddy's things, I was numb. Mama died while visiting her best friend Isabel, who she grew up with in Connecticut. They were going to have a girls' weekend in New York City. Mama was thirty-two and she was entitled to it, and Daddy thought she needed some time to let off steam. She'd been working so hard. He asked her to be extra careful because he heard New York was dangerous.

Mama was attacked by two men. She tried to defend herself, but they came out of nowhere, and one of them had a gun. He turned it on her and shot her.

He shot her. Anthony Fuller. Tony Fiore. Whatever his name is. And like the heartless, careless, stupid son of a bitch he is, he blamed his friend. Even testified against him. His friend is serving a twenty-year sentence. He didn't get the full twenty-five because he'd cooperated from the start, and now after almost sixteen years behind bars, I think he's up for parole.

I found out this information on my own. The internet is your friend, and I found out every detail of the murder and the trial.

Before I started college, when I was only eighteen, Matt and I hopped on a plane to New York and I went to visit Jose Sanchez, to face him, to let him see the daughter of his victim. Of course, he proclaimed his innocence—don't they all—and said it was his friend who did it, the one who testified.

"Tony Fiore" was a big deal in some Brooklyn neighborhood, and Jose thought it behooved his family to just shut up and do the time. Apparently, Tony Fiore had some sweetheart deal with the cops on top of that, and Jose was afraid for his siblings and his pregnant girlfriend. Jose was charged with manslaughter in the first degree. It was still a class B felony, but for the sake of his own safety in prison as well as the people he cared about outside, he cooperated. For that motherfucker Tony.

I care less about who pulled the trigger at this point. I wasn't a hundred percent sure I should believe a felon, but they were both there. One is paying a price, and one is living his best life. No fucking way.

Tony disappeared after the trial. It's amazing what information a regular person can find out about someone else, but still it wasn't enough. We needed more, and it turned out Matt was dating an EMT whose best friend was a dirty cop. Quid pro quo . . . Matt knew of some bad drug leaders from the club circuit, so there was a little exchange of information. One of the huge drug suppliers was raided, and Matt got a large manila envelope. New IDs for both of us, taken from dead people. I used mine and became Poppy Jade Walsh. Matt's is for an emergency. Besides those, we got a bunch of papers on Tony.

Quid pro quo.

There it was, all of it—Tony Fiore changed his name to Anthony Fuller. He had a lot of money now. Current address, Upper East Side, New York City. Trading stocks, working for some big Wall Street firm. Articles from fifteen years back, "The Guy Who Can't Lose." Everything he bought turned to gold. He fielded many employment offers before landing with Boswell Securities a dozen years back.

Not on my watch. The bigger they are, the harder they fall. After we sold the farm, I talked with Matt about the plan to make Tony Fiore pay. Revenge wasn't enough for him. Death itself wasn't either. I wanted him to grieve, to know loss. For him to give his whole self to me and understand what's going on when I take it all away. Only *then* do I kill him. Matt packed his things to come with me without a second thought. We were moving to New York, two peas in a pod.

Fast forward, it's Christmas morning with this stupid asshole. To play my big family life lie, I told him we were going to Dallas to stay with Mama and Daddy for a few days. He was thrilled to get to meet them. But *oooops*, our reservations got screwed up (knowing passwords is a good thing), and we didn't know about the canceled reservations until we were at the airport.

Instead of throwing a fit, I rubbed his arm and thanked him for trying and said maybe it's best if we don't waste the holiday arguing with customer service, that we could have a nice little intimate party of two, and he could meet my (nonexistent) parents another time. We went back to his place and "made love" (gag) while I dressed like a sexy Mrs. Claus, and he loved it.

Now I'm sitting by the tree, waiting for my presents, and I know they're going to be good ones. I make Anthony open his first, because I'm not a greedy bitch. I got him a men's spa day and two cashmere sweaters. See, Anthony? I have enough money to support myself and get you nice things. But see how I didn't overdo it with a Rolex? You're still so high above me. I need you more than you need me.

As if.

"Open yours now."

He's giddy as he hands me something thin, maybe four inches by nine inches. It's wrapped, and I'm careful not to tear whatever it is in half. How funny, we're *so in sync* because it's a gift certificate to a spa day as well. Not the same place, but that's not the point. I laugh *so hard* because we know each other *so well*.

The next box is enormous, and when I rip that one open, it's the newest Louis Vuitton bag. Not usually my style, but it'll fit well next time we see his boss and that absolute dishrag wife of his.

Then he hands me a small square box with a bow on top.

This is it. He's proposing. He was going to do it in front of my family in Texas because he's such a good guy. Skipped right over Phase Three (asking me to move in, even though Matt said I shouldn't until we were married), and now he's taking a hop, skip, and a jump right to Phase Four. I'm getting closer.

I can hardly contain my excitement as I tear it open and—

"Oh my God, Anthony, you shouldn't have. This is too much."

Asshole. Diamond earrings. Huge ones, at least two and a half carats each, but still.

He touches my face. "You're worth it. I love you." His soft lips land on mine. "Hey, I have one more thing for you."

Omigodomigodomigod . . .

Nope. The box is small, but it doesn't make sense for a ring. I try like hell not to show any disappointment, and I will not pressure him for the ring. It's going to be his idea when he proposes.

Curious, I tear this one open, and it's a key and a fob. I look up at him.

"It's your key. And your fob to the common areas and the rooftop. I'd really like it if you were here all the time," he says.

I smile. "Now I can let myself in without having to wait for you to get home from work."

He chuckles. "It's more than that." He grabs my hand. "I want you to move in. I want to live with you."

It's impossible to feel disappointed because things are progressing. It's Phase Three. It's all coming together. If this were real, he'd be a really good boyfriend.

"I'd love to."

We kiss like you see in the movies.

Matt is going to kill me for leaving.

17

KIM
NOW

Kim exited the country club. It was dark except for one of the cop cars that still had the lights flashing. No siren, no engine, just the lights like blue and red fireworks. Round and round. She stiffened on the sidewalk just outside the front doors. Eyes closed, she listened. For what, she didn't know. Something out of the ordinary. She'd read that taking away one sense can heighten the others. Maybe someone was in the bushes, waiting to ambush her. There could've been a dark figure in a hood, holding a knife.

She had no idea who The Stranger was.

She let out a breath, then forced herself to walk. One foot in front of the other, each step faster than the last, until she was just short of running. From twenty feet away, she hit her fob and the taillights on her car flashed. She was about to run to it, open the door, and slam it shut and lock it, but she tensed again. She stopped five feet away from her car, in the middle of the parking lot, and knelt down, checking to see if there was a body hiding under her car to slice her Achilles tendon, rendering her immobile and unable to escape.

Nothing.

Her door was open, but instead of getting in, all she thought about was someone in the back seat, crouching down, hiding, waiting to put a plastic bag over her head and suffocate her for not doing her job. Knowing there was no one under the car, and hearing nothing but her own heartbeat and the cicadas in the background, she opened the door. The interior light went on and she craned her neck to look, but there was no one else inside. She poured herself into her front seat and slammed the door shut and locked it.

One more minute.

Kim finally turned on the engine with pressed lips and tightly closed eyes, waiting for the explosion, which of course, she'd never know about. If the car blew up, she'd cease to exist, like a gust of wind from one second to the next. Gone.

The engine turned over, and there was no explosion.

So far.

She put the car in reverse and hightailed it out of the parking lot, going faster than she should've been.

Oh fuck. What if someone tampered with the brakes?

She released her foot from the gas and let the car slow itself down just enough that if she hit the brakes and they didn't work, she could open the door and roll out, letting the car steer itself onto the driving range.

Kim hit the brakes. The car came to a halt.

She was being paranoid, but with good reason. The Stranger knew where she lived.

Murphy. She had to get home to Murphy. If someone hurt him, she'd live the rest of her life like a cobra backed into a corner, ready to snap and maim, possibly kill, at any given moment. Even though she wasn't a killer. Anymore.

As usual, she parked her car blocks away from home, and her breathing was short and furious as she walked to her apartment. There were people out, of course—it was Friday night at the beach in the summer. Although she didn't live *on* the beach, she was only a ten-minute walk away. Parking by the beach was impossible to find, so lots of people parked near her place and walked to the strip of bars to party the night away.

Every time she passed someone, she thought, *Is this The Stranger?* But that was impossible. Everyone she passed had groups of people, girls in their short shorts and sundresses showing off their tanned legs and guys with their shirts buttoned only halfway to the top, exposing their pecs. How Kim wished she was one of them, in a group, going out to drink the night away because there was safety in numbers.

One more block to go.

When she turned the corner, there was a person standing under a streetlight about thirty feet away, between her and her front door. The person's back was to her, and they were wearing black pants and a black hoodie. From this far away, she couldn't tell if it was a man or a woman. It didn't matter. Death didn't discriminate and came in all forms.

Better safe than sorry. Kim crossed the street and continued to walk when she heard a loud noise.

"Come on, man, I'll give you cash! I just need to get home . . . No man, I don't do Uber . . . I don't know, on Bumfuck Street next to Fuck You Avenue . . . Look, I can be in front of Toadie's in five minutes . . . Thanks, bro."

Oh. Hoodie Guy was just a drunk looking for a ride. He hung up the phone and started walking in the direction of the beach, while Kim continued to go the other way. She stopped when she was across from her apartment and squinted to see if there were any strange envelopes in front of the door, or a booby trap above the door that would wrap her in netting to be easily dragged away by someone who wanted to harm her. So far, nothing. She darted across the street and stuck the key in the lock at record speed and slammed the door shut. Murphy barked.

"Murphy!" Kim turned around and sat on the ground, leaving her keys and purse on the floor. She pet him all over, looking for injuries. "Are you okay, good boy?"

Murphy did a cute little dance for her whenever she was gone too long. He kicked up his two front paws to kiss her, landed, and then did it ten times in a row. It always made her laugh, and she rolled onto her back while he crawled on top of her, licking her face.

"Are you okay, good boy?" she asked again. "I'm sorry I'm late." She said it like he understood her. Maybe he did. He didn't seem spooked, but she still proceeded to turn on every light in the house and check under every piece of furniture and behind every door. She was alone.

Kim knew he needed a walk, but he stood by his bowl rather than the door. First, she fed him dinner and then sat on the couch with him, waiting to see if there was going to be a random knock on the door or if a mysterious phone would start to ring from inside.

She put her head in her hands and finally thought about the events of the night. She almost killed someone. Tony was back. She almost killed Tony. Tony was engaged. Tony's fiancée was probably murdered. Someone else at the club, staff or member, probably did it. The Stranger was going to make Kim pay for not doing her job. Maybe not tonight, but that was almost worse.

She didn't know what to expect, or when it would come.

But it would come.

"You have to go pee, don't you, baby?" she said to Murphy like he was going to answer. In English. "Come on, let's go out."

Murphy stirred at the word "out," and Kim attached his leash to his collar. His little curly butt wiggled as he pranced to the front door. Once there, he sat, sensing Kim's apprehension. She touched the knob, then pulled back. She looked out the peephole, just to make sure no one was there. Never one to be afraid of the dark, now it felt suffocating. She hated that she had to go outside when someone was after her.

"It's not going to be a long walk tonight, okay?"

His chocolate brown eyes told her it was okay, as long as they were together. She opened the door, locked it behind her, and ran to the park two blocks away. She hovered under a streetlight while Murphy did his business. They were about to leave when Murphy muled. That was what Kim called it when he sat in one spot and refused to move, no matter how hard she pulled the leash.

Something spooked him.

Then the barking started.

Kim's adrenaline pumped through her body so fast she felt it, like she was waking from a nightmare. Murphy faced forward, then he stood, his tail pointing as his eyes seemed to zero in on something in the distance.

"Come on, boy." Kim's voice shook as she spoke. She tugged him to the side, away from whatever he'd been barking at. "Come on."

It took him a few seconds, but then he obeyed. He liked to run, and Kim made sure they ran at warp speed back to her apartment. Her keys were in her hand, and she fumbled with them trying to open the door. Murphy was acting normal.

She didn't seem to be in danger, but she knew she was.

Once inside, she locked, bolted, and chained the door. After she unhooked Murphy's leash, he ran into her bedroom—he knew after his night walk that it was bedtime. In the kitchen, Kim grabbed a bottle of water for bed. When she got to her room, Murphy was already settled into his doggie bed right next to hers. He was curled up into a ball with his favorite stuffed toy, a big fat porcupine, and Kim knelt down and pet his head.

"We're getting you fixed up soon, good boy."

If she had to return the money, Murphy would die in months. She wiped a tear away and kissed him on his head. Once under the covers, she decided that she needed sleep, and she would sort everything out tomorrow. She had to.

Then came the knock at the door.

18

PJ
THEN

It's the day after Christmas, the day Matt and I said we would spend together. He understood I had to stay with Anthony for the holiday, and Anthony understood I needed to spend today with Matt, since our "trip to Texas" was ruined.

"What do you have planned for me today, awesomesauce?" Matt yells from afar as soon as I walk in.

I drop my bag full of my Christmas presents from Anthony—the jewelry, the bag, the gift certificate, and a bunch of random sweaters. Also, these great knee-high boots I coveted. I take off my hat and gloves, and throw them on Matt's favorite chair, then unzip my coat and do the same. Shivering, I find Matt in the kitchen, pouring another bowl of Lucky Charms. He's not wearing a shirt, and his bare chest always reminds me of those few times we had sex before he came to terms with his sexuality. The hair not trapped in his man bun sticks up like he just rolled out of bed. I give him a huge hug, then hand him the milk from the refrigerator.

"Did you just get up? It's almost one. And aren't you cold?"

He pours milk over his breakfast and spoons some into his mouth. "Honey, don't act like you wouldn't be sleeping now if you weren't with him. I know the real you."

Guilty. I miss sleeping until noon most days. Now I have to get up early and do yoga. Yuck.

"Yeah, yeah. Early mornings and fancy shit isn't my wheelhouse."

He eyes the bag I dropped on the floor by the door. "And that is—?"

"My new Louis Vuitton bag. And oh, look at these." I move my hair away from my ears so Matt can see the huge diamonds that have taken the place of my small gold hoops that Daddy got me. I apologize to Daddy again in my head. *I promise they're going back in as soon as I kill the asshole.*

"Daaaaamn, girl. Go get yourself some cubic zirconias and let's pawn those today," Matt says. "That guy will never know the difference."

I chuckle. "Actually, he probably would. Don't worry, you can have them once I'm done with him. Pawn away."

Matt takes another spoonful, then sets the bowl down and grabs the Louis Vuitton out of the bag and holds it up. "This is tacky as hell."

"I know. You can pawn that, but make sure you get the exact replica first."

"Don't get any scuffs on it." He gently lays it on the chair. "Seriously, love bug, what are we doing today?"

Thankfully, it isn't as cold as it's been the past couple weeks, when it hit the low twenties. Matt and I are not cold weather people. "It's going to be in the low forties. I thought maybe we could go ice skating at Rockefeller Center and then get that frozen hot chocolate at Serendipity."

He raises an eyebrow. "So, you want us to be basic bitches today?"

"Basic bitches unite."

"Can we also go to Times Square and take a picture with an M&M? Maybe hit the wax museum?"

I laugh. "We're going to be basic, not tourists." We high-five. "I'll be ready to go in twenty."

Matt salutes me with his spoon. "I'll get in the shower as soon as I'm done eating."

We have a lovely afternoon, holding hands as we ice skate. Neither of us are very good at it, and Matt only wipes out once, though he takes someone else with him. He apologizes profusely and they start to talk, and then they spark. Turns out, the guy he leveled is a tourist here from Amsterdam, and they make plans for the next day.

"Just what I wanted. No commitment," Matt says later over frozen hot chocolate. "Did you think he was hot?"

"I liked his accent," I say. "And he was tall, so that's good."

Matt is six foot two and has trouble finding people the same height, which apparently is his type.

"Hey, I want to talk to you about something," I say.

"Speak, m'lady."

Suddenly, my mouth is dry, and I clear my throat. Several times.

"You okay?" Matt asks.

I punch my chest dramatically, hoping his worry will ease the blow I'm about to deliver to him. "Yeah, I'm good. Hey, so Anthony asked me to move in." Rip off that Band-Aid.

Matt drops his spoon with a clank, and whipped cream slides down the outside of his cup. His face drops. "You're leaving me?"

I grab his hand from across the table. "This was always part of the plan, Matt. I'll still pay my half of the rent; I'm not leaving you high and dry. Wouldn't you like the privacy anyway?"

"No. I like having you there." He leans back in his chair. Farther away from me. Creating distance. "I didn't think it was going to be as much fun as it is."

"It's obviously not forever. It's temporary, remember? Maybe after I get rid of him, we can move into his Upper East Side penthouse. I'll be the grieving widow, after all."

His lip twitches, and he waves a hand in front of his face. "Nuh uh. I like it downtown. It's my vibe."

"Have you even been to the Upper East Side since we've moved here?"

He shrugs. "No need. I watched *Gossip Girl*. Headbands and pet therapists and designer shit? No thanks. I'm good."

I don't want to lose him. I need him on my side, and I hate that I'm disappointing him.

"It's almost over. I'm everything he wants me to be. He'll propose soon, I'm sure of it."

He chuckles. "You do realize that when you move in with him, this fake PJ you invented, that's the person you're going to have to be twenty-four-seven. Are you sure you're going to be able to pull that off? I'm sure it's easy two or three days a week, but you're going to *live* there." He pauses. "You're going to *become* that person."

"No way. I just want him to suffer." I think back to that conversation in the prison with Jose. "I want him to know I'm her daughter right before I pull the proverbial trigger. I'll tell him I'm Paulina Jensen and that he killed my mother, and he thought he got away with it. But it's payback time." I take a spoonful of whipped cream into my mouth and lick my lips. "I want him to know he was tricked from the second I met him."

My phone vibrates in my bag, and I hold up a finger to Matt. It's a text from Anthony.

Oh shit.

> *Hey, baby. Someone owed me a favor, and I got us a ride on a private plane to Dallas tomorrow. I know how disappointed you were not being able to see your parents for Christmas. I can't wait to meet them. We leave from Teterboro at noon.*

"Fuck!" I say, a little too loudly. The lady with the two children next to me glares at me disapprovingly. "Sorry," I mutter.

"What happened?" Matt asks.

I hand him my phone and he laughs. "Good luck with that."

My brain is working overdrive to think of who can help me. Who would lie for me. There's really only one possibility.

"Call your parents. Now."

19
KIM
NOW

Her heart officially stopped with the bang on the door. Murphy barked—he knew she didn't get visitors late at night. In fact, she hadn't even brought a date back to her place since she and Nicholas broke up.

It happened again. *Bang, bang, bang.*

Kim wished she weren't so anti-gun at that very moment. It was a little late to realize she wanted one in her hand to protect herself, and everyone knew what happened to the guy who brought a knife to a gunfight. *Bang.*

"Come on, Kim, open the door. I know you're home because I still haven't set up that Tinder account for you."

It was her friend Maddy, and she slurred her words.

Kim jumped out of bed once she realized she wasn't about to be slaughtered. Murphy looked up at her from his doggie bed but decided he was still tired and rested his head back down. He wasn't in the mood for a visitor.

Truth be told, neither was she. But at least it wasn't The Stranger coming to collect. There was safety in numbers.

Kim was already wearing comfy shorts and a tank, presentable enough for company. Not that Maddy counted as company, per se. They met when Kim first moved to New Jersey and she had a bartending job at a dive bar, Night Shift, to supplement her income before she got the gig at the country club. Maddy still worked there.

Five years younger than Kim's thirty-three years, she had that perfect skin, shiny hair, and huge tits that the men loved on the person slinging their drinks. Combined with her almost black hair and fiercely light green eyes, she'd never have to rely on Tinder.

"Come on," Maddy yelled through the door while slapping it.

"I'm coming," Kim said. She ran to the door, and checked the peephole, just in case. When she opened the door, Maddy's eyes were red, and her black eyeliner smudged far below where it should've been. Her hair was disheveled, and one side of her face was redder than the other, as if she was leaning on her palm all night.

Kim flung the door open with urgency. "Are you okay?"

Maddy looked even worse without the peephole between them. "Of course, I knew you'd be home at midnight on a Friday. And no, I'm not okay. Jordan came in tonight with someone else. Asshole."

Kim held the door open so her friend could walk in. "You know I don't go out after my shifts. And what the hell was he thinking? Didn't you only break up, like, two weeks ago?"

Maddy grabbed a napkin from a dispenser on the kitchen counter. "Fucking men." She blew her nose. "Can I sack out here on the couch tonight? He texted me five minutes ago saying he was sorry, and she didn't mean anything and blah, blah, blah. I don't want him to show up at my place. Because you know my drunk ass would let him in."

Kim was honestly thankful for the company. She retrieved her spare blanket and pillow from the hall closet and handed them to Maddy. "Do you want to talk about it or sleep on it?" she asked as she grabbed some bottled water from the refrigerator.

"Definitely sleep." Maddy grabbed the water and twisted the cap, then took a long pull. "Thanks. We can go get breakfast when we get up. We'll go to that new place that opened on Fourth and River so we can sit outside with Murphster. This one is going to need a lot of grease."

Kim nodded. "Sounds good. I have a lot to talk about too. I ran into an ex tonight as well."

She decided not to lead with PJ's death. That was a conversation for mimosas. Maddy didn't need that tonight.

"Get the fuck outta here. Okay, lets pass out ASAP." Maddy twisted herself into the blanket on the couch. Kim knew she'd be asleep before her head hit the pillow. "The sooner we sleep, the sooner we can wake up and talk about all of it. Love you."

"Love you. Let me know if you need anything." She paused. "Or hear anything, like, strange."

"Don't worry." Her voice was already fading. "Jordan doesn't know I'm here."

No, but someone knew Kim was there, and the hairs on the back of her neck stood at attention like they were trained soldiers. It still scared the living shit out of her that she didn't know what to expect.

She went back into her room and shut the door. Murphy didn't stir at all. Before she turned off the light, she opened her nightstand drawer. The five thousand in cash was still there, another down payment for the murder that never was.

She was going to be in big trouble.

20

PJ

THEN

O kay, I won't lie. Flying private is amazing.

Anthony had a car pick us up at the apartment at nine in the morning, because we were expecting the normal holiday traffic that plagued New York City between Thanksgiving and New Years. After we got through the Lincoln Tunnel, we were at Teterboro airport in less than fifteen minutes. The car drove right up to the plane, and we walked on while someone else tended to our luggage. The day before, Anthony asked me what I wanted to eat for the flight, and I asked him what the choices were. He said anything I wanted. So, I got a two-pound lobster. Yes, for lunch.

When we land, it's at Dallas Love Field, just a couple of miles from the main Dallas/Ft. Worth airport. My stomach is in knots. I'm terrified that Mr. or Mrs. Mazzucca are going to screw something up.

Matt and I had a long talk with his parents yesterday. They agreed to hide all of Matt's pictures, obviously, since I don't have a brother. There are plenty of pictures of me and Matt with his parents, so I asked them to display what they had. *Look at PJ and her cousin!* It's foolproof. I also asked them to hide all mail and every reference with their last name, since, you know, we're the Walshes. They said they'd let me lead with any stories about my childhood, and they'd stick to generic talk about anything else.

Still, it's nerve-racking. I actually love that Anthony did this for me, because it's going to be fantastic to see Mr. and Mrs. Mazzucca. If this were a real relationship, he'd be a pretty good boyfriend.

There's a car waiting to take us the seventy miles to the Mazzuccas'. We get in, and Anthony puts his hand on my knee. I jump.

"Everything okay, baby?" he asks. "You must be so excited to see them."

I swallow, even though my mouth is dry, and it feels like sludge. "I am. I can't thank you enough for doing this." I grab his hand and squeeze.

The car pulls onto the interstate, and we head west. We're mostly silent, but as we get closer, I point out a few places along the way. *This is where we all went after prom! Right down that road is the water park we all went to in the summer! I had my first kiss on the swing in that park over there!* It's all so believable, because it's true. I'm really selling it.

Anthony doesn't seem nervous, not the way a guy usually is before meeting parents. Then again, he's ancient. He's probably done this a million times. During our *getting to know you* phase, we opened up the ex files. He said his first serious relationship was in high school with a girl named Kim and that they were neighbors, so he already knew her parents. He had two other serious relationships, one with Francesca for six months when he was in his upper twenties, and another with Jessica for two years when he was in his early thirties. He said he met her parents, but he and Jessica broke up because she was pressuring him for marriage, and he wasn't ready.

Sucker. See how I don't pressure you at all?

The car turns down Hickory Lane and I want to vomit but instead bounce around in my seat like I'm excited. The car pulls into the long driveway, and I forgot how much I miss it here. Matt's parents' house is at the end of a cul-de-sac and is surrounded by trees, making it very private. It's a sturdy Tudor-style home, three bedroom, two and a half bath, and they already know to say that this is their "empty nester" house that they bought when I went away to NYU for college.

Anthony knows I grew up on a farm and then went to New York City, so the whole suburban neighborhood would've been hard to explain. It's also good that I won't have a childhood bedroom for him to see, one that has all my old CDs and posters.

When the car stops, I give him a quick kiss and dart out of the car, where Mr. and Mrs. Mazzucca are waiting at the glass door. I run up to them, making a big show of hugging and kissing them before Anthony even gets out of the car. Because, you know, I'm so excited to see *my parents*.

"Thank you so much for doing this for me," I whisper to them.

Mr. Mazzucca is a dead ringer for Matt, tall and handsome at fifty. He squeezes me back, whispering, "I can't believe I'm letting this asshole into my house."

Mrs. Mazzucca slaps him on his arm. "Just do what she and Matt asked."

She's the closest thing I have to a mother now. She's three years older than her husband and a former Texas beauty queen. It still shows, which works out for me. We can say I got my looks from her, even though I resemble neither of them. Anthony won't notice. I smile at her and give her another hug. "Thank you."

Mr. and Mrs. Mazzucca don't know I'm planning to kill him. They just think I'm tricking him to take all his money because they know he's the one who killed Mama. They didn't know her, but they certainly knew my daddy when he was alive, so they like the idea of me taking revenge.

Anthony starts to come up the paved walkway.

"Showtime," I say.

He gets to the doorway, and Mrs. Mazzucca grabs him into a hug once he's in the foyer. "Anthony, it's so wonderful to finally meet you. We've heard so much about you."

He flashes his great smile, the one that disarms everyone around him. "Thank you for having us, Mrs. Walsh." He turns to Mr. Mazzucca and shakes his hand. "Nice to meet you, Mr. Walsh."

Mr. Mazzucca takes his hand and gives it a firm shake. The driver brings the two bags to the foyer. Anthony tips him and sends him on his way, confirming a 2:00 p.m. pick-up the next day. When you're flying private, a quick overnight trip is no biggie.

"Let's get you settled in your room, and then I have a spread for us," Mrs. Mazzucca says.

Anthony grabs the bags, and we follow her upstairs into Matt's room, since they use the third bedroom as an office space. Walking in brings back all the feels from when Matt and I used to hang out there all the time. We had sex in there a few times, but mostly we were listening to CDs or playing Mario Kart.

"Thanks, Mom," I say, and I have to stifle my laughter. "We'll be down in a sec."

She nods and leaves us.

"Are you sure they don't care that we're staying in the same room? I don't want to disrespect them," Anthony says.

Isn't he just dripping with chivalry. He really would be a great boyfriend.

"Nah, they don't care. It's not like I grew up in this room and my Barbie dolls are still lying around." Matt's Barbies might be. "They know we're in a serious relationship. I'm going to tell them that I'm moving in with you soon."

"Today? God, your father is going to kill me."

No, asshole, I am.

"They'll be happy I found someone so perfect." I smile.

Over antipasto, we talk about how we met, things we do, places we go. They ask him about his work at Boswell Securities, and I chime in about how terrific his boss Ron and his wife Carla are, even though he's a porky cheating pig and she's a plastic insufferable wench. But I'm good at faking things by now. I also tell a bunch of stories about my yoga practice, crazy clients, and other funny things that happen to me at my job, all courtesy of a Reddit thread I saw. It's going really well, and I don't even feel strange calling them Mom and Dad anymore.

"So, I have something exciting to tell you guys," I say and grab Anthony's hand. "Anthony has asked me to move in with him, and I said yes."

Mr. Mazzucca drops his fork. "What about Matt?"

Mrs. Mazzucca shoots him a death glare. "Her roommate will be fine." There's an edge to her voice, and she leans on the word *roommate*. "You gave him enough notice, right?"

They still love their baby boy, and they still worry about him in New York. Now, they're going to think I'm abandoning him. They have to know I won't screw him over.

"Yes, Matt supports the decision." He doesn't really, but this isn't his plan, it's mine. "I'll still be paying my half of the rent."

"I'm planning to cover it for her," Anthony says. "I know how close she is with her roommate. I haven't met him yet though. PJ said he's embarrassed for not having a career or a nice place."

"Yes, he's the best," Mrs. Mazzucca says. I just know her tongue must be bleeding from biting it so hard. Mr. Mazzucca too.

"Anthony's place is on the Upper East Side," I say. "It has a doorman and everything. I'll be super safe there, don't worry."

"Is it safe for Matt to be alone in the area you guys live?" Mr. Mazzucca asks.

"Perfectly safe." I widen my eyes at him, signaling *please shut up*, and then laugh. "Wow, you care more about my friend than your own daughter! I promise, everything is on the up and up. Come on, Mom, let's clean up."

Mrs. Mazzucca and I clear the table. Anthony stands to help, but I assure him he's a guest and *look at how wifely I am* and make him stay with Mr. Mazzucca, which may not be the best idea. From the kitchen, I hear him ask Anthony if he likes hockey. He answers that he's a Rangers fan, and Mr. Mazzucca says he's a Dallas fan and there's an afternoon game on. They retreat to the living room, which makes me happy. If there's a hockey game on, they'll be concentrating on that and not talking.

I already feel this charade cracking. We just have to get through dinner. I asked the Mazzuccas to make a reservation at a nice steakhouse that's about twenty minutes away. Anthony wants to take them to dinner to thank them for their hospitality.

After we finish cleaning, we join them to watch the game, then Anthony and I go upstairs to get ready for dinner. He opens his bag, and there's a long box on the top.

"Oh shit. I forgot about this. It's for your parents," he says.

"What is it?" I ask.

"You'll see."

He takes my hand, and I follow him down the stairs. Mr. and Mrs. Mazzucca are watching sitcom reruns on TV when he presents Mrs. Mazzucca with the box.

"What's this?" she asks.

"Just a little something for you guys for being so welcoming. Merry Christmas."

She looks at Mr. Mazzucca, who raises his eyebrows. She opens the box, and it's a custom wood carving, spelling out "The Walshes." On the bottom of the stand, there's a number carved into it.

"It's for your mantle," he says. "That right there"—he points to the numbers on the bottom—"that's the latitude and longitude of your town."

Well, that's thoughtful. He must've had it commissioned last month when I told him we were coming out here for Christmas, but this thing is completely useless. The Walshes don't even exist. They're the Mazzuccas and I'm Paulina Jensen.

"How lovely. Thank you, Anthony," Mrs. Mazzucca says. "You didn't have to do this."

She's got to be thinking the same thing I am, about how useless it is. But it doesn't matter that the carving's a complete and total waste of money. He has more money than God, soon to be all mine.

Dinner goes well. No more gaffes, and Anthony doesn't ask any more questions about Matt. Which is perfect, actually, because on the way home, Matt texts me.

How's it going, SISTERSAUCE?

I hold back my laughter and answer him immediately. *Perfect. This guy is an idiot, BROTHERSAUCE.*

I'm triumphant as we get back to the Mazzuccas' house. We pass on another coffee and decide to retire, since Anthony had planned a big brunch before we leave. It's near Love Field in the heart of Dallas, and he'll have the car take us to the airport after and then take "my parents" back home. When we get into bed (door open), he snuggles behind me and kisses my shoulder.

"Your parents are great."

"I know. I'm lucky." I'm so, so lucky that they did this for me.

"It's nice out here. Quiet. Maybe one day we can get a little place out here so we can see them more often. I don't want you to feel like moving forward with me will ever keep you from your family."

I turn over and look at him, and his eyes are pleading. Soft. Sincere.

Beautiful.

I never really noticed his eyes before.

"Thank you," I say. I kiss him and turn back over and sigh.

He really would be a great boyfriend.

21

KIM
NOW

After reliving the past night's death trauma at brunch with Maddy and Murphy, Kim went back to her apartment to hang with the dog for a little while. She let him get comfy on his favorite spot on the couch, his head on her lap, and even pulled a blanket over him despite the outside heat. The air conditioner from the living room window was set on medium, which was just enough chill that a little blanket wouldn't set you on fire. Murphy seemed to love it, snuggling even closer to her as if he wanted inside her clothes.

She kissed him on the head as she flipped through the channels, looking for bad '90s movies to watch to pass the day away. She'd promised Maddy she'd meet her out later for dinner and a couple drinks to distract her from Jordan, so for now, she just wanted to chill. She found *Beaches*. It would do; she could use a good cry.

Except that Tony's phone number was burned in Kim's brain from the night before, and she didn't know how to handle the situation as presently set. She couldn't tell him she was tasked to kill him, even if it shed light on someone who'd be after both of them. Someone killed PJ and it was very real.

Should she call him? This wasn't an etiquette question you might read about in *Cosmopolitan*. Headlines rarely said, "Tasked by a stranger to murder your ex? Five tips on how to get through it." She thought a text was impractical and impersonal, yet a phone call was too intimate. Who was she to call him less than twenty-four hours after his fiancée died? And it was done in her place of business, no less. There was no protocol for this.

She decided on a text. That could be misinterpreted easily but explained away as "it didn't translate over text," so she went for it.

Hey, Tony, it's Kim. I'm so, so, so sorry—

Nope. She deleted the extra *so*'s because my God, what overkill.

Hey, Tony, it's Kim. I'm so sorry about last night. I got your number from the computer; I hope that's okay. I'm here if you need someone to talk to. Again, I'm sorry.

Should she end it with *xoxox?* No, she decided against that and hesitated before her thumb smacked down on her screen to send the text. *Screw it.* She settled down farther into the couch to waste away the afternoon with Murphy.

Kim petted his curly head, then maneuvered onto her left side. Murphy squished into her back, and her hand traveled down the right side of his body, up again, down again. Every time she got near his head, she kissed him right near his ears.

"I'm sorry. I love you. I'm going to fix you," she whispered to him.

No matter what it took.

Five minutes later, her text went off, and Tony's name popped up. It took her by surprise, and when she opened the text, it said: *Thanks for this. I'm still numb. I'm at our summer house not too far from the club. If you want to come by, I could use the company. I still can't believe any of it.*

Kim bit her lip. How would it look if she showed up at Tony's house, the house he shared with PJ, mere hours after PJ was killed? Again, *Cosmo* didn't give protocol for these situations. It wasn't like she had a sexual interest in Tony, not anymore—that part of her life was over. But to any outsider, she was the ex who showed up at his house after his fiancée was murdered at her workplace. Optics could be cruel.

And the police were probably watching.

Still, it wasn't like Ron or Cunty Carla gave a damn about him. They were getting divorced anyway. Tony barely knew the Xiangs and the Hernandezes. His family was back in Brooklyn. Actually, she had no idea about that. Where was his family now that he had money? Did he set them up somewhere else? It was sobering to realize that her Tony, her old love, was a complete stranger.

The Stranger.

Kim didn't know when she was going to have to pay them back. The last contact she'd had with The Stranger was a couple days ago, when she picked up the pill of powder and the vial of sweet liquid and was ordered to destroy the phone.

Better to get out of the house. She texted Tony back.

What's your address?

An hour later, Kim pulled into his driveway. He was ten minutes away from her apartment but on the other side of town. "Across the tracks," if you will. The haves versus the have-nots. His house was a classic beach style for the Jersey shore, light blue with white trim and paved walkways. It was across the street from the beach, and as she got out of her car and craned her neck, she was able to make out the rooftop lounge area. She pictured Tony and PJ sipping coffee, watching the sunrise, or sipping cocktails, watching the sunset. What a nice little life he'd made for himself.

Except for the enemies he'd made. The ones that got his fiancée killed, and the ones that almost got him killed.

She rang the bell, and Tony opened the door. His hair was sticking up like he'd just woken from a nap. He wore sweatpants and a New York Rangers T-shirt, and he held the door open for her to come in.

The first thing she noticed was the wall of windows at the back of the house, at the end of the kitchen, looking over the pool. The ceilings were high, and a curved staircase led to the second floor. The décor was beachy, with pictures of sand, sunsets, and dolphins. But it was tasteful, not tacky. Something you'd see in a magazine, where the look was perfect but something you'd never be able to replicate.

"Nice place," Kim said as he led her to the kitchen.

To the right was a dining area with wainscotting, and to the left was a living room. Both had pale blue walls with white crown molding. The living area had white furniture with beige throw pillows, and the pictures on the wall were large renditions of aquatic life. More dolphins, but also manatees, whales, and stingrays. An obligatory navy-colored anchor-shaped clock hung above a fireplace.

Tony pulled out a stool at the kitchen counter, and Kim sat down. Tony sat next to her in silence.

"Are your parents or Maria coming down?" Kim asked.

He shook his head. "I've had a hard time with them. They thought PJ was a gold digger, and they never accepted our relationship. I didn't even let them meet her until after she moved in, but they were so cruel to her. Maria called me a poseur; told me I 'went Hollywood' because I didn't come back to the neighborhood. Did you know she married Vincent Colletta? My mother purposely destroyed PJ's—ugh. I don't want to talk about it. Forget it. Anyway, I haven't spoken to any of them in over four months, so they don't know." He swallowed. "They'd honestly all be happy that she died." He choked on the last words.

Wow. Maria and Kim were tight back in the day, when everything about her was so different. After Kim left for the West Coast, she didn't want any part of the old drama and unfollowed all of them on Facebook. And she never seriously thought of searching for her old friends once the rest of social media started taking over.

Still, Kim couldn't believe Maria married Vincent—her old boyfriend's best friend. Maria was tough to deal with back then. She'd stalk her boyfriend's ex-girlfriends and try to start fistfights with them all the time. Kim couldn't imagine the drama that went down in the neighborhood when Maria hooked up with Vincent.

It made Kim wonder if his family had anything to do with PJ's death. Tony specifically said they didn't like her. In fact, he said they'd be "happy" if she died. And with Maria always acting like a thug, Kim certainly didn't put it past her to take someone out for messing with her family.

People in the old hood held grudges for years over disrespect, but she didn't think they'd ever hurt Tony. She doubted someone in the neighborhood would want both Tony and PJ dead on the same night, or if these old acquaintances even had any idea where he was.

Unless his parents or Maria let the cat out of the bag on his whereabouts after meeting PJ. Tony *did* have some enemies back then. It made sense that Jose Sanchez, from his jail cell, could've been masterminding this with his friends on the outside.

"Do you talk to anyone else from back home?" she asked. If The Stranger was someone from back home, she wanted to know what she was dealing with. *Who* she was dealing with.

"Nope." He looked around the space surrounding them. "It feels so empty here without her. We just closed on this place right after we got engaged. It was going to be our summer home. She was in the middle of decorating." His eyes misted over. "I don't know what to do with all her stuff upstairs. Or worse, at home in the city. I can't—I just can't—"

He placed his head in his hands and wept. Kim, used to making herself at home where Tony lived, stood and went to the other side of the counter and opened the refrigerator. Thankfully, he had bottles of water in there, and she grabbed two and took them back to the counter.

"When are you going back to the city?"

"I don't know. I want to wait until after the autopsy, which they said should be complete tomorrow. God, they're going to have to cut her open. I've seen those cop dramas and hospital dramas on TV." He choked back another sob. "I know what they're going to do to her. They're going to gut her like a fish."

He cried again. Kim touched his arm out of habit.

"I'm so sorry." She swallowed, but she had to fish for information. It could save her own life. "Do you think anyone would want her killed? Did you have any enemies that wanted to see you hurt?" Or dead. "Was anything going on at work? That was some show with Ron and Carla last night."

He looked at her with surprised eyes. "You think this was on purpose? They said it was probably an allergy."

So naïve, but she'd let him think that. It kept her safe. "I don't know why I said that. I'm sorry."

Tony sighed. "Ron's been all over the place. I knew he'd filed for divorce, but they were playing some charade. I have no idea why. He was messing around with someone else and just trying to appease Carla until the papers were final." He closed his eyes for a minute and scrunched his face up for a millisecond that only Kim would notice. He'd just recalled a bad memory. "Ron and Carla wouldn't do this to me. Especially Carla. I think she has some sort of crush on me. She made passes at me all the time. It was kind of uncomfortable."

Kim's eyes widened. "Did you tell Ron?"

He shook his head.

Maybe Carla wanted PJ dead. But did Ron find out something else that would make him want to take care of Tony? Maybe it was a husband/wife one-two punch. One last thing to do together before they split up.

Kim didn't stay long, but she assured Tony she'd be there for him. He promised to keep her posted. On her drive home, she wondered what it was going to be like with Tony back in her life. Would he be though? They'd reconnected over the worst of situations, so seeing Kim might be a trigger for him later. She wasn't going to push it either way. He had trauma to deal with first.

Kim parked the car and walked to her apartment to nap before dinner with Maddy.

No such luck for a rest. There was a manila envelope in front of her door.

22
PJ
THEN

Matt is upset with me for leaving our apartment, even though it was my plan to move in with Anthony. Soon, it will be back to business as usual. Roomies until one of us settles down for real.

I don't have much stuff here, and it all fits into two wardrobe boxes and six medium-sized boxes I bought from U-Haul. I didn't even need to hire movers; Anthony sent someone with a truck to pick it up and take it to his place. The two men hauled it all away, and now it's just me and Matt and none of my stuff surrounding us. The place looks so big without little ole me.

I'm only leaving two things here. The first is a small stuffed bear that Matt won for me at the county fair when we were dating in high school. The other is a picture—it's a selfie I snapped of us right after we graduated, and despite Matt being the one with the talent, it's my favorite picture of us and he knows it. I had it printed and blown up into an eight by ten, and I even bought a glass frame and hung it up on the wall, like I'm Mr. Fix It. This is where it belongs. I still have the digital copy to look at whenever I want.

He's eating another bowl of cereal, even though he knows I'm taking him to lunch in an hour. I got us reservations at a very-hard-to-get-into brunch place on the Lower East Side. This one has velvet ropes and a DJ and transitions easily from bottomless mimosas to dancing on leather banquettes with sweaty strangers. Matt's favorite.

"Don't fill up on Lucky Charms," I say. "You know we have a big day ahead of us."

"Yep. Got it."

He's been short with me this week. I told him Anthony wants to meet him, and he refuses. Matt seems to think I'm getting soft for Anthony and that I actually *want* to live with him and play girlfriend. I don't. It's a means to an end.

I shower and pull on jeans and a tight, low cut sweater that I kept from the movers. I have a separate set of toiletries at Anthony's place, so at least my shower gel was here, as are my moisturizers and eye creams and body butters. Matt doesn't like flowery or fruity smelling things, so if I was stuck using his body wash or his generic Walgreens moisturizer, I'd be itchy all day. Pair it with the outside cold, and I'd look like a lizard.

From my messenger bag, I pull out my notebook, the one thing I absolutely couldn't send with the movers—this can't fall into the wrong hands. I'll hide it when I get to Anthony's place, because God forbid he sees it. I crane my neck to the bathroom, and I hear the shower running. Matt will be ready to go in about fifteen minutes, which gives me time to look it over again. He's the only one who's seen it, and he even helped me with some parts.

Phase One has pictures of Anthony from when he did interviews on television regarding investments. I'd grabbed them from social media. Underneath, I listed all the facts I could find out about him. His real name, his likes and interests, that kind of stuff.

Phase Two has a couple of selfies of us that I took, with big hearts I drew around them in the pages. That was the *I love you* accomplishment. Yeah, he loves me all right. I stare at one of the pictures. I see it in his eyes, how he's looking at me, and I notice my dead eyes back at him. He's a target, nothing more, nothing less.

Phase Three has pictures of his apartment building and pictures of the inside. What will soon be *my* closet and *my* bedroom and *my* view. I detail how I'm going to live there, maybe with someone I actually love.

Turning the page to Phase Four, I already have pictures in there of my dream engagement ring. I'm sure Anthony will ask me what I like—he's a good boyfriend like that—and I casually slide my fingers over the images. I want an oval, because that's the same one Mama had. Of course, mine will be ten times the size, but I want the same one she had, one that was ripped off her finger after she was shot. It was never recovered; probably went straight to a pawn shop.

I wonder how Anthony is going to feel sliding it onto my finger knowing how he tore the a similar one off someone else's.

My Phase Five pages are filled with images of legal documents, last will and testament, living wills, proxy medical stuff—nothing I really understand, but that's why I'm going to get a good lawyer as well. I've written out exactly what I want to be included in and how I'm going to get it done.

I turn the page to Phase Six, filled with wedding dresses, wedding cakes, and flower choices, listing all the things I want to see at my fake wedding. Getting married is going to be so fun!

Then Phase Seven.

Dead.

I found a book that's primarily for writers about which poisons to use in their fake deaths. What a treasure trove of information! It tells you not only what to mix them with, but how long they'll take until they act, plus what the effects will be and where to get them. Anyone who wants to murder someone has an entire universe of knowledge in that book.

I took pictures of a few of the pages—no sense in getting caught with the book, you know, just in case—and have them listed here. I picked ten that were fast acting, twenty minutes or so, and wrote next to each how to administer them and what the side effects are. Strychnine sounds gnarly, but it's too cruel, even for him—I even write that next to it. It seems a good dose of arsenic is fast acting, as is simple antifreeze. The best part is, the arsenic won't show up in an autopsy unless they're truly looking for it, and the antifreeze will evaporate from his system in hours, before an autopsy is performed.

On other pages, I have pictures of private boats that we can take on our honeymoon. I can dose him and push him overboard. Or I can slow dose him with something else and then stick his head in a bucket of water to drown him. Tie his dumb ass up to one of those donut life savers and dip him in the ocean. I'll jump in for a second too, just to get wet and look like I tried to save him, then get out and call for the Coast Guard. *I tried everything when he fell over, but he drowned! I even got him the donut! I thought I saved him, but the water was so rough . . . Oh my God, not on our honeymoon!*

Wah, wah, wah.

Matt, with his false ID, will bear witness. *Oh no, I saw the whole thing, she tried and tried and tried to revive him!*

The only reason I'm going through with the wedding is because if I kill him right after he changes the will, well, come on now. I'll go to jail for killing him no matter how careful I am. The investigation would center on me and me alone.

"Five minutes," Matt says.

I snap the book shut and tuck it back into my bag, then give myself a final once-over before we leave.

The brunch place is alive. There are people everywhere, and it's standing room only as bodies mush between tables. I got us a reservation at the bar instead of a table, but now people are crowding us, shouting their drink orders next to our faces, and bumping us handing over their credit cards and cash. We finish eating right before the DJ starts, and everyone looks at us like we're about to get up. Nope. We got prime real estate and we're not moving.

"I think I'm going to bleach my hair," Matt says.

I nearly spit out my martini. "What? Why?"

He nods to the music as he looks around. "Time for a change. You're moving on with your life, maybe I should too."

I grab his arm. "Come on, Matt. Once we're engaged, I'll push for a fast wedding. I'll do it on the honeymoon." My eyes mist over. I hope Mama understands, wherever she is, that I'm doing this for her. And Daddy, because he was never the same after she died. "Then life is back to normal."

"What's normal anymore?" He sips his Cosmo.

"We'll have his money. We can do anything. Stay here, start over somewhere else. Even go back home."

"I have plenty of money. I've been selling all that expensive shit he gives you. I was right, he's too stupid to notice the fakes. I can't believe he thinks he bought you that piece of shit Louis Vuitton I got on Canal Street for fifty bucks."

I laugh. It's true, and Anthony constantly showers me with things I never ask for.

"You know I'm still going to see you all the time. Are you sure you don't want to meet him?"

He scoffs. "After what he said about me not having my shit together? Fuck no. That asshole thinks he's better than me. Go live your fantasy life and leave me out of it."

"Matt, you're still with me, right?" I worry he's faltering from the plan. "You're supposed to be my witness. If I charter a boat and push him off, you happened to be in a nearby boat and saw me struggling. If I poison him, you watch me try to revive him. If I stab him, which I won't because that's disgusting, you know it was self-defense because I've been telling you about physical abuse from the beginning. You have to promise you'll be there for me."

He pulls the joint he has tucked behind his ear and rolls it between his fingers, then puts it back and nods. "I will. I love you, awesomesauce."

"I love you too." I smile. "I'll even bleach your hair for you."

"Girl, no. You know how I get. That needs to be done by a professional."

We finally decide to get up and dance. He doesn't even leave me when a really hot guy tries to pick him up. It's the last day, the last hour, the last minutes of us being roomies. For now. We both know I have to leave soon and go sleep in my new apartment.

The goodbye is quick. A *see you later*, as Matt puts it. He's right though. I have dinner plans with him in two days.

I get in a cab and go to my Upper East Side palace. Once there, I use my new fob to enter the building and wave to George, my new doorman. I press the button in my new elevator to take me to my new apartment. When I use my new key and open my new door, I see Anthony has covered the entire floor with rose petals. There's a bottle of champagne and two glasses on the table.

"Welcome home, baby," he says and walks over and gives me the biggest bear hug and kisses my forehead. "I'm so happy you're here."

He'd really make a great boyfriend.

23

KIM
NOW

Kim shuddered while staring at the manila envelope at the door. Of course, she looked around to see if anyone was watching her. She'd done that more in the past week than any other time in her life. She got that unsettled feeling, the one you got when there was a cop behind you, even though you'd done nothing wrong.

But she had done wrong.

With her keys positioned as weapons between her fingers, she headed to the door, even though she was certain she wouldn't be attacked in broad daylight. When the keys jingled in the lock, Murphy barked.

"I'm coming sweet boy," she whispered.

She kicked the envelope into her foyer, and it made a thudding noise as it did cartwheels down the front hall. *Another burner*, she thought.

Murphy jumped onto her, looking up at her with his sweet dark eyes. The weight of her decision crushed her. She was going to have to give all the money back, and it was poor, sweet Murphy who was going to pay with his life.

She knelt down to his level and hugged him. "I'm sorry, baby. I promise Mommy will figure something out."

How did she get here in her life? Thirty-three, single, and her best friend was a dog who was going to die because she didn't have any savings. She'd tried like hell to hustle more freelance work. To be honest, she was bored most days. She'd begged for more shifts at the club, but all they had for her was Wednesdays, Thursdays, and Fridays.

With little social life, everyone who worked there knew Kim was the go-to girl if someone wanted a night off. She'd pick up anyone's shift, but for some reason, everyone had been so damn responsible lately. She'd been sure once the summer hit, a lot of the younger staff would rather be out partying on a Saturday night instead of serving a bunch of uptight rich folk. No such luck.

Kim stared at the envelope and then ripped it open. She was correct—it was another burner. Setting it on the counter, she didn't know how long she had until the phone rang, or what her punishment would be. She had a sudden urge to drive to Brooklyn, to the old neighborhood. She never asked her parents for a loan for Murphy because she knew they didn't have it, and she hadn't seen or spoken to them since she went up to visit for Easter, so it would be a little presumptuous.

At least Tony made something of himself. Seeing his reaction to PJ's death was something she'd imagine from the leading man in a romance movie. This Tony wasn't familiar to her anymore. Tony, with his millions of dollars and his New York City place and his spectacular beach house.

Poor PJ. Kim still couldn't get the image of her dead contorted body out of her mind.

She couldn't ask Tony for a loan, could she? That would get her out of trouble. She could pay back The Stranger and still get Murphy fixed. She was sure he'd loan it to her. The timing was just awful . . .

Nope.

Kim made some iced tea and sat on the couch to flip through Netflix before she had to get ready for dinner with Maddy. Surely it was okay if she left the house and didn't answer the phone if it—

Ring.

Fuck.

She had to answer it. Time to face the music. She thought for a second about being combative when she picked up, but she was afraid The Stranger was at her door, ready to pounce. She went with old faithful.

"Hello?" Like she didn't know who it was. Burners didn't show up on people's doorsteps randomly. Well, except for that first time. Look how that turned out.

"Kim," the electronic voice said.

She waited for her berating, for them to tell her in detail how she was going to be killed, with pain. It felt like an hour passed before they spoke again.

"How did it go? I assume the job is done?"

Kim put her hand over her mouth so she wouldn't scream—at that point she could've screamed from fear or excitement.

The Stranger didn't know she'd failed at the task. They didn't know Tony was still alive.

This was a test. Now what? Did she lie to them? No, that wouldn't fly when she got caught. And she knew she would eventually. She looked at Murphy and decided to buy time.

"I didn't do it. Not yet," she added quickly. "Something else happened that interrupted me."

The silence was deafening. She looked at her front door, waiting for someone to bust in, guns blazing. Until it occurred to her that The Stranger wasn't here. Not right now. They dropped the envelope with the burner and left. Or better yet, paid a delivery service to do it. Maybe she was never in danger the way she thought she was. If they were here, they would've known what happened last night—that only one of them was dead. That only one person they tasked to murder an innocent person was able to do it right.

"What happened?" the voice asked. "You were paid to do a job, and to do it last night."

Kim began to panic—she knew it was time sensitive. "I know. And I will. Next week, I promise." Kim had no idea if Tony would be there next week after PJ's death. And she wasn't going to do it anyway, but she needed time to figure out the situation. But The Stranger had to believe that she would. "Someone else was killed at the club last night, and there was mass chaos. His fiancée, PJ, died."

Silence.

"Did you arrange that too?" Kim held her breath. "Why did you want them both killed?" She released her breath and gulped. "What did they do to you?"

Click.

The line went dead.

24
PJ
THEN

Anthony is being really sweet, holding my hand and caressing my arm in the town car that is taking us to his parents' place in Brooklyn. I'm "meet the family" status. I've only lived with him for a few weeks, but it's been great. I'm playing wifey material perfectly, assuring him I don't have to go to fancy restaurants every night and instead cooking him dinner. Thankfully, Daddy was a good cook, and it was something we used to do together while I grew up motherless.

Daddy's favorite to cook was pasta e fagioli, which he called *pasta vra zhool*, which is really the only Italian he knew besides *ciao*. He made it in the colder months and always said it was a good dish to stick to your ribs, meaning it would warm me up from the inside out. It always did. He sauteed the little tube-shaped pasta with the bacon, beans, and onions and let it sit for hours. It was super thick and delicious. I remembered his recipe to a T. I made it for Anthony one night, and he said it was the best he'd ever had and that his whole family was Italian, so it was a huge compliment.

Anyway, I made a fresh batch to bring to his mother, because that's what nice people who are meeting the family for the first time do. Homemade is always more thoughtful than store bought, and getting the Italian mother to like me has got to be the last step before he proposes. Anthony knew how hard I worked on the meal and how much it meant to me to bring Daddy's recipe to his family—even though he thinks my daddy is Mr. Mazzucca.

The car pulls up to a house in a neighborhood called Sheepshead Bay. The house, like the others, is modest, brick, and two floors with a porch. All the houses are too close to the ones on either side. I can't imagine growing up in a place like this, especially since my childhood home was on over a hundred acres. The thought of being right on top of your neighbor and having everyone know all your comings and goings is claustrophobic.

I grab the ceramic Le Creuset baking dish that I bought for the pasta e fagioli. I planned to leave it with his mother as a gift. That shit is expensive. Almost a hundred and fifty bucks for a place to keep leftovers? I'm used to the plastic Rubbermaid ones with the red tops you get in the grocery store. Five of them for six bucks. Done.

We're only here for dinner, so the car is going to wait outside. Anthony has his arm around me as we walk to the door. We stop on the porch, and he pauses.

"I don't know if I should ring the bell or walk in." He laughs. "Screw it, I always used to walk in before." He pulls the screen open and then opens the door. We're in a little vestibule that has another door, which opens to the main living area. "We're here!" He gives my shoulders a good squeeze and kisses my temple. "I love you."

"Love you too." I've been on autopilot saying it back.

The house looks like it's been updated inside. The floors are hardwood, and to the right, there's a fireplace and a bar setup, with two semicircular off-white couches facing each other and a cocktail table in the middle. A huge screen TV is mounted on the wall to the left. Farther in, there's a dining room table that could rival Ron and Carla's, with seats for twelve people. It's not as nice as theirs though. This one is heavy. Ornate. Tacky. The kitchen is in the back of the house, and that's where the noise is coming from.

A woman emerges. She looks like she's in her early thirties, so this must be his sister Maria. Her eyes and her curly hair are dark like Anthony's. She's petite, wearing jeans, knee-high boots, and a red turtleneck. I can see the layers of heavy Kardashian-style makeup from the front room.

"Tony," she says, then looks back into the kitchen. "They're here."

The talking stops, and then everyone else pours into the dining room. Another man around Maria's age comes out. He's in jeans and a New York Giants sweatshirt that's either too small or he doesn't skip many meals.

Anthony's father is tall like him, with hair that's more salt than pepper. His mother looks like an older version of Maria, except her hair is a bit frizzier and harshly box dyed, and she has a sauce-stained apron wrapped around her waist.

They all stare at me with raised eyebrows and pursed lips, and I shrink.

"Hey, Mom, Dad, Maria, Vincent—this is Poppy Jade. PJ. My girlfriend," Anthony says as we take off our coats and hang them on the hooks by the door.

There's a round of *heys* and head nods, and then they converge around Anthony for hugs, blowing right past me. He shakes hands with his father and Vincent, and his mother gets to him first for hugs.

"How's my baby boy?" She reaches up and grabs his face. "Look at you, still all cleaned up." It's not said with love or admiration. Why does she look so disappointed that her son is wearing a button-down shirt? Her head swivels in my direction. I smile as she looks me up and down. "More Hollywood, I see."

Was that an eye roll? Fuck you, lady. Now I want to kill him just to make you blubber like an idiot. I stick the dish out to her in a friendly manner rather than dumping it over her head.

"Nice to meet you. I brought some homemade pasta e fagioli for you." I even say it the way Daddy did.

"Mmm. Tony tells us you're Irish and German. But I'm sure it's wonderful anyway. Call me Theresa." She smirks as she hands the dish to Maria. "Put this on the counter."

"Yep. Be right back," Maria says and leaves without saying a word to me.

"Hello, PJ. Call me Frank." Anthony's father looks back at his son. "So, come on in." He sits on the couch and picks up the remote. "NFL playoffs are on."

That's it. That's all I get from him. His name.

"Yes, come with me," his mother says. "We'll get the boys some snacks and drinks."

I'm no goddamn man-maid, but I smile as she links arms with me. Vincent and Anthony join his father on the couch so they can get lost in pigskin world. After he's seated, Anthony looks at me and winks. I blow a kiss back at him because I have to.

In the kitchen, my dish is tucked into a back corner of the counter, under the cabinets. Jesus, why didn't she just cover it with a towel? *Be gone, Devil Dish from the Irish and German girl!* There's a big pot of water boiling, and another large pot next to it, covered with sauce splashes. Good ole Sunday dinner in Brooklyn. Maria is flipping through a magazine. When I walk in, she doesn't even look up, but she talks.

"So, how did you two meet?" She turns a page, reading *Us Weekly* reality TV bullshit.

"Last summer at NYU when he was giving a talk on investments. I had just graduated—"

"Clearly." She flips another page. The mother smirks again.

I don't care about these people. This relationship isn't real, but come on, what's with all the hate? Still, I stammer. Why do I care if they hate me?

"I—I'd just graduated." I blink and shake my head, losing my train of thought. "Anthony was giving a speech and—"

"Right. *Anthony.*"

Ooof. "Yeah. Anthony. I—we hit it off. I guess you can say the rest is history."

"Quite the upgrade moving in with him, huh?"

"I—I—" I don't even know what to say to that. "I'm used to having a roommate, I guess."

"Nice purse." Maria nods toward the knockoff Louis Vuitton bag that Matt gave me in place of the real, pawned one. Of course, she thinks it's the real thing. She doesn't live this lifestyle.

"Thank you. It was a Christmas gift."

"Must be nice."

Never in my life did I want to watch a football game more than I do at this moment. I glance toward the living room, but the couch isn't visible from where I am. Anthony can't see me beckoning to him. Why I'm even doing that, I have no idea.

"Grab those bowls." Theresa points to two orange plastic bowls on the small table in the corner. They're older than I am. I do as she says and bring them to her. She pours peanuts into one bowl and chips into another, then jams them back at me without a look. "Go give these to the boys."

I want to tell her that no, I'm not her little bitch to dump on for the day, but I still want them to see me as acceptable. So, I take the tray to her two fucking man-children—her husband and her son-in-law, because Anthony is better than them—with a smile.

"How's it going?" Anthony whispers.

"It's fine." My voice wavers. *Ugh. Why?!*

When I get back to the kitchen, there are three beers opened on the counter. His mother nods toward them. "You forgot those."

My first instinct is to grab one upside down by its neck and pour it all over her. "No problem, Theresa." Sweet as honey.

I take all three and go back to the living room and place them on the table. Frank and Vincent don't look up as they grab them and sip. No *thank you*, no nothing. Anthony grabs my hand.

"Thank you, baby." When he glances my way, he notices the tears in my eyes, the ones I've been trying not to let surface, but damn it, this is harder than I thought. "You okay?" he mouths without a sound.

I blink them away and nod, then turn around and go back to the kitchen for the rest of the torture.

It's my job to set the table, cut the bread, separate the sausage from the meatballs and the ribs, put them all in separate bowls, toss the salad, grab the wine from the rack—two reds on each side of the table because "real Italians don't drink white on Sundays," whatever that means. Two Chiantis and two Cabernets bookend the food spread in the middle. When it's time to eat, Theresa and Frank take a head spot each while Anthony and I sit across from Maria and Vincent. I say my usual quick prayer in my head and pick up my fork.

"We say *grace*, here," Theresa shakes her head.

"Hey. Stop it," Anthony's voice has an obvious edge, like he's speaking through clenched teeth.

Thank you. My heart jumps at his defense of me, and that shocks me.

After joining in on their prayer, I wait until everyone else has picked up their utensils before I dare make that mistake again. The conversation is like Anthony and me aren't even present. It's all about Maria's job teaching English for high school freshmen, Vincent's job at the utility company, how they've decided that the time is right for kids, Theresa's book club and bridge games, and Frank's nights playing competitive darts at the bar a couple blocks away.

They never ask me about myself, but they certainly make assumptions. When Maria talks about her teaching job, she always casually looks over at me and says *you remember, right? Freshman year hasn't been so long for you.* When Vincent talks about his job, he makes sure to look at me when he says he's got to *keep the internet running for people who twerk on TikTok.*

Theresa makes sure to roll her eyes and nod her head when talking about her book club and her card games because *young people don't do either anymore,* and Frank asks if I play darts *like all the kids do.* Anthony senses the same thing, the complete discomfort they're causing me. He rubs my leg affectionately under the table to soothe me.

When dinner is finished, Theresa says, "Oh, we didn't heat up that stuff you brought. Let me get it."

That *stuff.*

It's the first time I feel like a part of anything in this household. I'm surprised she doesn't say it's past my bedtime. Theresa leaves, and thirty seconds later, there's a crash and everything stops. Then we all rush into the kitchen.

My pasta e fagioli is all over the floor, and the Le Creuset baking dish and cover is in pieces.

"Sorry. It slipped," Theresa says flippantly.

Look, this is all fake to me, but I want to cry. I have no idea why this scene is affecting me the way it is. The mess is in the middle of the kitchen, so I really doubt it "slipped" off anything. Did she really come in here and slam it on the floor? Why does she hate me that much?

Flabbergasted, I stare at my hard work. There it is, Daddy's recipe, as garbage on the floor. It's insulting to Daddy, and I can't take it anymore. I don't know why it happens, but I break down. I actually start to cry, and I mean every tear that slips down my cheeks.

"Damn it, Mom. Did you do that on purpose?" Anthony asks.

"Of course not, *Anthony.*"

She did. She threw it on the ground like trash.

"Apologize to my girlfriend. Now." His voice is stern. He sensed my unease earlier and now he isn't messing around.

Theresa stares at him without a word. No one says anything. They're all against me.

Anthony turns to me. "Get your coat. Go wait in the car. I'll be right out."

I do exactly as he says and leave the kitchen without uttering a word to any of them. As I'm closing the door, I hear him rattling off at them. Defending me. Telling them that I'm everything to him, that he loves me and I'm his whole world, and he will not allow me to be disrespected that way, and that they shouldn't expect to hear from him until they all apologize to me.

He's fuming as he gets in the back of the car. As much as I see the anger—the clenched jaw, the fire in his eyes—he's nothing but soft with me. He lifts my chin. "I'm sorry about that. It won't happen again." He kisses my lips.

I open my mouth and kiss him back, grabbing the back of his neck. I want to. It's been a long time since anyone defended my honor. I dated in college, sure, but nothing was ever serious because I was always so worried about Daddy and his health. This feels like what I always imagined a real adult relationship would be.

It feels real.

"Thank you," I say.

"I won't let anyone treat you that way. Not my family. Not anyone."

His arm is around me, and I lean my head on his shoulder. "I love you."

For the first time, I say it before he does, and I try like hell to squash down the feeling that I really mean it.

I fail.

25

KIM
NOW

Two days have passed since Kim last heard from The Stranger. She didn't know what to make of it, and she was still scared all the time. She jumped at every shadow; she shuddered at every noise. Even her alarm clock terrified her. Sleep hadn't come easy, but the nightmares were the worst. Her mind was locked in a jail cell, on death row, where she sat and waited to be executed. She wouldn't even know which one would be her last meal, so she'd savored them all. Just in case.

She thought back to how it all went down. How she agreed to do it and how she got her hands on the poisons. In retrospect, whoever thought of it had a foolproof plan.

Kim had gotten a call from The Stranger every day after their first contact. Every day, there was a different burner at her door, and she'd always been instructed to destroy the previous one. Each time, she went as far as to drive two or three towns away to drop it in someone's recycling can, or off a bridge, or in a public garbage can on the street. She never wanted to answer the new phone, but she felt compelled to do it. And truthfully, though she hated to admit it, she had begun to mull The Stranger's proposition over.

It all came down to Murphy. The day she had planned to tell The Stranger to find someone else to do their bidding, Murphy had another seizure. That one lasted for over five minutes while Kim cried, holding his furry body tightly so he wouldn't hurt himself. It was almost like he was begging her, his soft brown eyes fixated on hers, saying *Mommy, please, please help me. Do whatever you have to do, I don't want to die.* When he came out of it, he curled his entire body onto her lap and placed his head on her shoulder, breathing quickly with relief. She hugged him and rocked him, and he looked at her with such love, such devotion and loyalty, that she'd decided she had to do whatever it took to keep him alive.

The next call, she just said, "Okay." The Stanger replied, "Await further instructions."

Two more days went by in agonizing silence. It was the day before PJ's murder when another burner was delivered. When it rang, she was told to go to a local chain pharmacy. In the candy aisle, she was instructed to go find the bags of mini Snickers. In the back, underneath all of them, there would be a plastic grocery bag that she was to take with her. Then she had to buy something from the pharmacy—anything—so it looked like she'd been a regular girl running daily errands.

It was all public. No dark meetings on a park bench, no fishing paper bags out of abandoned garbage cans.

With her reusable tote on her shoulder, she followed the instructions. Apprehensive, she grabbed a small plastic basket by the handles and filled it with a nail polish, Windex, and Dove Body Wash. Her mouth was dry as she searched for the candy, and she could barely swallow. When she got to that aisle—aisle twelve, she'd never forget—no one was in there.

She tried to look like she was doing nothing wrong, she was just grabbing a snack. People did it every day. In front of the Snickers, she paused. Her hands tingled. Everything was going in slow motion when she dug underneath the neatly packed bags, and sure as shit, there was a plastic grocery bag wrapped around itself on the very bottom. She grabbed it and tossed it into her tote without looking inside. Then she picked up a bag of the mini Snickers and placed them in the basket so nothing was conspicuous.

Waiting in line, Kim glued her eyes to her phone and scrolled social media. She wasn't *really* reading and retained nothing she saw, but that was what everyone else in line did and what she'd do on a normal day. She paid for her items in cash—no trail. The cashier rang up her items and pushed them to the side for Kim to put into her tote. She did that, then placed the plastic bin under the register, and she was on her way.

She practically ran home. Locking the door behind her, she emptied the tote bag and unwrapped the plastic grocery bag. Inside was another burner and twenty-five hundred dollars in cash. It was a mix of all bills, mostly twenties and fifties, some fives and tens. They weren't all fresh, crisp, and banded while facing in the same direction. Somehow, that made it trustworthy to her. It was like whoever did this wasn't a professional hitman or hitwoman, just someone who wanted someone dead.

Someone who'd been saving up for it.

She stared at the cash, then stared at Murphy. It was all for him. She had to kill a stranger. Saving her dog made her the opposite of a monster.

She thought back to a show she saw as a child, reruns with her parents or at spooky sleepovers, called *The Twilight Zone*. There was one particular episode that stuck with her—a man showed up and offered a woman money, a couple hundred thousand dollars, and if she decided to take it, then a stranger, *someone they didn't even know*, would die. All the main character had to do was press the button.

She contemplated it for days before she finally did it. She'd been pushed to the edge with bills and responsibilities and had finally had enough. She pressed it. The man again showed up at her door, delivered the money, and asked for the button back. She argued that it was dangerous, that it needed to be destroyed, and the man said not to worry, it was going to someone else.

Someone she didn't even know.

Someone who, when they got the button next—if they decided to push it and take the money—would ensure the main character was the next to die. Killing someone else always sealed your own fate. Your own death. For *money* of all things. It was made into a movie in the mid-2000s, starring Cameron Diaz.

What if a stranger was hired to do this to her? Would they go through with it? Would they need the money to save someone's life, just to take Kim's in return?

When the new burner rang, the one in the grocery bag, she knew she was in neck deep. It rang the same day she was supposed to poison Tony. The Stranger gave new instructions, now at a local grocery store. She was to go to the organic vegetable department, and under all the green beans, way down at the bottom of the bin, there would be a small paper bag for her to take. Same situation—grab the bag, put it in the basket, and buy a few items of her choice.

No biggie.

Kim fished under all the beans, the deepest vegetable bin, until she found the bag, threw it in her tote, then grabbed a sack of potatoes, two boxes of gluten free orzo, non-GMO peanut butter, one box of organic oatmeal, and a quart of organic milk. As she placed everything on the conveyor belt to pay in cash, again, she waited for the men in blue to ambush and arrest her. Tell her that they'd been following her for days and that she was going to jail for attempted murder. But hey, with the burners and no trail, all she had to say to defend herself was that she'd accidentally grabbed something that was in the bin, and by the way, what was even in there?

Foolproof. For everyone involved.

When she got home, she emptied the small paper bag. One pill with a powdery substance, and one small vial of liquid. Another twenty-five-hundred dollars, this time all in hundreds, a mix of the old white ones and the newer blue ones, held together with a simple paper clip. They certainly knew how to settle her apprehensions. Holding the cash, twice, gave Kim a sense of certainty—she still had the bank account and more to come.

Kim had eyed the poisons. The powder from the pill could be used in a glass of bourbon, the vial of liquid on dessert—The Stranger had already told her it was sweet tasting and could be used over ice cream or mixed in with a pudding. The "mark" would never notice.

She could use both if she was unsure. If she really wanted to get the job done to The Stranger's satisfaction.

She'd used neither.

What she wanted to know was who killed PJ. It was obviously a targeted effort on them both.

It was a Monday, and Kim wasn't due into work until that Wednesday, but paychecks always came on Mondays. She hadn't stepped foot into the club since PJ's death three days ago. She wondered if it would look the same. Kim parked her car, ran into the lobby, and then to the right near Dana's office to grab her check. She wanted to get in and out and not have to pass the bar room. Still, her eyes flicked over that way to the left, where it happened.

No one would ever be able to tell that something sinister had gone on just a few days before. There was no police tape, no body bag, no cones indicating evidence markers. What she saw instead were golfers having lunch, laughing over beers, and clinking wine glasses to celebrate who broke eighty that morning.

"Hey, Kim, how are you doing?"

It was Dana who interrupted her gaze. "Oh, hey, I'm fine. Still a little rattled." *Understatement of the year. Act normal.* "How are you? What happened after we all left?"

Dana blew out a breath. "God, it was so horrible, right? I feel terrible for Mr. Fuller. They had to physically remove him from the body bag. We got him an Uber home. I thought maybe Ron or Car—I mean, Mr. or Mrs. Boswell—would offer to take him, but they didn't. I guess those two had a big fight when I was in the kitchen with the detectives. Did you see it?"

Kim nodded. So much drama Friday night.

Dana's eyes widened. "Anyway, the detectives came back Saturday and interviewed everyone at the pro shop, plus the two new caddies we hired, and the rest of the waitstaff and bartenders that weren't even here on Friday. It was probably an allergic reaction, and I think they were just covering their bases. Obviously, no one here had anything to do with it."

Change of subject. "Crazy about Mr. and Mrs. Boswell, right?" Kim said.

"Yeah, Lucy filled me in. Who knew?"

Kim thought back to a few days before, at Tony's beach house, where he'd told her that Carla had made advances toward him. How badly did she desire him?

Enough to kill?

Even worse, Kim couldn't shake the feeling that this was the second homicide Tony was involved in. Once was an accident, twice was a coincidence, and three times was enemy action.

Was someone else about to drop dead?

26
PJ
THEN

This bed is so comfortable that I don't want to get up and get out, but I promised Matt we'd have brunch today. I blew him off for dinner this week because Anthony hurt his shoulder at the gym. Of course, I couldn't tell Matt that and I feel awful about telling him I was sick, though he knows I'm prone to sinus infections. Poor Anthony couldn't do much with his arm in a sling, so I didn't want him to be alone. He relaxed and didn't have to do a thing.

He told me he kept the sling from almost a decade ago when he tore his rotator cuff playing in a charity hockey game. I didn't know Anthony liked to play hockey. When I asked him about it, he told me how they all played it on the street in Brooklyn when he was growing up and that he was a big New York Rangers fan. I knew that from a passing conversation or two, and I remember him telling Matt's father about it when we were in Texas and they were discussing the hockey game that was on television.

I prop my head into my hand and listen intently as he describes shoveling snow off driveways as a kid and teenager to save enough money to go to the Rangers games. He said that he and a bunch of friends from the neighborhood would buy the cheap seats and take the subway into the city by themselves, as young as twelve years old. They were street smart, and their parents trusted them. The'd take a bus to the Kings Highway subway station and ride it straight into the city, a block away from Madison Square Garden. To this day, he goes as often as he can, though now he goes to something called the Delta Club with free food and alcohol. I'm sure he pays through the nose for that "free" stuff.

Where I grew up in Texas, football was the big thing, namely high school and college football, just like you see on TV. I never got into hockey, but Anthony's passion for it makes me want to go to the next home game and get a foam finger and a flag to wave.

"Take me to a Rangers game," I say.

"Anytime you want. You'll love it."

He's tickling my shoulder, and my head is on his chest. We're still in the afterglow. I've not only been enjoying sex with him lately, but I've been craving it. I know I'm screwed. My mind is completely twisted. On the one hand, I've spent so much time and energy on the plan, and everything I've wanted has worked in spades. On the other hand, it makes me feel weird now.

He hasn't spoken to anyone in his family for a month, after we visited and they disrespected me. He adores me, and he'll do anything for me, and despite what's in my head, the relationship is real. Maybe I can use him and abuse him and become a gold digger and then break his heart into a million pieces. I can still just *hurt* him, not kill him.

But I don't want to hurt him at all.

Maybe I don't have it in me to be a killer. I'm not like him.

Him, Anthony, who killed my mother. I need to focus. I didn't come to New York to become a mush ball. I came here for a reason.

"I have to go. I'm meeting Matt for brunch," I say.

"Oh. Right." He rubs his stubble, then the back of his neck. "Can I come? I really want to meet him."

"I—" I need to make up an excuse. Matt will legit kill me if I ambush him with this guy. No matter how twisted I am inside, Matt fucking hates him. He still thinks *I* hate him. I'm afraid he'll see through me. "I think he wants to talk about a relationship problem. Next time. Sorry, we just kind of have opposite schedules now. It's a little harder than it used to be." I kiss him on the cheek and jump up to shower.

My hair is due for a wash, but I don't have time to blow it out right now. I tie it up into a high bun even though it's still freezing out and I'd rather use it as an extra scarf, but it's an oily mess. My outfit consists of a black cashmere sweater and black leather pants. This new wardrobe of mine sure does make me look like I belong where I am, on the Upper East Side. Minus the oily hair.

In my closet, I can't find my new Chanel bag, one that I'm actually going to keep. I won't let Matt sell this one and get me a knockoff. It's not on the shelf I've dedicated for it. Pursing my lips, I start taking everything else off the shelves in case it's hiding behind something. Other bags fall to the floor as I frantically knock things over, and finally, I see it under a sweater, one I must've thrown in a passionate and heated encounter with Anthony.

Checking my watch, I realize I'm going to be late to meet Matt. I leave everything scattered on the closet floor to clean up later. The whole thing could use reorganization if I'm being honest. When I moved in, I didn't have much. As Anthony got me more clothes, bags, and shoes, I kind of stuck them in places all willy-nilly. I need to make sure everything is in its rightful place. Clean. Rows of bags, shoes color coordinated, clothes separated by season.

I step over the mess and close the closet door, then exit the bedroom. Anthony is relaxing on the couch, reading the Sunday issue of the *New York Times* with his bare feet on the cocktail table. Ew. Sometimes, he attempts the crossword puzzle. I laughed inside a few weeks ago when he left it on the table and I glanced at it. Nine letters, and the hint was "animal with pockets" and he put *squirrels* when it was clearly *marsupial*. He pluralized it for no reason, and hello, squirrels don't even have front pockets like a kangaroo. For a smart guy, sometimes I think he's an idiot.

Stick to that thinking, PJ, I tell myself.

"I have to go. I'll be back in a few hours," I say.

He curls a finger and smirks. I trot over to him and kiss him, letting my lips linger, and I hate myself for it.

"Do you want me to make reservations somewhere for dinner?" he asks.

"No, that's okay. I'll cook or we can order in. It's freezing outside. I won't want to go back out again."

He laughs. "You and your thin blood. It'll be warm soon enough; the beginning of March is always unpredictable weather. I called Monty when you were in the shower. He's waiting downstairs so you won't have to brave the elements. He'll wait around and take you home too."

Monty is the driver that Anthony has on call. It's Anthony's car, a black Lincoln like all the fancy rich people use. He bought it a few years ago to squire around town with a hired driver. He lets Monty use it for personal stuff as long as he's available to take us anywhere with thirty minutes notice. Anthony doesn't make him wear a uniform or one of those stupid hats, but he does like that Monty opens and closes the door for us. At this point, I'm extremely grateful that I don't have to stand in the twenty-degree temps and try to hail a cab, or worse, trek all the way to the Second Avenue subway. Not in these new leather boots.

"Thanks. I appreciate you calling him." I do, I really do, and that's the type of guy Anthony is—a really good boyfriend. My heart stabs me with terrifying, electric pains, because I've been lying to myself. How long could I go on this way? Matt was right, and living with Anthony twenty-four-seven was a bad idea. I've become who I was pretending to be.

As promised, Monty is parked right in front of our building, and he gets out and opens the door when he sees me. I get in the warm car and tell him to take me down to my old neighborhood where Matt still lives. We're going to a restaurant a few blocks away from his apartment. As we get closer, I realize how much I miss it here. Especially the nights with Matt and greasy Chinese food from the twenty-four-hour delivery place we always ordered from when we had too much to drink. Having known him more than half my life, I miss the little things.

Matt is sitting at the bar when I walk in, and I run up to him and give him a huge hug. It feels good to have my arms around someone I know I love no matter what. His hair is down, out of the man bun, and it's just past his shoulders now. Still not bleached. His beard is thicker too. He usually keeps it pretty trim, but he lets it grow out a bit during the winter months. He looks good. I plant a big kiss on his cheek, and he makes a face and wipes it off with a cocktail napkin, leaving a slick mark on his scruff. He always thought I used too much lip gloss.

"Gross." He grabs another paper napkin and tries again. "Feeling any better?"

"Yeah. It was another sinus infection." He helps me with my coat, and I take the seat next to him, where he has a mimosa waiting for me.

"You look good. And you're warm. The subway is four blocks from here."

"I know. I—" *I have a fancy car with a fancy driver take me everywhere.* He doesn't know all the details of the life I live now. I've been keeping things from him as I sort out my shit. *Shit* being my feelings. I don't want Matt to turn on me. I can't have that. "I took a cab. You know that asshole will give me money for anything."

"Must be nice." His lips are pursed. "Any closer to the ring?"

I sip my mimosa and shake my head. "Not yet. Let's order, I'm starving."

After we both devour our omelets and we're on our fourth mimosa each, Matt's demeanor changes. Before, he was acting like regular old Matt, singing awfully with the music, making fun of everyone around him, and flirting with the bartender who is clearly straight. Now, he tears at the napkin still on the bar from the lip gloss incident. Nervous.

"I've been debating telling you something."

My eyebrows raise. "Oh?"

"Yeah."

"*Yeah*," I mock. "Well, you can't bring it up like that and then say nothing, so just get on with it."

He sighs. "When you guys were with my parents in December, pretending they were your parents, he asked my dad for permission to marry you."

My heart leaps, for the wrong reasons. I hated him with a passion back then, but the last month since we were with his family has been so strange. "Oh. Good. So we're on track."

His eyes narrow. "What was that?"

"What was what?"

"You smiled."

"Of course I did." I take another sip and avert my eyes. "This is what we wanted."

"No, lover, it wasn't your evil smile. You looked . . . happy."

"That's because I am. It's almost done."

Matt stares at me, and it feels like worms are fighting to the death in my stomach. He shakes his head and looks down. "You're falling for him, aren't you?"

"Are you crazy?" *God damn it.*

"That's not an answer. And you paused for like a whole second before you answered anyway." He lifts his head back up. "I see you less and less. You take forever to return my texts, and when you do, you don't ask me anything about myself anymore."

"Yes, I do."

"No, you don't. It's all generic bullshit. 'Did you get laid last night?' and 'How's Starbucks?' like you care about either."

Now it's my turn to put my head down. I can't look at him. "I'm sorry. I do care about you."

"But you care about your relationship more now."

"It's not real. You know I have to pretend it's real. I need him to trust me."

He looks at the bartender. "Check, please."

"Matt, don't be like this."

The bartender drops the check. I glance at the total, just over seventy-five dollars. Gotta love bottomless mimosa brunches. Matt reaches into his pocket and throws down a hundred-dollar bill.

"Courtesy of the Anthony Fuller fund," he says, reminding me he's been living high on the hog selling everything Anthony buys me before he replaces it with a replica. "After all, that's what we want, right? His money."

"And revenge." I try to say it with conviction, but my voice falters.

"Right. And revenge. Because you seem to have forgotten that he fucking killed your mother." He stands up and places a hand on my shoulder. "Good to see you today." Then he walks out.

"Wait!" I throw on my coat and go after him. He's ten feet away from the door when I get out there and call his name. He turns around, and the look he gives absolutely guts me.

It'll never be hate with him and me, but this is worse. It's disappointment. "Matt, wait."

In the worst timing in history, Monty exits the black Lincoln idling outside of the restaurant, heads to the other side of the car, and opens the passenger door. "Ready to go, Ms. Walsh?"

Matt looks at him, at the car, then back at me and shakes his head. "Have a nice ride to the Upper East Side." He puts his knit beanie on his head and shoves his hands in his pockets before walking against the whipping wind toward home.

27

ANTHONY
THEN

The Sunday crossword puzzle was stressing Anthony out, so he decided to take a walk. He usually went to the gym on Sunday mornings, but since he hurt his shoulder last week, he'd been taking it easy. PJ would be at brunch with Matt for a few hours anyway, and he never minded the cold. He missed taking walks with her around the neighborhood, but she didn't do cold, and he never wanted her to feel uncomfortable. He was the luckiest man alive, having such a young, beautiful, smart woman as his girlfriend.

Checking the weather on his phone, Anthony found that PJ was right, and it was freezing out today. He grabbed his cashmere coat, a hat, and a scarf and headed outside. The air was crisp, and the wind was brutal, but he breathed it all in even though it felt like he was being stabbed in the lung. With his sunglasses shielding the wind from making his eyes tear, he headed south. His leather gloves were in his pockets—a nice surprise—and he put them on as he walked.

It smelled like snow, even though there was nothing in the forecast. The quaint stillness of the neighborhood made everything look like a Norman Rockwell painting. The buildings, the sky, even the people looked like they'd been coated with a sepia filter as his shoulders hunched toward his non-destination. Ten blocks turned into twenty. Anthony turned west. It was like he was on autopilot as the quiet neighborhood turned into the bustling Sunday shopping, and before he knew it, he was outside Tiffany.

Muscle memory took him there. He was going to do this.

A gloved gentleman opened the door for him, and he went inside. As he browsed the cases, he smiled softly at everyone who'd offered to help him. Was he really going to buy her a ring? Eyeing one of the cases that held cocktail rings, he found a beautiful one, plain but big, that would look amazing on her dainty finger. It was a huge stone, probably five carats, but it wasn't a diamond. It was an octagon shape and glowed a very soft mint color. He smiled as he saw matching earrings, less than a carat each, hanging from a silver strand.

PJ would love it. She loved everything he got her. Still, he moved past the area and found himself on the third floor in the engagement ring section. A saleslady sized him up in his double-breasted Versace cashmere coat and beelined toward him—they were trained to sniff out wealth. She wore glasses and had her medium-length brown hair tucked behind her ears. Her white collared shirt popped under a black V-neck sweater. Her smile was genuine, yet he saw the money signs in her eyes.

"Can I help you find something today?" she asked.

"I hope so. I don't have an appointment. This is kind of spur of the moment," Anthony said.

"Sometimes, you just know when the time is right."

He nodded. "Yes, you do. I didn't know I was going to end up here today, but now that I'm here, I don't want to waste the chance."

"Excellent. I'm Claire, and you are?"

"Anthony Fuller." He took off his gloves and shook her hand.

"Excellent, Mr. Fuller. Do you have anything particular in mind?"

"Something special, just like her."

Another smile. "Do you have a budget in mind?"

No, he didn't have a budget since this entire scenario was as shocking to him as it was to Claire. What did they used to say? Three months' salary? That was a bit much to spend on a ring, especially since he'd showered her with jewelry all the time. Still, he wanted her to know what she meant to him, so the bigger the better.

"I want something as close to perfect as you can get. Oval." He'd remembered that much. She'd always mentioned how much she loved oval rings. "Three carats. Diamond pavé band. Platinum."

Claire mentally calculated next week's paycheck in her head and nodded. "Follow me."

Anthony tucked the blue bag into his breast pocket before he left the store. Monty was with PJ, but he couldn't risk walking all the way home with a ring that cost him almost a quarter million dollars. He didn't even want to risk walking to the corner to hail a cab. Instead, he waited inside until his Uber X pulled up to the front. He made sure to check the plate—front and back—before he got in. He couldn't take any chances.

The smile on his face, the one no one could see but he could feel, was genuine. He'd never been so content. In the past, he wasn't even sure he wanted children, but now he thought of PJ as the mother of his kids. It was a good feeling to have. Settled. Family. Love. Stability.

When Anthony walked into his building, his doorman stopped him and told him he had a package. He waited at the podium while George went into the back room, and he returned with a large cardboard box. Looking at the return address, he saw it was from Saks. Ah, it must've been the Stella McCartney purse he'd ordered for PJ. She had this way of looking at things, with a sparkle in her eye, so he knew she wanted it when they were window shopping. It was the same sparkle she used to look into his eyes.

With the box under his arm and the ring still snug in his coat pocket, he took the elevator up to their home. Once inside, he hid the ring in the safe in his office—PJ didn't have access to it. It was mostly business papers, his will, and a copy of his parents' will, even though he was sure all of that would be changing in the near future. Screw them—if they couldn't accept PJ, he didn't need them. He'd moved past them and their ego-driven bullshit long ago.

Anthony opened the Saks box and decided to place the bag front and center on PJ's display wall in her closet. She was going to be so surprised. He'd had one of the bedroom closets redone before she moved in. It was the smaller one; however, it was still a walk-in and big enough. She didn't have much to start, but he filled it up for her fast. It was more of a woman's closet now, with a place to hang dresses, shelves with drawers, that coveted shoe wall. His was bigger, full of suits and polos and even had one of those glass and mahogany chests in the middle that housed his cuff links and watches.

When he opened her door, it looked like a bomb went off. Things were all over the floor and the shelves were a mess. He wanted her to notice the bag immediately, so he tidied up a bit, making sure he didn't invade her privacy.

Until he saw something sticking out of a messenger bag on the floor. His name and his picture were on the cover.

Anthony opened it and started to flip through it, starting with Phase One. Awww. How they met. He'd heard of younger people documenting things like this, and it was going to be a book about their relationship, one they'd cry over at their fiftieth anniversary.

Then he turned the page.

Just what the fuck was he reading? This was no storybook romance. It was a kill book. With details, about how she was making him fall in love with her, to get his will changed. To marry him. To—

What?

Oh, and that was how she thought it was going to end?

First, his heart broke into a million pieces. He wouldn't cry, but the ache in his chest was physical, so much so that he clutched it like he might be having a heart attack. It couldn't have all been a lie, could it? He pictured her smile, her cuddling him, the way she kissed him when they left his parents' house. He couldn't have gotten it all wrong. No way.

Then, he flashed back to their first meeting, her dreamy expression and how she took him to a steakhouse. She drank bourbon that he loved. Everything about her was exactly what he'd ever wanted.

It was all meticulously planned, and his heart rate increased, his face turning tomato red as the blood flow drew to the surface. It hit him—he'd been played since day one. Before that—she'd clearly done her research on him, with articles about him and his successes that came out a year before they'd even met.

That bitch. She manipulated him. She played with his feelings. And she planned to *kill* him? On their honeymoon?

He'd see about that. In his mind, he already had his strong hands around her tiny little neck, and the thought of crushing her grew into a feeling far more pleasing than the thought of having sex with her. He'd started considering how to get away with it.

Or . . . maybe it would be more fun to make her think she was winning this bullshit game. Tony Fiore would climb out of the shadows when she'd least expect it.

28

KIM
NOW

Kim was lucky enough to win a design contract the week after PJ's murder. She'd applied online and submitted a bid to do a logo and marketing materials for a coffee shop that was opening forty-five minutes north of her.

The place was under renovation in a strip mall, and the entire transaction was done online, aside from one phone call from the owner, Ted, to let her know she'd been hired and to go over a few concepts. He'd told her they'd planned to cater to Gen Z, like most businesses did these days. The establishment was called Cool Beans and was cashless, with Instagram and TikTok worthy designer desserts, and local one-person-bands were invited to play on Thursday nights when they stayed open until 9:00 P.M. It wouldn't be open for another few months, after renovations and inspections, so she had time to come up with a couple of ideas.

Kim was thankful for the distraction, even though her subconscious was seeping into her designs. One idea had frost on top of the word "Cool" in the store's moniker, but she thought it looked too much like powder. The poison powder that she was supposed to mix into Tony's bourbon. Another idea had icicles dripping off the word, but she thought it looked too much like the vial of sweet liquid she was supposed to pour over his dessert.

She hadn't heard from Tony since she was at his house the previous weekend. She hadn't heard from The Stranger either, and she was due at work tonight.

Frustrated with her inability to come up with a kick-ass design, she decided to go to the club a little early. Wednesdays at the bar weren't entirely busy, but truth be told, she was still afraid to be home, not knowing when another envelope would show up or when another call would come in.

She fed Murphy dinner, a combination of his dry food and some homemade chicken soup that she cooked for him every week. She stored it in the refrigerator and gave him a hearty ladleful every morning and every night. He knew when she went to the specific cabinet where his food was stored and heard the rustling of the dry kernels that it was food time. He got up from his bed—slowly—to follow her.

"Hey, good boy." She patted him on the head, then scratched behind his ears. "We need you all strong for your surgery on Monday."

The surgery Kim hoped he'd be getting, if she still had the money for it . . . and if she were still alive by then. She mixed everything into his bowl and filled up his two bowls of water—he was a thirsty little thing—and changed into her all black ensemble to face the scene of the crime.

When she got to work, she went straight to the employee break room and saw an unfamiliar face. He was younger than her, tall, with very light blond hair, clean cut with sharp edges. He wore a polo with the club's logo over the heart and white pants and matching white shoes, which he was in the process of removing for beat-up sneakers. He smiled at her; she smiled back by pressing her lips together and giving him a nod.

"Hi. I'm Terrence, one of the new caddies." He offered a hand, one that still had a golfing glove on. "Call me Terry."

Kim hesitated. She'd been reading about how criminals were lacing everything you could think of with fentanyl. They'd leave hundred-dollar bills near someone's car so the stuff absorbed into their skin immediately, rendering them helpless. Then they'd be robbed, their car stolen, maybe worse if they were a woman. Human trafficking was at an all-time high. She still didn't trust anyone she didn't know and eyed his outstretched hand.

"Oh, sorry." He clumsily removed the glove, threw it in his locker, and stuck it out again. Well, he touched it and didn't fall into a convulsing pile of garbage, so she shook his hand.

"Hi. Kim. Waitress." She placed her purse and flip-flops into her locker and retrieved her black heels. "Welcome to the madhouse."

His eyes widened. "I heard. I had to talk to the cops, and I wasn't even here the day it happened. I mean, I was . . . I work Tuesday through Friday, but I was gone by five o'clock. I've only been here a month. What a nightmare."

"I was serving them. It was . . . Ugh, I don't even want to talk about it." Kim didn't know this guy. He could be The Stranger for all she knew.

"I'm sorry. Dana said it was disgusting. I can't even imagine."

He turned toward his locker and scrolled through his phone, shielding it with the door. Just then, Kim's phone beeped, and she jumped. She side-eyed Terry, who looked at her suspiciously. Not malicious-suspicious, just curious as to why she was so high-strung. His eyes drifted to her phone, where Murphy was her screen saver.

"Awww. Cute dog," he said.

"Thanks. He's—" She stopped because she hated saying it. "He's sick. He's supposed to have surgery next week." She squeezed her eyes shut, falsely assuming it would keep the tears in, but one escaped. "Sorry." She wiped it away and glanced at her phone and was relieved to see the ping was a text from Maddy. She berated herself for being paranoid, thinking Terry the caddie was texting her from a burner to tell her she was next to die.

Can you come to the bar when you get off tonight? Something strange is going on. I'll be here till at least eleven.

Well, if that didn't make her paranoid, nothing would.

What do you mean? What's going on? Kim texted back.

Three dots. Then nothing. Then three dots again.

I heard some people talking. About the club, and about that girl dying. I think at least one of them knew her.

Kim thought her heart actually stopped. She had to place her hand on it and hold her breath to make sure she felt it beating.

It was The Stranger. She was sure of it. And now they were stalking Maddy.

She wasn't in the clear. Not yet.

29
PJ
THEN

I scurry into the building—the wind has really picked up. I texted Matt five times on the ride home, but he hasn't answered me yet. If I don't have Matt, I don't want to cling to Anthony as the only alternative. I text Matt for the last time as I'm in the elevator.

I've been a little mixed up, and I'm sorry. I love you no matter what, awesomesauce.

It bothers me more than it should when he doesn't write back immediately. But he will. We're soulmates.

I open the door, and Anthony is sitting at the table, in jeans and an NYU sweatshirt, when I know for a fact that he didn't even go there. He *thinks* I did. His hands are folded. "How was brunch?"

"Good." I take off my coat and unwrap the scarf from my neck and hang them both in the closet.

"I want to talk to you about something."

It's just now that I notice his demeanor. He's sitting at the table without a prop—no magazine, no book, no newspaper. No work files. No food. No coffee. Sitting there, staring straight ahead like a psychopath. How long has he been like that? He didn't know when I'd be getting home. Even though his jaw is slightly clenched, I go over to him and kiss him on the cheek and take the seat next to him.

"What's up?" I ask.

"Hang on." He stands, goes into his office, and returns with his laptop. He opens it up and clicks a few buttons and turns it toward me. On the screen is a picture of a beach at sunset. The sky is a fiery red, with dark grey and yellow clouds flitting in the sky. The beach sand looks pink, either because it *is* pink, or it's a reflection from the sunset. There are palm trees off to the side, and the whole scene looks like it was taken from a high floor of a balcony.

I dent my eyebrows. "What am I looking at?"

He grins, goofy and sideways. "Our villa. I booked us a trip to Maui next month." He exhales and leans back in his chair. "I could use a break from the office. I just hope it's okay for you, with your yoga clients. A month's notice should be long enough. Tell them you'll be gone for ten days."

A smile breaks out on my face. "Really? Hawaii?"

I've never been to Hawaii, and I've always wanted to go. I was going to bring it up as a honeymoon destination when the time came, but here we are. A surprise vacation. I jump up from my chair and hug him. I can't help it.

Anthony picks me up, carries me to the bedroom, and places me on my feet in front of my closet. The door is closed, because I kicked everything from the floor inside and shut it before I left. No one needs to see that mess.

"Open the door," he says.

I don't want him to think I'm a slob. "I have some reorganization to do," I say sheepishly. "I made kind of a mess earlier looking for the bag I wanted to take to brunch. I planned on cleaning up when I got home." That's the truth.

He rubs my shoulders and opens the door. Everything is exactly as I left it, except in the center is the Stella McCartney bag I was eye fucking through the window when we were on Fifth Avenue a couple weeks ago. My mouth hangs open.

"You like it?" he asks.

I turn around and kiss him, then push him on the bed to thank him. It hasn't been the normal, mechanical, Oscar-worthy sex the last month. I find myself really enjoying it. Craving it. Craving him.

The sex this afternoon is rougher than usual, but that's okay. He's a great boyfriend and I love him. Which makes me a monster, really.

I can't believe I fell in love with him.

When we're finished, he says he's going to take a steam—we have a steam shower and a sauna in the master bathroom. I get out of bed, tie my hair into a bun, and throw on a robe. Not the sexy silky one, but the fluffy comfortable one because despite the heat being on, the bedroom is usually colder than the rest of the apartment. Anthony likes to keep a window cracked open for fresh air. It's good for snuggling under the down comforter, which is heaven, but times like now it's annoying because it's cold as shit. I have to clean the closet. I swore to myself I would.

First, I take my new bag off the shelf and hook it over my shoulder, then unfold the top flap and hold it in my hand as I pose in the full-length mirror. I really love it, and it's going to look great with my Diane von Furstenberg wrap dress and Manolo heels. Maybe this will be my outfit next weekend when we have to meet Ron and Carla Boswell for dinner.

Ugh, I hate that plastic fake-ass wench. Ron's not much better, but at least I don't have to deal with him. It's just going to be the four of us, so Anthony and Ron will be talking shop and I'll be fighting off Carla's venom, just like the first time I met her. She's a shark in the water, and she smelled blood. She knew from the second she met me that there was something in her surroundings that didn't belong, and she intended to fillet me with her razor-sharp teeth. She didn't get there but hey, *if at first you don't succeed, try, try, again.* I know I'm still on her radar.

I place the bag back on the shelf and start to gather my belongings from the floor. There are a few dresses that fell off the velvet hangers. I hang everything back up, I rearrange my shoes, and I clear my shelves for what I think should be front facing. My Stella bag, natch.

The last thing I see on the ground is my messenger bag. The corner of my kill book for Anthony is sticking out of the edge.

Shit.

My heart tugs, because I hate that I even made this thing, yet I don't have it in me to destroy it yet. I grab for it immediately, hoping he didn't see it, but no, it's all good. It's in the same place I left it when it fell when I tore apart my closet this morning. All Anthony did was put my brand-new Stella bag on the shelf, looking at my closet through love-fogged eyes to give me a present like he normally does. He never saw the kill book.

If he did see it, he wouldn't have booked a dream trip to Hawaii. Quite the contrary; there's no way he would've let me walk out of here alive.

30
KIM
NOW

Kim was terrified of her shift. Everyone must've been, because there were only about half the number of people dining that usually come in on Wednesdays. While the club was no longer under suspicion, no one wanted to be next. Kim decided for her own safety to wear a pair of rubber gloves that the chefs used when they were chopping vegetables. She looked like a serial killer, but she didn't care—she didn't want to take the chance of touching something that traveled through her skin and into her bloodstream to kill her.

No incidents had happened since PJ's death last Friday—but the hesitation was there. No one sat in that corner of the room, even though all the police tape and evidence markers were gone. Those who weren't there had obviously heard about it, and Kim wondered how long it would take for everyone to forget about it.

She acted normal, greeting everyone by their Mr. and Mrs. last names and exchanging pleasantries before she read the specials. Aside from a sympathetic comment or two, no one brought it up. No one had gotten to know Anthony or PJ yet, and while what happened was awful, it wasn't like anyone there had lost a good friend.

Kim was thankful for the slow night, because she was able to get off at nine instead of ten. The place was a graveyard by then. Only Lucy and the chefs had to stay, in case anyone came in for a late meal, which she didn't think would be the case.

She tore into the employee locker room and changed back into her flip-flops and a tank top. Once in her comfy clothes, she undid her ponytail and ran a hand through her hair, then took yet another agonizing walk to her car, waiting for someone to jump out of the bushes. She had to go see Maddy before the bar closed and find out what the hell she'd been going on about, saying someone there was talking about PJ's death.

There were no attacks from behind and no chloroform over her mouth, her car didn't explode, and her brake lines weren't cut. She drove ten minutes to the other side of town where Night Shift was located. It was a complete dump but had a barrage of regulars and the occasional frat boys pregaming with two-dollar shots and three-dollar beers before heading to the beach bars, where drinks cost significantly more.

After locking her door and making sure the lights chirped twice, she walked inside, her flip-flops sticking to the floor, as usual. The place wasn't *filthy*, per se, but they didn't exactly have a maid service to clean up all the drinks that spilled throughout the night. It was the closing bartender's job to mop, but sometimes, they just wanted to get home and did a half-assed job. The layers of tequila and beer were apparent as Kim thwacked her way to the bar.

The place was dark, save for a few overhead lights and the twenty neon signs advertising beer, bathrooms, and cigarettes. Some flashed, some didn't. Slipknot played on the jukebox, and three men sat around the bar at the far corner, not speaking much, drinking their amber-colored drinks out of thick glasses. A young couple in their early twenties appeared to be on a date, the guy cheering on the girl at the old Pac-Man arcade game next to the pool table. No one was playing pool, but the balls were scattered on the green velvet as if someone abandoned a game in the middle.

Maddy was behind the bar, wiping it down with a wet rag. Her black hair was half up with the bottom curled, and she'd been heavy-handed with the black eyeliner again. She wore a vintage Guns N' Roses tank top with black denim cutoffs, the kind that fringed gray at the edges.

"Hey," Kim said.

Maddy threw the rag into a bucket under the bar. "Kim. Good, you're early." She widened her eyes and nodded her head to the other end of the bar, where no one sat.

Kim followed Maddy's orders and took a seat on a stool with snaggled red polyurethane and white stuffing peeking out. Maddy grabbed a Corona and a lime and slid it down the bar for Kim. She grabbed it, squeezed the lime, and shoved it down the neck before taking a sip. Maddy knew it was the only beer she drank, but only when there were no other options. Night Shift wasn't exactly a wine place. Everyone there would look at Kim like she was wearing a tiara if she ordered a cabernet in a place like this.

"So, what's up? What happened?" Kim asked.

Maddy laughed. "I swear, I never even would've noticed them or paid attention to them if it didn't look like they were trying so hard *not* to be noticed. They both wore hats and kept their heads down."

Kim nodded. "Did you get their names?"

"That's another thing. They kept calling each other their names over and over, like they wanted to be known as those people in case anyone asked. It wasn't natural. 'Oh, Kenneth, do you want fries, Kenneth?' 'No, Patricia, I think chicken fingers. You like those, right, Patricia?' It was so weird."

"It was a couple?"

"I think so. He had his arm around her sometimes, and they were talking too close not to be doing something shady—I've seen it all here. They were probably having an affair. Why else come into this dinky little place? I didn't see a ring on either of them, but they were definitely acting like they fucked before, and now they were trying to hide in plain sight."

"Huh. What did they say about PJ and the club?"

"That was when I started to pay attention. I heard the guy say 'PJ'—you said that was the girl's name, right? The one who died?"

Kim nodded again.

"Well, my antennae went up because it's not a common name. Then he said something about the country club and an autopsy, and it's just not regular conversation I get in my bar, you know? I pretended to scroll through my phone and pretended to be texting, but I was really trying to listen. The woman kept saying something about *the plan*, and he kept saying he needed more time. They ended up getting the fries and the chicken fingers, and when they ate, they didn't talk much. But when they were leaving, I heard him say not to reach out until he did, that he'd figure it out. Once they got outside, he broke left and she broke right, like they didn't even know each other."

The plan. It was The Stranger. And the plan was bigger than Kim thought.

"Do you remember what they looked like? At all?"

"She had blonde hair, unless it was a wig—you never can tell these days. Big ole fake titties, but otherwise she seemed tiny, in one of those velvet matching sweatsuits from like two decades ago. He was kind of hot, but he dressed like a dork. Dude was wearing Crocs and jorts. Jorts! That, plus a navy-blue Reebok T-shirt. He had dark hair and dark eyes. You could tell they were trying so hard not to be who they really were." Maddy shrugged. "Who knows, maybe it was some of that role playing shit. I just thought the entire scene was weird."

Kim sipped her Corona, racking her brain, trying to think of anyone from the club who would match that description.

"Anything else? How old were they?"

"She was definitely older than him, tons of noticeable Botox. Oh, and he had a sleeve of tattoos on his left arm."

Kim caught her breath. Tony?

It had to be Tony. What was he doing in a dive bar with another woman so soon after PJ died? What *plan* was the woman talking about? Who was the other woman? What was he involved in?

Then it hit her.

The other woman was Carla Boswell.

31

ANTHONY
THEN

"**Y**ou ready to go, sweetheart?"

Every time Anthony had to call PJ a term of endearment, his rage inside grew. He waited by the door, checking his watch every few seconds. She finally emerged from the bedroom and walked into the kitchen. She wore a tight black and gray wrap dress, something expensive that he undoubtedly paid for. The new Stella McCartney bag he gave her on the day he bought that fucking ring was over her shoulder. Her heels were so high she'd almost be his height. She was lucky she was hot; it was the only thing that saved her from having the life choked out of her little neck every night he had to sleep next to her. Look at her, living her best life, faking *everything* while having this evil plan to kill him.

She stopped and gave a *ta-dah!* twirl, something he used to find breathtaking whenever she was dressed up for a night out. Now he saw her for what she was—a gold digger and con artist. His family had been right from the jump, but he couldn't let them know that. He had to keep up appearances exactly as they were while he figured out how to handle her. That meant treating her like a queen and maintaining that his family was awful. Not telling anyone at work.

He'd already sent her wine glass to his "guy" to have her prints run, and the results would be in on Monday. He didn't believe a word out of her mouth, a clench out of her body. He didn't believe her real name was Poppy Jade Walsh—why would she tell the truth about that?—but he'd get to the bottom of all of it.

He dramatically put his hand over his heart while regarding her as she spun around. "You're radiant." *Bitch.*

She smiled, her puffy lips curling in a way that usually gave him a hard-on, but now all he saw was a fragmented grin from a funhouse mirror.

"I wanted to look nice," she said. "I read about Per Se, and I know it's impossible to get into." She walked up to him, still a few inches shorter even in those heels, and lifted herself to her toes to give him a peck on the lips. "You're so good to me."

No shit. "Ron got the reservation. I suppose he's still the toast of New York. Part of it, anyway."

The week before, in a meeting that was on Anthony's calendar as a scheduled discussion about the new SEC regulations, Ron told Anthony that he was planning to divorce Carla. It had been a long time coming. He said they'd basically lived separate lives for the better part of two years.

Unashamed, Ron also divulged information on his various affairs, sweat glistening from his chubby face as he got into the details. Money really could buy anything, Anthony thought, as Ron regaled him with tales of strippers and twentysomethings he had met at bars. Carla, he'd said, was clueless, and if she did know anything, she turned a blind eye to it in favor of a charmed lifestyle that included money, status, and an unsurmountable number of bags and shoes and vacations.

Anthony faked sympathy and asked Ron why he didn't just leave it as status quo, since he was getting away with it. Ron said he wanted to embarrass Carla. Nice guy.

Anthony knew PJ didn't exactly favor Carla, and he really couldn't blame her. When he loved PJ, Carla was terrible to her. Now, he couldn't care less if Carla wanted to take the bitch down a few notches, but he was going to have to try *really* hard to pretend he cared otherwise. He'd hoped he was as good of an actor as PJ.

The weather had been cooperating lately, defrosting winter winds into more suitable springlike temperatures. It was sixty degrees when they left the apartment, though it would probably drop fifteen degrees by the time they left the restaurant. As much as Anthony wanted to watch PJ suffer and complain about being too cold, he still had the car take them door to door. Because that was what Anthony Fuller would do for the woman he loved.

PJ had no idea she'd been dealing with Tony Fiore as of late.

When Monty pulled the car to the front and let them out, Anthony gripped PJ's hand as they approached the infamous blue door, which he opened for her. Her eyes lit up at the entrance.

"Wow. This is beautiful."

She was a good actress. He almost believed that she cared.

They were led to a table overlooking the park, naturally, where Ron and Carla were already seated. Ron stood to shake Anthony's hand, then kissed PJ on her cheek. Carla rose from her chair—unusual for her to make concessions for anyone, but Anthony was sure it was so she could show herself off in her skintight bandage dress. She'd do just fine as a single cougar. Then she did the opposite of what Ron did—she shook PJ's hand but kissed Anthony, like he knew she would.

"Don't you look scrumptious? I could just eat you," Carla whispered.

The years of innuendos weren't lost on him. Especially not now. Not now that he knew the Boswells' divorce was imminent and PJ was a liar who he was going to leave broken, homeless, and penniless with only the H&M clothes she came with. Maybe he was as bad as Ron; he wanted to embarrass her too. When it all went down, he'd find a way to do it in front of Carla. PJ would hate that the most.

Still, Anthony kept up appearances all through dinner, lovingly stroking PJ's hand and complimenting her yoga business. If that was even real . . . Where did she go in the mornings when she was supposed to be doing private training? She also surprised him by saying she wanted to volunteer for animals or something. And that she wanted to start a website to help old people by doing errands for them for free. She was laying it on too thick—*look at how great and selfless I am.* She was really gunning for that ring. Phase whatever in her book about how to murder him.

Don't worry, darling. I'm proposing in Hawaii. You'll get your dream wedding. You'll be getting everything you want.

So she thought.

Carla was predictable with her insults to PJ, very passive aggressive. When PJ showed off her new Stella McCartney bag, Carla said, "That's nice, if you like that basic color." When she reapplied her lip gloss after dessert, Carla said, "That gloss is great. You're a bit too young to pull off a red lip." The usual.

As they prepared to leave, Ron brashly announced he had to "tap a kidney" and PJ wanted to wash her hands. She was never able to get the stickiness off after she popped the top of her crème Brulée with a manicured finger that Anthony paid for. Jesus, he probably spent close to half a million dollars on her already, if he counted the ring. The dinners, the hotel rooms for one-night staycations, the spa every week, the clothes. He wanted to kick himself for becoming such a cliché.

He should've known it was too good to be true. He'd get the money back for the ring, that was a no-brainer. And he'd find someone to sell all her shit online and recoup some money that way too. He didn't need it; he just didn't want her to have anything from their time together.

One thing was for sure, he'd never fall in love again. Now that he thought about it, the only person who ever really loved him was his ex-girlfriend, Kim. She was the only one who knew him before he made thirty million dollars. He fleetingly wondered what had happened to her after she left for California. She didn't want the drama anymore. He almost admired that. His memory of Kim stopped cold when Carla approached him.

"Hey, you," she said in her *I want to be sexy voice*. She'd always used it on him. "How are things going with PJ?" When she said her name, it was spoken like she was spitting out blood after taking a punch to the face. She'd hated all his girlfriends, but PJ in particular.

Anthony had to stay in character. He even smiled. "Excellent. I'm going to propose soon." He made a *shhh* face, placing his index finger up to his pursed lips.

Her eyebrows raised, as much as the Botox allowed. "Is that so?" She looked toward the bathrooms to see if one of their beloveds were going to crash her flirt party. "Marriage isn't all it's cracked up to be, you know. Why don't you just stay single? And have fun?"

As she said *fun*, she put her hand on his forearm.

The thought finally crossed his mind about going to bed with her. Despite social interactions, Ron was his boss, not his friend. Carla would be free to do as she wanted soon anyway. And Anthony wouldn't even consider it cheating, because PJ wasn't real. The whole thing was fake from day one.

A better thought was maybe he could use Carla to get back at PJ. Wouldn't that rub his girlfriend in all the wrong ways.

"You know what, Carla? Call my office on Monday."

32
KIM
NOW

When Kim returned home from Night Shift, it was a little after nine thirty. She didn't stay for more than the Corona Maddy had given her, feigning fatigue from her first night back at work since PJ's death.

Thankfully, there was still no manila envelope waiting for her at the front door. She changed into comfy shorts and put her flip-flops back on to take Murphy out for a walk. She wasn't as frightened as she'd been every other time she'd left the house the past week.

After talking to Maddy, she had a feeling she knew who was messing with her—Tony—and he wouldn't hurt her.

She exited her apartment and walked without fear to the park Murphy loved. The humidity had broken a bit, and she was able to inhale a huge gulp of dry air. She wrapped the leash around her hand twice to make sure she had a good grip, even though Murphy didn't pull. In fact, she could walk him off leash and he wouldn't leave her side, but she'd read horror stories about other peoples' dogs off leash attacking innocent ones. Better safe than sorry.

She felt so safe she didn't even flinch when a guy in his twenties approached with his own dog, some sort of Labrador mutt. As the dog and Murphy checked each other out, butt sniffs and all, Kim and the guy gave the typical greeting to each other, a head nod and a quick hello, while talking more to their dogs than each other.

Awww, Murph, you made a new friend!

OK, Atticus, let's leave him and his mom alone now. Let's go home and get a treat!

Why did she suddenly feel safe? Tony was The Stranger. He had to be. He certainly had the money and connections to pull off this little cat and mouse game he'd been playing with her. And he had to know that Kim worked at the country club and that she wouldn't do anything to harm him.

Did he do it to take focus off him because he poisoned PJ? He seemed to really love her, in the few interactions she'd had with Tony since they were tossed back into each other's lives. She didn't think he could fake the sincerity of the feelings he'd emoted since it happened. But what was he doing at Night Shift with Carla Boswell, if that was, in fact, them? Were they in on something together? The more Kim played with the scenarios in her mind, the more nothing made sense. She'd have to go straight to the source and try to figure it out from there.

Despite the new sense of fearlessness, she was relieved that an envelope didn't show up in the fifteen minutes she'd been out with Murphy. When they got inside, she refilled his water and poured herself the last of the cabernet that sat on her kitchen counter. As Murphy drank sloppily, she sat on her couch, grabbed her phone, and sent a text.

> *Hey. I know it's late, but I just wanted to check in on you and see how you were doing with everything. Let me know if you need anything.*

Then she backspaced and changed it to *Let me know if you need a friend.*

Right now, she wanted answers. Three dots appeared instantly. Kim's stomach warbled as she waited the agonizing minutes before the text popped up.

> *Peej and I had talked about our wishes when we got my will changed and she got a living will with after life care. She wanted to be cremated, so that's what I'm doing. No funeral. Maybe a memorial service later after I've processed this. The autopsy didn't show any of the regular toxins, so they think it was an allergic reaction. Everything has been a mess. I don't know when I'm going back to the city. I don't know about anything anymore.*

Then another quick text.

> *Thanks for checking in.*

Was that it? A heartfelt text full of emotion, then an *okay-cool-thanks-peaceout*. Kim typed back and hit send before she could stop herself.

You can come over if you need to talk.

No response.

Good. She didn't know why she sent that text. It was after ten o'clock at night, and he was her ex, and he just lost his fiancée, and he might have been terrorizing her.

She put *Schitt's Creek* on Hulu and started watching it from the beginning—again, for the tenth time at least—and right when David and Alexis started telling each other to get murdered first, her phone beeped.

What's your address?

Oh shit.

33

ANTHONY
THEN

Anthony was in the office by seven thirty on Monday morning. He tried to spend as much time away from PJ as he could, not knowing if he was more embarrassed or pissed off at the fact that he'd been duped. He didn't much like playing pretend the way she did—a little girl and her games. *A few more months*, he kept telling himself.

He'd booked that trip to Hawaii with the intention of mock proposing, following all the phases in her ridiculous book. He'd even change his will, have it notarized with her there and subsequently filed with the courts, and change it right back and have it refiled without her knowledge. It was none of her business. He'd marry her all right, just so she'd think she'd won. And the next day, before they'd even left for the honeymoon, he'd pull the rug out from under her. The annulment papers would already be drawn up by his lawyer.

She'd never get to kill him on their honeymoon.

The only thing that bothered him was the *why*. People didn't go to those lengths just for money. Sure, he was worth close to thirty million dollars, and she wouldn't get anywhere near that much in a divorce, but was *murder* worth the extra money? Maybe he was second, third, or fourth in a line of people she'd done this to before; a black widow. What did she have planned to cover her own ass?

He tapped his pen on his desk for a good half hour, letting the sound put him in a trance. His two televisions were on MarketWatch but muted, and every once in a while, he'd flick his eyes up to see the ticker scroll on the bottom. He really needed to pay attention to the futures if he was going to add more money to this firm, and therefore, his pocket.

His pocket. Not PJ's.

It was an hour later when his office phone rang.

"Anthony Fuller," he answered.

"Mr. Fuller. It's Damien."

He sat up straighter. Damien. His *guy*.

Anthony looked at his watch. "You're earlier than I expected. Did you find anything?"

"Are you sitting down?"

He gulped. He didn't like the sound of this. "Go on."

Damien drew in a deep breath. "Well, for starters, her real name is Paulina Jensen, not Poppy Jade Walsh. She grew up in—"

"Stop."

Anthony needed a moment when the realization of who she was hit him like a heavyweight punch. She didn't go after him for money after seeing him on CNN. She wasn't a starry-eyed student who targeted him after listening to his speech at NYU. She wasn't a black widow. She was Paulina Jensen.

It all made sense. He knew exactly who she was. *She* knew exactly who *he* was. She didn't want his money; that was just the icing on the top of her revenge cake.

How long had she known about this? About him? How long had she been planning this entire elaborate scheme?

Sweat gathered at his temples, and he grabbed a tissue from the holder on his desk. "Damien, can I place you on a brief hold?"

"Sure thing, Boss."

"Great."

Anthony hooked the phone on the receiver and pinched the top of his nose. Pushing his chair back from his desk so fast he almost hit the window behind him, he stood and tried to walk at a normal pace to the bathroom. That proved impossible. People in the office looked his way as he moved swiftly past everyone, bumping into desks as he turned corners. In his haste, he forgot the key to the executive bathroom, but he didn't care. He went to the public one that was used by regular traders and guests. Inside, there were Formica counters instead of marble, no mahogany shelving or soft lighting or tasteful decoration. A cannister of paper towels hung attached to the wall. Plastic stalls. No scent of lavender throughout.

Sterile. Antiseptic. Basic.

He didn't care. He ran to the sink and turned on the water, one of those awful sinks with the handle you had to push every five seconds to keep the water coming out, unlike the

chrome faucets with constantly flowing water in the executive bathroom. He kept trying to get a stream of water to
splash on his face but had to do it one hand at a time, hot then
cold, hot then cold. He yanked a few paper towels to dry his
hands and face—itchy, unlike the soft, laundered towels he
was used to—and wiped the back of his neck.

Paulina Jensen. The daughter of Monica and Harold
Jensen.

Monica was dead, and he started to see the forest for the
trees. He killed her, all right. Still, he suspected it wouldn't
make a difference to PJ who ultimately pulled the trigger.
Jose was paying a price for it, but Anthony never did, and
PJ—Paulina, whoever—wanted revenge. Jose did Tony a favor
by taking the fall. He had no choice. *Tony* had street power
back then, and Jose didn't want his family to be in danger.

But, if Monica Jensen was dead, who the hell did he have
dinner with in Texas? Anthony had asked Damien to investigate everything, so he'd better have that answer.

Washing his face proved futile since the sweat wouldn't
stop dripping down the side of his cheeks, so he brought a
few of the scratchy paper towels back to his desk. When he
returned to his office, he closed the door behind him before
he picked up the line with a shaking hand. "Sorry about that.
Continue."

"Right. Okay, so her name is Paulina Jensen, born to
Monica and Harold Jensen, August 24, 1999, in Cades Point,
Texas. Raised in Cades Point, Texas. Mother died March 16,
2006. Father deceased as of December 2019. Paulina attended
Texas Tech, graduated May 24, 2021. Previous address listed
as Hester Street in New York City, current address listed as

East 79th Street, New York City. No arrests, no felonies, no convictions, credit score of 745."

Anthony's breathing was shallow. "And what about the address I gave you?"

Damien flipped pages on the other end of the line. "Oh, right. That belongs to Peter and Susan Mazzucca, purchased June 2009. One son, Matthew, born February 22, 1999. Peter is—"

Anthony tuned out as Damien went into Peter's job as an accountant and marrying a former beauty queen. *One son, Matthew.* That had to be her friend Matt—her former roommate. They were in on this together. Those were *his* parents, not hers. Now it all made sense why the father cared so much about what was going to happen to Matt when PJ—*Paulina*—moved in with him.

Despite everything he'd learned already, his heart ached. He'd spent so much effort trying to pick out a perfect present for them. The Walshes. The hand carving with their longitude and latitude. They'd accepted it and placed it on their mantle.

The Walshes didn't exist.

They'd all faked it so well. Anthony didn't have a mirror on the wall across from his desk, but he could guess the tomato color of his face. The steam coming out of his ears like a cartoon character. The pressure in his cheeks like he was an atom bomb about to blow. The crazy behind his eyes when it occurred to him that PJ didn't know his exact brand of crazy, but she would.

"Areas of income?" Anthony asked.

He heard pages flipping again. "Right. After Harold's death, there was an offer on his land, which had been willed to Paulina. The sale closed in September of 2020. Two point one million offer, four hundred thousand or so left on the mortgage. After applicable fees, Paulina got just under one point six million."

Paulina. The whole thing was so weird to him. She really was a bitch; she didn't need his money at all.

"And the yoga business?"

More pages flipped. "Nothing on record as income. Just interest and investment dividends. Not much annually. She seems to be burning through the money fast. I guess she's young enough to make it back."

Was anything about her real?

"Is there anything else?" Anthony asked through a clenched jaw.

"Nope. Anything else I can do for you, Boss?"

A feeling of familiarity swept over him like a broom. The only woman he'd ever trust was the one who knew him before he made his money, and he yearned for that connection again. He didn't know what he'd do with the information if he got it, but he'd decided he needed it, just in case.

"Actually, yeah. I'm going to email you the last known address of someone in Brooklyn. All I know is that she moved to California fifteen years ago. I want to know where she is now. What she's up to. Her name is Kim Valva."

"I'll await your email. Is that it?"

He was sure he'd need Damien again. This was war. "I'll keep you posted."

Anthony hung up the phone and started to make a list of everything else he'd want researched. Her friend Matt. His parents. Her elementary school teachers, her soccer coach, her fucking sorority sisters. He had to know every single thing about the real her, whoever that was. Anything that would give him an edge. His rage was interrupted when his phone rang again.

"Anthony Fuller."

"Hi, Anthony. It's Carla Boswell."

A sly smile broke onto his face. "Carla. I'm so glad you called."

Let the games begin.

34

KIM

NOW

Why did she text Tony, and why did she give him her address? Unless that was his play, and he knew it already because he was The Stranger. He was going to be at her door in less than ten minutes. She didn't even prepare what to say to him, or how to find out why he was at Night Shift talking about PJ's death with someone who was probably Carla Boswell.

In her bedroom, Kim put a sports bra on under her tank top and pulled on loose-fitting pajama bottoms with a drawstring waist. After all, it was ten o'clock at night during the week. She shouldn't be all dressed up, like she was waiting for Tony to come by. Like she cared what he thought of her attire. She sent him a random text asking if he was okay, that was all it was. Still, she ran a brush through her hair and used mouthwash and flossed. She pinched her cheeks to give her face some color—adding makeup this late would look too desperate. Desperate, or eager? Didn't matter, she was neither.

When the knock came at the door, she jumped. Murphy lifted his head, but then went right back down. It was after his bedtime, but it was always in the back of Kim's head that he was getting weaker. She had to remember, all of this was for him. She looked through the peephole, and Anthony was there. She opened the door.

"Hey, come on in," she said.

"Thanks."

He walked in and went to the left, into her kitchen. He, too, was dressed very casually in jogging pants and a crisp white T-shirt. He'd really grown into a man. He'd always been handsome, as much as you can be through high school and your early twenties, but now there was more to him. The silver strands in his scruff, which looked so much better on him than being clean shaven. His stature was different; he'd held himself with more confidence, and it showed, even now in his worst state.

She closed the door behind him, and they bumped into each other while attempting an awkward hug. Tony held on a little too long, a little too hard, and Kim stepped back and detached.

"How are you handling things?" she asked him.

He shook his head and rubbed the back of his neck, his T-shirt *just* lifting above his pant line, exposing skin. "I don't even know. A week ago, we were planning a wedding, and tomorrow I'm setting her on fire."

Ugh. She saw the anguish in his face. The defeat.

"How's her family doing?" Kim grabbed her glass of cabernet that she'd been working on when she sent him the text to come over. She lifted it to him as if to ask, *do you want some?* and he quirked up a lip. *Yes.*

Their silent language.

Kim found another glass and wiped the rim on a cloth, then set it down and opened another bottle of red and poured. She handed it to him, and he took a sip before he answered.

"They want me to send the ashes to Texas. The Walshes were lovely. I only met them once, but they were very welcoming. I don't know why they didn't fly in, but I guess they're in shock."

Kim pressed her lips together. "Do you have any right to keep her here? Legally?" *Keep her here.* Like they'd be going dancing on Friday nights.

"She was my fiancée. I thought that was enough. I was able to make the decisions because I was in charge of her living will, but I guess because I didn't yet have that ring on my finger, the *Walshes* want her with them."

He sounded angry. She tried not to judge; she hoped to never be in his position.

Kim gestured for them to sit on the couch. Murphy stood and gave him a good sniffing, and Tony pet his head and scratched him behind the ears before Murphy decided Tony was cool and waddled into the bedroom to go sleep in his doggy bed. She wanted to have a real conversation with Tony and find out if he was at Night Shift with Carla.

"So, what did you do today?" She thought she'd be able to detect it if he lied. She knew him well enough.

"You know. Just stuff. I worked remotely for a bit, and I tried to find someone to get rid of her stuff in the city."

He paused. She'd detected a bit of an edge to his voice. "It's too painful for me to go back and pack it up myself. Everything reminds me of her and the life we were going to have."

"How are Ron and Carla handling it? I assume you've spoken to them since the . . . accident."

To be fair, unless he had something going on with Carla, there was no reason for him to talk to her about it. Ron was his boss, and Kim was sure they'd kept in contact while Tony wrapped up all the loose ends dealing with PJ's death. The police might've been done, but Kim knew what was going on behind the scenes with The Stranger.

"They're going through their own shit with their divorce right now. I haven't talked to them about it. I just told Ron I wouldn't be in this week."

He sipped his wine and seemed to be contemplating. He shifted his place on the couch ever so slightly, and Kim knew it was a tell. He was lying. That had to be him and Carla at Night Shift. How could she get him to admit it?

She decided to go with shock. "Did you know I worked at the country club before you joined?"

"What? Kimmy, that's insane."

Was it though? She hadn't seen him in fifteen years, and she knew he was lying about something. Stuff like that, it was muscle memory. It snapped back like she'd started lifting weights again, where everything seemed to fit like there was never a break in the process, no matter how long it had been. She knew him better than she remembered.

Kim shrugged. "It's an awful coincidence. Have you tried to contact me recently?" *Are you The Stranger?*

"Kimmy, my life is completely different than the one you remember. Nothing is the same. I'm not the same. I mean, I don't want to say I forgot about you because it sounds terrible, but I'd moved on from you, that was for sure."

So had she, but hearing him say it stung. Like using hand sanitizer only to discover a paper cut. His left eyebrow did that thing, and she didn't believe him. "Me too. I've had serious relationships. I even lived with someone."

"Really? What happened?"

She hated talking about her relationship with Nicholas. They were together almost two years, and she never pegged him as the type to hurt her. Even the way they met was out of a storybook—she'd spilled her coffee on him when she'd turned around too quickly and subsequently asked him to send her the dry-cleaning bill. He'd later used the opportunity to ask her out for coffee if she promised not to pour it on him. The romance books call it a meet-cute. It really was, until it wasn't.

"He got his coworker pregnant. He moved out over a year ago. We don't keep in touch." She looked toward her bedroom. "All I have is Murphy. They call him a rescue dog, but he's the one who rescued me and now . . ." Her voice cracked. "He's sick. He has a cancerous tumor, and I can't afford his surgery. He's supposed to have it on Monday, but my funding just fell through."

She couldn't stop the tears from pooling over and falling down her cheeks, and she wiped them with the back of her hand. Her *funding* falling through would be the least of her problems. Being killed for not doing the job by taking Tony out was worse. However, she still hadn't been asked to return the money. She hadn't heard from The Stranger since the day after PJ died.

Unless she'd just let him into her home.

"I can help, you know. I can lend you the money," Tony said.

She blinked and squinted her eyes at him. "I can't let you do that."

"Oh, so you'd rather let him die? Come on, Kimmy."

She shook her head. "I can't. I mean, how would it look? Your fiancée dies and days later you're giving ten grand to your ex-girlfriend, who was there when your fiancée was killed? It's going to look like we're conspiring something."

He took an extra-large swig of his wine, draining half the glass. "I can give you cash. No one would know." He bopped her on the nose, like he used to do a long time ago. Not only did that mean it was a pact, but it was a sign of affection. Of love. "Our little secret."

Their eyes were locked. They shouldn't have, not then. Kim wanted to know if he lied about being at Night Shift, but she physically couldn't pull away. She tried, but it was like sleep paralysis. She was completely immobile, and it didn't help the wiggle in her stomach that he didn't look away either.

It took her by surprise when he leaned into her, and a bigger surprise was that she still didn't move. She closed her eyes and braced for it. Right before their lips met, Murphy came out from the bedroom and barked at the door.

"Murphy, stop." The trance broke, and it was the first time she was able to move. She scooted back and covered her lips like a shield. "Oh my God, what were we about to do?"

Tony also scuttled backward. "I'm sorry. This was my fault. Talking about PJ dying and wanting to help you, I just fell into old—"

"No, it's my fault too. Talking about Nicholas and lost love. We're both vulnerable."

Murphy continued barking at the door, then facing them, then back at the door.

"I think the pooch has us figured out," Tony said, chuckling. He finished the last of his wine. "Thanks for the invite. I feel so comfortable with you, Kimmy, but maybe I shouldn't be here. I'm going to go. But hey, stop by this weekend. I'll have cash for you. I promise."

The Stranger always had bundles of cash. He was playing her, and she didn't know why.

They stood and she walked him to the door. He stopped and turned to face her, a look in his eye that was simultaneously fifteen years old and fifteen minutes old. He smiled and stuck out his hand. "Good to see you tonight."

She shook it. "Good to see you. And I'll pay you back. I promise." With what, she had no idea. She'd figure it out. "Good night."

Murphy scuttled out of the way when Tony opened the door, then looked at the ground. "Oops. Sorry. Something was leaning against the door." He squatted down and picked it up, then read the front before handing it to her. "Just a manila envelope with your name on it."

He handed it to her, and she felt the hard plastic contents.

"Thanks." She closed the door behind him and waited.

Oh shit.

35
PJ
THEN

I can barely keep my eyes open, but I have to. I've heard the sunsets in Maui are second to none. Being on a plane for like, twelve hours, isn't helping, in addition to the time change. In my brain, when we landed, it was after eleven at night, though it's just past six here. That was after heading to the airport before 6:00 a.m. Our first-class seats were mini beds, which was super cool, but I couldn't sleep. Not even a quick catnap like Anthony took. He fell asleep several times, but I used my inability to relax to read gossip magazines and watch a gazillion movies. My eyes were strained for many reasons.

Staring at the purple and orange sky from our balcony calms me. With the light breeze and the smell of coconuts in the air, I'm in heaven.

Anthony kisses my neck from behind, his arms wrapping around my waist. "I've only seen one other thing as beautiful as this in my life. I'm glad I get them both at once."

I sigh, leaning backward into him. "This is perfection. I love you so much."

I hate myself, because I do. I also hate that Matt has all but stopped speaking to me. He knows me better than anyone, and when we had dinner last week, he sniffed the love on me like a drug dog at the airport. Like he'd said before, he knew I was going to turn into who I was pretending to be once I was with Anthony twenty-four-seven.

After coming clean, I told him some of the intimacies in our relationship, the little things Anthony has done and how he worships me, and that he should be happy for me. I told Matt that maybe we should have a reason to doubt Jose Sanchez's story. The man was convicted of murder, for God's sake. How do I know he wasn't lying about what happened when me and Matt visited him in jail five years ago?

I pleaded with Matt to meet Anthony, to see for himself what kind of a man he is, but he refused, because whether or not Anthony pulled the trigger, he got off scot-free and it wasn't fair. Told me to figure out if I'm Poppy Jade Walsh or Paulina Jensen.

I can be both. Paulina can forgive. Paulina can be Poppy Jade. I always was a *PJ*.

"We should order room service and get a good night's sleep," Anthony says. "The time difference is crazy. We can wake up nice and refreshed on Island Time."

"That sounds perfect. What are our plans for tomorrow?"

He gives my shoulders a rub. "I thought the breakfast buffet and just relaxing. Doing our own thing until we fully adjust. We'll probably need one full day here. We can lounge by the pool, get tan, go shopping; whatever you want to do."

I turn around and hug him, breathing in the scent on his neck, *his* scent, the one I love even through the airport and plane and travel smell. "I want to see dolphins."

"There's a whale watching tour and a dolphin tour. We can stop at the concierge tomorrow and grab all the brochures. I want to do the hike up the Road to Hana. There's a ton to do here."

"Ten days of activities. I can't wait."

He kisses me and thumbs my cheek. "Plenty of time to relax too. I needed a break from the office. I told them we went to Paris and I wouldn't be calling in all the time. Let them think I'm in another country."

"Ha. They think you're five hours ahead, but you're really five hours behind? That could make for some interesting Zoom calls."

"Nope. I told them to leave me alone for two weeks. I deserve it."

"Yes, you do." He works so hard, all to make a life for me. For us. And I wanted to kill him over something a convict said. "Hopefully they have yoga here. I'd hate to fall behind." I feel bad for lying to him this whole time, stuffing my face with French pastries and drinking coffee when he thought I was doing private training.

"There's a state-of-the-art gym. I'm sure they have classes, or at least a room you can use. Things are pretty Zen here."

"Right. You've been here before."

He told me he brought an ex-girlfriend here about a decade ago. They stayed in a room at the Ritz, and we're in a two-bedroom villa at the Andaz. He told Matt's father he was planning to propose to me. He's got to be planning to do it here, in the most romantic place in the world. At least it feels that way right now.

"Let's order some food, and then take a long, hot shower," he says. "I can't wait to demolish that big, beautiful bed."

We go inside, and off to the left of the enormous main room is a sitting area with a desk. On top there's a thick leather-bound book that contains all the hotel's attractions, and in the back, there is a room service menu. We order the works, complete with expensive champagne.

After eating and a soapy, steamy shower, I tell Anthony I need to get ready for bed. He leaves me to my own devices, and I unpack the vacation-sex required lingerie, complete with thigh-high stockings, garters, and heels with feathers. I'm exhausted, but I want to make love to him. It's our first night here and I want it to be special.

It is. The look on his face is priceless when I come out of the bathroom.

The next few days are a dream. Still no proposal, but we do a lot of romantic things. Morning walks with coffee, sunset dinners on the beach, cocktails at the Four Seasons, visits to the lavender gardens. It's exactly as I pictured it would be.

Until it isn't.

We just finished dinner at Mamma's Fish House and are perusing the dessert menu when *Oh my God, are you kidding me?*

"Anthony and Poppy, is this really happening?"

It's Carla Boswell, in a sapphire-blue dress cut down to there, the deep V-neck pointing to what she wants everyone to see, even if it's below her belly button. Her near nakedness is on full display, and that sweating, dumpy husband of hers is behind her, his eyes narrowed at our presence. He thinks we should be in France eating croissants.

Anthony squeezes my hand under the table. I know that means he wants to take the lead and I should just follow what he says. Fine by me. I can't make up a thing right now.

"Ron, Carla, what a surprise!" Anthony lays it on thick. "What on earth are you doing here?"

"I could ask the same thing," Ron says. "I thought you were in Paris."

Anthony wipes his mouth with a cloth napkin and stands. Kisses Carla, who grabs him too close as usual, but *eat your heart out, you'll never have him.* Then he shakes hands with Ron and holds his hand out as if to offer them the remaining two seats at our table. *Ugh.*

After everyone is seated comfortably, Anthony grabs my hand and looks at me lovingly. "We were in Paris for a few days, but it got so cold, and poor PJ was uncomfortable." He kisses my hand. "I wanted to show her a nice time, so we came here. Landed yesterday morning. Wasted twenty-four hours traveling, so yesterday sucked, but we're good now." He clears his throat and directs his attention to Ron. "How were you able to leave the office with me out for two weeks?"

Ron purses his lips. "Because I own the damn company and I can do what I want, when I want."

"I wanted to come," Carla interjects. "Spur of the moment. Who knows the next time I'll be able to see Hawaii? We got a suite at the Ritz."

This is one of the only times I can legitimately one-up this bitch. "Oh, that must be adorable! We have a villa at the Andaz."

She's seething so much I can almost see her Botoxed face move. Only a little though. She grabs Anthony's glass of water and sips. "Any special plans while you're here?"

Well, that was awfully familiar, drinking out of his glass. "We've already—"

"We have so much on the agenda, but we just relaxed today," Anthony interrupts. Whew. I almost mentioned the fifty things we've already done, which is obviously impossible if this is our first full day.

"You guys have great tans for one day," Ron says, staring at me. He faintly licks his lips as he scoots his chair a little closer to me and takes a deep breath. "I love the smell of the air here. So tropical."

If I didn't know any better, I'd think he was about to pee on my leg.

I nod. "The sun is so strong here. It's my first time. I should've used more sunblock. Lesson learned." Silence. Awkward. I look left to right. "Where's the waiter? We should probably get the check." So much for the chocolate souffle I was eyeing, but Ron has always made me uncomfortable. I never said anything to Anthony about it when I was playing a part, but maybe now I will. Things are different.

Anthony rubs my forearm, then grasps my hand and kisses it again. "Right. It's time for bed." He says it devilishly, and I think Carla's head is about to explode because she has to go to bed with doughboy Ron. "How long are you guys here?"

"The rest of the week. I guess we'll be seeing you around," Carla says.

"Maybe. I have a lot of activities on the brain. And this is our first real vacation together, so we want to be alone as much as possible. Just me and Peej, a nice romantic getaway."

I love him. He knows Carla is trying so hard to get under my skin, and possibly his, but he won't allow it. Plus, he said he wanted a break from work. Complete insanity that his boss showed up at the same place. What are the chances? It's not like Anthony has social media and tagged us.

I did though. Uh-oh. They might know exactly when we got here. Is Carla stalking me?

Or worse. Is Ron?

36
KIM
NOW

After Anthony left, the dread set in. Of course, she ripped the envelope open to find a burner phone. And for the first time, a small, handwritten letter. The letters were meticulous, like they came from a typewriter. She doubted a handwriting expert would be able to pin this on anyone in court.

> He's not who you think he is. The job will be finished with or without you. Await my call.

With shaking hands, Kim searched her junk drawer in the kitchen until she found the lighter that she used to light candles and set the piece of paper on fire over her sink.

The "job." Did that mean just Tony, or was it still a one-two punch that it was supposed to be both him and PJ, but now it was going to be him and her? She had no right to ask questions. And The Stranger wasn't going to give her answers anyway.

Kim took the burner into her bedroom and placed it on her nightstand as Murphy camped in the doggy bed. She shut off the light, got under the covers, and stared at the darkness above her. What was Tony thinking, trying to kiss her so soon after his fiancée died? What was she thinking, preparing herself for it, and then agreeing to take his money? She never got answers on if it was Tony at Night Shift earlier today, or if it was Carla with him. Kim had dismissed that he was The Stranger, but he could've left that envelope at her door when he got there, only to "discover" it as he left. Or he was working with Carla, or whatever woman he could've been at the bar with, and they were setting her up, with one half of the cohort team dropping it at her apartment while Tony fake seduced her inside.

And she fell for it. Was she an idiot for believing anything Tony said or did?

Her mind drifted back to things she hadn't thought about since she was a teenager. The way Tony charmed everyone in their old neighborhood. The rotten things he'd done. Not just the murder-adjacent thing with Jose, but everything else. The constant fistfights, the illegal gambling ring, the intimidation—hell, even some adults were afraid of him. What was his secret? Did people ever change, or did they just learn to hide things better?

Tony had so much more at his disposal now, with his millions of dollars and his high society position. He could have the entire internet scrubbed of Tony Fiore. He probably already did, lurking in the shadows to pop up when anyone would least expect it. But a new haircut and tailored clothes didn't hide "Tony" from "Anthony"—not in Kim's eyes.

Or he could be as innocent in all of this as PJ was. He probably wanted to kiss her tonight simply because she felt like home to him, and home was what he needed with everything going on in his life.

If Murphy hadn't started barking, what would the kiss have led to? She didn't think either of them would've stopped. Once his tongue was in her mouth, it would all rush back. Not just him, but the feeling of being desired, wanted. She needed hands on her breasts, in her pants. It didn't matter if it was Tony or someone else. She hadn't gotten laid in almost nine months, after a one-night stand that she forced herself to have with someone she pulled out of a bar after wallowing about Nicholas for months. Maddy was right; she needed to get back out there.

She would. After Murphy was okay. Right now, he was the only man she had room for in her life.

Her eyes felt heavy, and she was about to drift off when the burner rang and startled her. She jumped up and reached for it.

"Hello?"

"Listen to me very fucking carefully, Kim Valva."

She sat up straighter—she was in trouble. The computerized voice, full of anger and contempt, wasn't playing around. She stiffened, the hair on the back of her neck standing up.

"Anthony Fuller is a dead man. His relationship with PJ was a scam. I have proof. You will finish this, or you're next. Do. You. Understand. Me?"

Kim's blood ran cold. She screwed up. She'd known this for the past week, but now it was time to pay. In her panic, she let it all out. "I'm sorry. I knew him from a long time ago, and I couldn't do it once I saw it was him. I don't even have the poison anymore, I got rid of everything once his fiancée died that night. I didn't know what was going on. Everything happened so fast." She talked a mile a minute.

There was silence on the end of the line, and then a fierce bang on her door that made her yelp. Murphy barked, then jumped onto the bed and curled up next to her. Protective.

"Don't answer that," the voice said. "It's me. Want me to prove it? Three bangs, right now."

Bang.

Bang.

Bang.

Kim gripped Murphy as if he were her lifeline, which at that moment, he was. Her heart was going into V-fib with the amount of adrenaline coursing through her. She wasn't a tough girl anymore; she wasn't the type to jump up and open the door and confront The Stranger. Instead, she stayed with her head buried in Murphy's fur, eyes squeezed shut.

"I know where you live, Kim," The Stranger said. "I know where you walk your dog, I know where you work, I know who your friends are and where they work. I will make sure you're blamed for PJ's death, and I'll make sure you're blamed when your friends start getting hurt. I will make your life fucking miserable if you don't finish this, are we clear?"

She nodded.

"I said *are we clear*?"

"We're clear." Her voice shook.

"Await further instructions."

The line went dead.

37

PJ

THEN

We wake up on the last day of our vacation. I couldn't have asked for a better ten days in my life. Every sunset, every meal, every time Anthony grabbed my hand to lead me on a trail in the woods made me fall more in love with him.

Our flight is at eleven o'clock tonight, so this is the last hurrah. Three more meals, and the next time I wake up next to him, it'll be on the plane when we land in Newark. I'm lying next to him, on my left side with my right arm and leg draped over him. He tickles my hair. Major bedhead, considering we *really* took advantage of our last night in paradise.

A bonus, we hadn't run into Ron or Carla the rest of the time we were here. Ron reached out once, asking us to dinner, but Anthony knew I didn't want to go and made an excuse about being on a sunset helicopter tour that night. Which we had already done before the phone call, so we'd be able to recount the details if asked about it.

He kisses the top of my head. "Hey."

"Hey." My voice is hoarse.

His soft brown eyes say everything I'm feeling, and I mentally kick myself for ever wanting to hurt this wonderful man. Before we left, I googled everything I could find about the trial from fifteen years ago and looked at all of it with a fresh set of eyes. It was obvious that Jose did it. Jose murdered my mother, and Anthony dropped him right from that point on. Even testified against him, his old friend. He changed his entire life. He wanted to make everything right, become a better man. I believed a fucking convict over Anthony. Matt would eventually see; I'd make him come around.

Maybe this all happened for a reason. Maybe Mama took one for the team, knowing what I'd do to avenge her death, but in the end, making me the happiest woman alive.

Anthony jumps out of bed and pulls on his boxers, then strides out of the bedroom and over to the desk, and opens the room service menu. "Same as the rest of the week?" he calls out to me.

I nod, but he can't see me. "Yes, please." An egg white omelet with peppers and onions for me, hash browns and white toast on the side. Anthony had been bouncing between poached eggs with whole wheat toast and Belgian waffles with extra whipped cream. Which made for at least one really fun time. We always split a plate of crispy bacon and a pot of coffee.

He places the order and comes back into the bedroom, then into the bathroom to brush his teeth. I rise and do the same, side by side at our own sinks. He winks at me while my mouth is foamy with toothpaste. I spit and rinse, use my mouthwash, then saunter over to him and hug him, his hard muscles resisting against me. I snake my hands up his biceps and squeeze as his hand drifts down my back onto the curve of my ass.

He reaches under my chin, lifts my face, and kisses me softly. "I want to talk to you about something important."

All business. What now?

"Okay. What's up?" I ask. Should I be nervous?

He takes my hand and leads me back to the bed, then sits on it and pats the space next to him. I take it and regrip his hand. Our fingers intertwine, then he grabs my other hand and does the same. Two bodies, joined as one.

"I never thought I'd meet anyone like you, Peej. I'm the luckiest man in the world."

There are stars in my eyes. "I'm the lucky one."

He gulps, then grins. "Remember when I left for a few hours the other night?"

I nod. He'd surprised me when we were lounging in our private lanai, sipping fruity cocktails and vibing out with the breeze. It was around four in the afternoon, and he looked at his phone and said he had to go and would be back in a little while. Came back around six thirty, apologized, and told me he had some urgent work things he had to take care of. I didn't mind because we'd spent every second together and I knew how important his job was to him.

"Well, it was at that moment I made an impulse decision."

"Oh?"

He slides down to the floor and faces me on both knees, still holding my hands, until he disengages one. He reaches for the handle on his nightstand, opens the drawer, and pulls out a small square box. A robin's egg blue box.

Oh. My. God.

He lifts one leg so he's only on one knee and takes a small black velvet box out of the blue one and opens it. Inside is the biggest, clearest, brightest, most beautiful oval stone I've ever seen. Just like Mama's, only grand. I notice pavé diamonds all around the band as he takes the ring out of the box and holds it up in front of me.

"Poppy Jade Walsh, I love you with all my heart. Will you marry me?"

I scream YES before I faint, because it feels like I'm going to. My arms are wrapped around his neck and I refuse to let go. Tears fall down my cheeks, and I grab his face with both hands and kiss him while his hands tear at my underwear and lift my nightgown over my head.

My new plan is coming together, and I don't need a scrapbook for this one. It's been in my head since I was a little girl. Meet my prince, fall in love, get married, have babies, and live happily ever after.

And I'm going to have it all with the love of my life.

38

KIM

NOW

By Saturday morning, Kim hadn't heard from The Stranger since the last terrifying phone call on Wednesday night. The new burner hadn't rung again, there were no new ones delivered, and she worked her shift on Thursday and Friday without incident.

Last night, it was the regular crowd at the corner table in the bar room, minus one—Ben and Emiko Xiang, Hector and Wendy Alvarez, and Ron Boswell. No Carla. Not after that disaster announcement about the divorce and her throwing a drink at his face. Looked like Ron got to keep the friends in the split. He was the one with the power, after all. They all ate and drank, forgetting that just a week before, there was a tragic death in that very spot.

Kim wondered where Carla was and planned to try to follow up on her hunch about the mystery couple at Night

Shift. She had to stop at Tony's house to pick up cash for Murphy's surgery, for when she'd be forced to return all the money she'd already taken. She decided that was going to be her play—return it all. Walk away like nothing had ever happened. She didn't know who The Stranger was, and she didn't want to be involved in what was coming, so she shouldn't be a target any longer. Since she'd destroyed every burner that had been delivered and burned the note, there was nothing left except the bank account, and she planned to give up the password if she ever got another phone call. Let them take it all back.

She also wanted to warn Tony that someone was after him, and she didn't know how to do that. Not without outing herself and what she'd been tasked to do. And how she almost went through with it. It couldn't be as simple as *hey, watch your back, someone might have it out for you too.* She needed to be creative.

After walking and feeding Murphy, she got a text from Tony.

Stop by whenever you want. I'll be here all day.

She replied, *Thanks. I'll be there within the hour.*

Despite her old bad feelings toward Tony, she couldn't shake the desire she'd felt the other night. Her former fury was rooted in teenage angst, and she was surprised at how quickly she was able to let it go as a mature adult. That didn't mean she wanted to start up again with him, and she didn't want to be alone with him, just in case. She grabbed her phone and tapped.

Hey, is it okay if I bring Murphy? His surgery is on Monday, and he's been acting a little off. I don't want him to be alone.

It was only half true, but she thought it was a good way to not fall into bed with him. He wrote back, *No problem.*

After showering and putting on a pink cotton sundress and white sparkly flip-flops, she loaded Murphy into her car and drove to Tony's beach house. When she pulled into the driveway, her heart tugged for PJ and the plans she'd made in her new, grand home. Kim didn't have to know her well, or at all, really, to know it was a beautiful life lost too soon.

Why?

Kim opened the back door and Murphy jumped out, tail wagging. He probably thought he was going to get to go for a swim in the ocean again. The dog-friendly part of the beach wasn't too far from where Tony's house was, maybe a quarter mile. Murphy probably recognized the scent and was preparing for a day of soaking himself, playing with the other dogs, and rolling in the sand.

"Come on, good boy," she said as she grasped his leash and headed up the paved walkway to the front door.

Tony opened the door before she got there. There was a huge smile on his face. "Hey, Kimmy." He looked down at Murphy, who remembered him from the other night and shoved his head under Tony's outstretched hand for some scratches. "Come on in."

He held the door open wide, and Kim entered behind a curious Murphy. "Don't worry, he's house trained."

"It's okay. I still love dogs. Remember Koko?"

Kim smiled at the memory of Tony's old chocolate lab, the best ninety-five-pound lapdog in the world. Koko had to be put down just after her sixteenth birthday, when Tony was nineteen. She didn't know which he took worse—that death, or the one of his cousin in the car accident in the snow. Kim knew he'd been devastated over Koko, though he didn't cry in front of her over *an animal* the way he did over William's car crash. Appearances and all, and Tony never wanted to look weak.

She unleashed Murphy and let him run around the first floor, smelling everything he could take in. He paused for an inordinate amount of time near a blanket that was rumpled on the corner of the couch, his nose buried in the soft wool.

"PJ loved that blanket," Tony said, his eyes misting over. "She used to wrap herself in it all the time and sit in that exact spot." He seemed rattled, his unblinking eyes staring at nothing before he gave his head a little shake. "I can't believe it's all over."

"I'm sorry," Kim said. "I know I keep saying that."

He touched her arm, then quickly removed his hand. "I know. It's all anyone can say."

"Have you told your family yet?"

He shook his head. "I'm going to call them when I get back to the city tomorrow night."

"Oh. You're going back already?"

He shrugged. "Life goes on. I have to get back to work. Figure out what I'm going to do with the rest of my life."

She took in the space around her. "Are you keeping this house?"

"For now. Probably for the rest of the summer to enjoy the club and have a haven out of the city, but I'll either sell it or rent it out after that."

Life goes on. Enjoy the club. Those didn't seem to be the feelings of a grieving fiancé, and Kim's internal antennae went up. "Hey, did you—" She stopped. She couldn't just come out with *Did you go to Night Shift with Carla fucking Boswell last week?* "Did you really think it was an allergic reaction?"

"Of course." It was said matter-of-factly. "What else could it be?"

His face changed. It was a Tony Fiore face, not an Anthony Fuller face. Not that she knew Anthony Fuller so well, but she definitely remembered Tony. It was the same expression he'd used in the past when people doubted his whereabouts, his alibi, whatever bullshit story he'd told to keep himself out of trouble.

Except Kim knew he was usually lying back then.

"That's what the experts said, and I have no reason to doubt them. Do you want some coffee?"

"Sure." He'd changed the subject at lightning speed.

Moving into the kitchen, he took coffee beans from the refrigerator and measured them in a cup, then poured them into a grinder. The noise startled Murphy when Tony turned the machine on, and he tucked himself close to Kim's legs. Tony took the grounds and pushed some buttons on a fancy contraption she'd seen in high-end coffeehouses—the ones that did it all. Regular coffee, espresso, cappuccino, and everything in between.

"Actually, can you make mine a cappuccino?" Kim asked. It had been a while since she'd had one.

"Sure." Anthony opened the fridge again and scanned the contents. "Shit. I'm out of milk."

"Oh, don't worry about it. Black coffee is fine."

"No, wait one second. There's a Wawa that's a couple blocks over, just a two-minute walk away. I need more bottled water anyway. I'll run out and grab everything. I can be back in five minutes."

"It's okay. You don't have to—"

"I insist. I'll be back before you miss me."

He grabbed keys off a hook near the kitchen entrance and walked out the door.

Kim felt like a fish out of water. Why would he leave her in his house? Kim wasn't really a stranger, but it seemed too familiar. She didn't know if this was one of those new smart homes that was riddled with cameras, so she sat in the same spot and scrolled through her phone. Two minutes had gone by when she noticed Murphy was no longer at her feet.

"Murph?" she said. "Where'd you go, good boy?"

She looked around the surrounding area, but she didn't spot him. She got up and walked through the living room, again admiring the decoration. Salt life perfection. There was an open door toward the back of the room, and she went in. It was an office, and Murphy sat on the floor, staring at the window that looked onto the front yard. She was afraid of him barking at a passerby who was innocently jogging or heading to the beach with their surfing equipment.

"Come on, boy. Let's go."

She directed him to the door, but curiosity got the best of her when she saw Tony's desk. It was neat, with a small desk lamp, a printer, and a thin laptop. A pile of magazines and books sat in the top left corner. She thumbed through them. *Architecture Digest, Cigar Aficionado, Whiskey Advocate.* My, how he'd changed from fantasy football magazines and gaming literature. On the bottom was a bound notebook with a picture of him and PJ on the front.

She glanced at the window and didn't see Tony coming from down the street. She didn't want to snoop, but she opened the book and began reading. Kim's heart tugged when she saw girly handwriting—definitely PJ's, since she remembered Tony's chicken scratch—talking about how they met. It was toward the middle where things started to look sinister. Pictures of fire, the grim reaper, knives, guns, pictures of Tony with his face X'd out.

What was she looking at?

Kim squinted and her mouth went dry. Her heart raced as it became clear. PJ wrote this entire book, and it wasn't a keepsake. It was a detailed plan about—about what? She immediately opened her camera app and took pictures of the remaining fifteen pages to examine in further detail when she was alone. There were a few loose typed-up pages folded and tucked into the back of the book, so she took pictures of those as well without looking at them. She slammed the book shut and piled it under all the magazines, lining it up perfectly like it was before. Then she put her hand under her sundress and wiped down the desk so there were no smudges.

"Come on, Murph. We have to go."

He listened to her and walked out of the office, tail wagging, oblivious to what Kim just saw. That made two of them. Murphy ran to the kitchen and sat obediently near the barstool where Kim was before she found him in the office. She shut the door behind her. Wait. Was it open? It had to be; Murphy was in there and he didn't have opposable thumbs to turn a doorknob. Was it wide open, or cracked? She didn't know. She hoped Tony didn't know either as she left it open ten to twelve inches before she took her seat back on the stool.

Tony still wasn't back. With her heart beating out of control, she opened her phone and started expanding the pictures she took with her thumb and forefinger, reading them carefully. Several pages had lists of accidents. A boat wreck. Drowning. Poisons. So, so many poisons.

Was PJ going to try to kill Tony?

And if she was, he found out, which could be the only explanation of the possession of this book.

Did that mean Tony killed PJ first? Or did he find this in her stuff after she died? What the hell was going on?

Kim's hands were shaking by the time Tony came in a minute later, and she still hadn't read all the pictures in detail. She pretended to be scrolling on her phone. She was sure she was white as a ghost, and she tried to steady her trembling lip. *Nothing is wrong.* She cleared her throat. "Everything cool?"

Tony set the bag down. "I didn't know if you liked regular or skim, so I got both. You weren't exactly a coffee drinker when you were a teenager." He took a quart of each from the bag, along with four one-liter bottles of Smartwater, which he placed onto a pantry shelf. He went to a separate cupboard and took out two mugs and placed them on the counter next to the machine.

"Regular is fine. Or skim. Whichever you want. Don't go to any trouble." Kim wanted nothing more than to grab her dog and get the hell out of there. "Regular is fine." However, she had to play this cool until she could figure out what was really going on.

"I'm just taking mine black. So it's no trouble."

She watched his every move as he prepared the cappuccino, making sure he didn't try to spike it, and kept the conversation light and friendly, and away from PJ. He clearly didn't want to talk about her, but Kim was positive there was something nefarious going on between him and Carla. Still, she refused to bring up the Night Shift talk she'd previously sworn to get the truth about. Playing nice was hard while samurais were having an all-out kendo battle in her stomach.

After twenty minutes, coffee cups empty, Tony stood. "Oh. I have the cash for you. Ten thousand, you said, right?"

Kim wanted to vomit. "Yes. I swear I'll pay you back as soon as I can. If you want me to sign a contract, I can give you monthly payments. With interest." She didn't want to give him a reason to kill her. She was already starting to think he'd killed PJ, and it always niggled at her that maybe he'd killed before.

"I trust you. And it's only ten grand."

Only ten grand. *Imagine being able to say that,* she thought. She wished Murphy was a bad boy so she could have him sic 'em right into Tony's balls. "Thank you."

He walked across the living room and into the office, and less than a minute later came out with a stack of neat hundred-dollar bills with a paper band around them and handed it to her.

"I hope Murphy is okay." He touched her upper arm. "I'm sorry you're going through this."

He had the same look in his eye that he had Wednesday night. He wasn't even trying to hide it anymore. Kim did her best to return a longing look, the *Oh, I want to, but we can't right now* look, because the truth was, she was terrified of him.

"Thanks so much for this." She tossed the bills into her bag. "I really have to go." She decided to test him before she left. "I have a bunch of stuff to do today. Errands, a freelance project, and I'm having dinner with my friend Maddy. She finally got a night off work. She works at a place called Night Shift." His face remained blank. "It's not too far from here, actually. You ever go there?"

He shrugged. "Never heard of it. But I don't much do the dumpy dive bar thing anymore."

"Right. You're *Anthony Fuller*." She tried to say it in a teasing, playful way, but as she hooked Murphy to his leash, she broke out into a sweat.

She never told him it was a dumpy dive bar.

39
PJ
THEN

We've been back from Maui for two days, and I'm finally adjusted to the time change and back into the swing of regular life. My heart aches that I have this gorgeous rock on my left hand and I haven't even told Matt yet. I texted him a bunch of times asking to get together, but I always got one- or two-word answers as excuses why he couldn't see me. *Can't,* *busy,* or *Not tonight* or *Working late* and once, just *Sorry, no.*

It truly breaks my heart, but I have to make him see the light.

It's Monday morning, and Anthony left for work at 7:00 A.M. He said he had to catch up after being out for so long. All I want to do is flop back into bed, hike up my sleep mask, and count sheep, but I get up and get dressed. The weather is finally getting springlike, and while it's going to hit the low seventies today, it's early and still chilly. I put on a T-shirt and jeans, and then a long-sleeved cashmere wrap sweater over it. I can always tie that around my waist later if it gets warmer and I'm still out.

Bypassing Monty, I decide to take a cab down to the Lower East Side. I have my key from when I lived with Matt, and there's no way in hell he's up yet. I just have to pray he came home last night, because he'll still be in bed, dead to the world. I punch in the code for the front gate, the metal cage-like door swings open, and I walk up the three stories to my old home. I push the key in the lock and the door opens. Thank God Matt was always too lazy to use the chain—that was always on me. A girl in New York City and all that.

The place looks different. My favorite selfie of us hasn't moved, but Matt has framed and hung some of his own shots on the walls, and they're so good that they look out of place in the small, unrenovated space. Some are color, some are black and white, but they all capture New York City in a way that only he could. Matt isn't interested in taking shots of Soho or swanky rooftop bars or the Financial District. All his pictures are from his eye.

After scanning them all, I find my favorite and it takes my breath away. It's a shot of six strangers at a bus stop. Three are sitting on the bench, and three are standing. All of them are scrolling through their phones oblivious to the world around them, except one older Black lady, who appears to be looking up, staring at something in the distance that gives her pure joy. Her smile is captured perfectly on film. It's not even a toothy grin, or that her lips have moved much at all. It's all in the eyes.

My hand is on my heart when I hear movement in the bedroom.

"Hey, awesomesauce." I try to remind him that it's *me*. "Be decent when you open the door."

The movement stops for a few seconds. I picture him on the other side, trying to decide whether to pretend he isn't home or resign and face me for the first time in months.

"Hang on," he says.

When the door opens thirty seconds later, Matt is still pulling on his blue pajama bottoms. His hair is pulled back into a bun and his beard is thick and dark. His eyes float to mine as he rubs them. "You're tan."

"Hawaii." I can't elaborate on the importance of that trip yet. "I missed you. Why haven't you been answering me?"

A shrug. "Been busy."

"Yeah, I got that from your super wordy texts."

He walks past me and into the kitchen, where he takes a bowl down from one cabinet and cereal from another. Turning the box upside down, he empties the last of it into the bowl and opens a drawer for a spoon, which he drops into it with a clank. He turns to the fridge and opens a new container of milk and pours, then carries the bowl to his favorite chair in the living room.

I'm still standing near the bedroom door. He didn't even hug me.

"Why are you here so early?" He eats a spoonful of cereal, then puts the bowl down on the end table and rubs his eyes again.

"Because I knew if you came home last night, you'd definitely be here at this hour. Remember, we sleep till noon?" I say *we* even though I haven't slept until noon in five months. It totally sucks. But it was something we did when we lived together.

"How did you know I came home? Do you have spies on your payroll now? Did you implant a microchip in my mimosa for me to swallow a few months ago? Did you bug one of the gifts he got you that you knew I'd keep and not sell?"

"That's not funny."

"Kind of is."

"You've been taking so long to get back to me, so I went by Starbucks a few days ago. They said you don't work there anymore."

"I don't."

"What are you doing now?"

"I'll figure it out. I'm fine. You, on the other hand . . . "

"Matt, I really wish you could be happy for me."

He undoes his bun, then runs his fingers through his hair and ties it back again, closer to the bottom of his neck; more of a ponytail than a bun. "I really wish you remembered that he killed your mother."

I blow out an annoyed breath. "We don't know it was him. He testified against Jose Sanchez, he turned his life around after, and we're so quick to take a convict's word over Anthony's. Plus, you didn't even know my mother. I don't know why this bothers you so much."

Shit. I legit never should've said that.

"No, I didn't know her. I know you." He grabs the cereal bowl and puts it on his lap. "*Knew* you."

I find myself hiding my left hand from him as I walk over, then sit cross-legged on the floor next to him. "I miss you."

"Yep."

"I really wish you could be happy for me. Will you please meet him? Please? If you still decide he gives you the creeps or whatever, I'll listen. But right now, it's hard for me. You don't know him."

He eats silently. All I hear is the chewing, then he rubs his eyes for the third time. "I'm tired."

I nod. "What did you do last night?"

"I was out with Derek."

"Oh. Who's that?"

"The guy I've been seeing for three weeks."

This rips my heart out. The fact that Matt has someone important to him and I didn't even know about it. I try to hold back the tears.

"That's great. Where'd you meet him?"

"Swipe right."

"Can I see a picture?"

"I don't have any."

"The photographer doesn't have any?" He's lying to me. He doesn't want to let me in. I scan the walls again. "All these shots are terrific, Matt. I'm so proud of you. Have you tried to get a showing?"

He shrugs. "For what? My hobby? I'm a barista."

"Former." I touch his forearm. "You know you're more than that. You should try to get an agent."

His eyes fly to my hand. I touched his forearm with my *left* hand. Shit.

"Wow," he says.

I snap my hand back like I touched a hot stove. "It's not what you think."

"Oh, really? That's not an engagement ring? From the man you *love*?"

A tear drops down my cheek. "Matt, please. You don't know him. Can you please have dinner with us this week? Bring Derek. I'd love to meet him."

"I think we're beyond meeting each other's lovers. We live separate lives now." He finishes the last of the cereal and drinks the rest of the sugary milk from the bowl. "You're an uptown girl. What do you want with me anyway? I'm just your pathetic, gay childhood friend."

"Is that what you think is going on? That I don't value you anymore just because I fell in love with someone? If it wasn't him, eventually it would be someone else. Are you saying you'd never be happy for me?"

He frowns. "I just thought it would be someone like us. Dive bars and billiards and party brunches. Not some finance douche. Not him, for the love of God. You've changed."

"How, exactly? I still try to hang out with you all the time. We've always done the same things. I never tried to take you to some country club or social club or a function of any kind. I'm exactly the same with you, and that's all that should matter. What's different about me besides my wardrobe?"

He stands and walks to the kitchen and puts the bowl in the sink to wash later. He turns and places his hands on the counter, keeping his head down. "I don't know. I just don't know how to act around you anymore."

"That sounds like a *you* problem."

"It's just been different since you left. Like, you left to go do this whole plan we worked on for a year and then you just abandoned it because you got butterflies in your stomach one day. Remember, I gave up my entire life in Texas to move here and do this with you. And now I feel like the one who's abandoned."

"You always said you loved New York."

"I do. Whatever, PJ. It's separation anxiety. I'll be fine. You want to be in love and marry him, that's fine. But if you want to kill him, you know where to find me for your alibi."

I gulp. After Daddy died, I was angry. All I wanted was revenge, to have a place to aim my anger. I remember how Matt and I sat around together, painstakingly putting together the plan in the kill book.

Who was that girl? All I know is it's not me anymore. And I must bring Matt back from the brink. He couldn't hurt a fly; he was always doing it for me.

"Will you have dinner with us this week?"

He scratches the back of his head. "I can't this week. But I will next week."

"Promise?"

"Yes. But if I still don't like him, I'm not going to be your bridesman or man of honor or whatever. I mean it, Peej, I won't even go."

That hurts more than anything else he's said or done in the past few months, but I understand. I have to make sure Anthony is on his best behavior.

So, I wait. I begrudgingly wait eleven whole days before Matt is finally free and able to meet us for dinner. After a lot of contemplation, I decided on cooking dinner at our place. I think he'll feel more comfortable in a casual setting. Originally, I wanted it to be easy for Matt and sought out a "regular" place down on the Lower East Side, but then

Anthony wouldn't be at his best, and let's face it, he's the one who needs to make an impression. I didn't want to go to some chichi place that Anthony usually likes because then Matt would feel like a fish out of water and accuse me of being someone else. So, I thought it best that we just have dinner and conversation here.

Our cleaning lady comes every Friday, so the place is fresh and smells like a mix of lemon and something spicy, but I can't place it. Not cinnamon, maybe nutmeg? Almost Christmas-y, but without the bite.

I set the table beautifully, with the good china and the cloth napkins. The chicken is roasting in the oven, and I prepared twice baked potatoes and a mix of caramelized carrots with balsamic glaze over green beans. I'll cook those once Matt arrives so everything can be ready to eat at the same time. Also, I thought it would be something fun to do together over wine. For dessert, I ordered from a patisserie a couple blocks away. I got a dense German chocolate cake and a dozen red velvet cake pops dipped in white chocolate and garnished with smashed Lucky Charms cereal and marshmallows—a special order that Matt would appreciate.

Anthony looks scrumptious. He originally wore a button-down and a tie, but I told him it was too formal and it would make Matt uncomfortable. He changed into beige slacks and a navy golf polo from some country club in Connecticut.

"I'm thinking about joining a country club," Anthony says. "Ron and Carla belong to a beautiful one in New Jersey by the beach."

"New Jersey?" I don't mean for it to come out confrontational like it does. I just can't picture Carla at the Jersey shore if the TV show is anything to compare it to.

"Yeah. You know they have a house down there. They invited us down on the first Saturday in May so we could check it out." He pauses, then smiles. "We should check out the area anyway. Maybe we'll find a nice house to use for the summers."

Don't people like *us* summer in the Hamptons? Oh God, Matt is right, I'm insufferable. I'll never tell him what I just thought. "That sounds great." Except the visiting with Ron and Carla part.

My phone beeps. It's Matt, and he's not telling me he's on his way.

I'm not coming. We have to talk.

"Everything okay?" Anthony asks. He must've seen my face drop.

I laugh nervously. "Mm-hmm." I type back, *Please don't do this to me.*

He writes back, *There's something you should know about your fiancé.*

He's pulling this shit again. I'm in the middle of rage texting something when another text comes through. It's a picture, and it's downloading.

I stop typing when I see it. The accompanying text says, *This is him, right? I took this earlier today.*

It's him all right. Kissing Carla Boswell.

40
KIM
NOW

Kim raced home from Tony's house, eager to upload the pictures she took onto her tablet so she could see them better. She needed to make sense of it, of what she saw, because if it was what she thought it was, then nothing that happened over the past few weeks was an accident.

She let Murphy off his leash and refilled his water, then forwarded all the photos to her email so she could open them on her Surface Pro. Once they were all loaded, she started from the beginning. Phase One, as it was called, was manipulating Tony into meeting and falling in love with her. Why? She was pretty enough and young enough to be a regular gold digger—why the elaborate plan that ended in *murder*? Why did she want to kill him?

And who was Matt Mazzucca? His name was in the book as a friend of hers. It got more convoluted by the second. Every page she swiped to was more bizarre than the last.

Toward the end, some of the last pages were typewritten notes, a report on someone named Paulina Jensen. Who was she, and why would PJ have an entire history of her parents, her schooling, even her credit score? There was a header at the top: "Prepared by Damien Lightfoot, DLPIA."

A very quick Google search showed that was *Damien Lightfoot Private Investigative Agency.*

The next typewritten page . . . Oh shit. Kim's name was on it.

It was a page much like the one for Paulina Jensen. Where Kim graduated high school, where she went to college, her work history, and recent addresses. This was PJ's book—why was she looking into Kim? PJ knew she worked at the country club. Was PJ The Stranger?

No, she couldn't be. The Stranger contacted her after PJ died.

At the very bottom, there were a few dotted lines, and in super tiny font, it said REPORT COMPLETE FOR ANTHONY FULLER.

What? Anthony hired Damien for these reports? That was why they were tucked in the back. They weren't part of this big plan concocted by PJ.

Kim started to put it together. PJ wasn't who she'd claimed to be. She was Paulina Jensen, not Poppy Jade. *PJ.* Anthony must've found this book, realized what PJ had planned, and turned the tables on her. And likely, whoever this Matthew person was, unless Tony took care of him too.

Kim hoped this had nothing to do with her. If this was Tony's sick way of getting rid of his fiancée and nudging his way back into Kim's life, he was barking up the wrong tree. It made sense now. Tony didn't randomly run into her at the country club—that report was prepared in April, two months ago. He knew where she lived. Where she worked.

Kim started her own Google search. It led her to the right place immediately.

Paulina Jensen was the daughter of Monica Jensen, the woman killed in Tony and Jose's robbery gone wrong all those years ago. PJ was out for revenge, right from the start. All of it was connected.

But why her? Why was it up to Kim to poison Tony? And she still didn't know what Carla's role in this whole thing was, but she had to find out.

And then, if ever she was saved by the bell, it happened. The burner phone rang.

She was armed with information, and this time, she was going to use it. She was no longer afraid.

"Hello?" she answered.

"Kim." It was the electronic voice. "I'm giving you a location for the new poisons. You'll pick them up tomorrow morning, and you'll get the job done this week."

"No, I won't." She was defiant in her tone. "I'm going to give you the money back—every cent. And you're going to listen to me, because now I'm the one with the power."

Silence. But they didn't disconnect the call.

"Who are you?" Kim asked. "I know PJ's real name was Paulina Jensen. Is this Matthew?"

"H-how do you know those names?" It was the first time she heard doubt from the voice.

"Because I saw PJ's plan book. The name Matthew was in it."

"Where did you see that book?"

There was no confusion from the voice about what Kim was talking about. It hit her. The Stranger knew about the book. "I was right. This is Matthew. Tell me the truth, and I'll tell you what I know. Otherwise, I'm hanging up."

"Don't hang up."

The voice wasn't electronic anymore. It was a young man's voice.

41
PJ
THEN

The last thing Matt texted me was *Don't let him know you know. Tell him I'm sick. Act normal. We'll get together tomorrow and game plan. We'll get through this, awesomesauce.*

My Matt is back. And so the fuck is Paulina Jensen. She never should've gone away to begin with. The rage has got to be all over me, so I casually fake a yawn and cover my face with my hand as I turn away from Anthony to sip my wine. I need to dull the Paulina inside me before she grabs a knife and stabs this asshole in the throat.

I try to steady my hands and not let my voice shake, because the truth is, my heart is broken. That fake old bag Carla Boswell? She's twice my age! Ugh, how long has that been going on? I feel like such a fool. But I know I'll get over that real fucking fast. How fast? Well, I'll say this much: He dies before I marry him. I have to get him to change his will as soon as possible, but there's no way I'm staying with this asshole and pretending to love him for another six months.

"Oh, man. Matt just tested positive for Covid. He needs to stay home for a few days. He can't come tonight."

The look on Anthony's face was pure remorse. "Oh, honey, I'm so sorry. I know you were dying for us to meet." He stands and comes over to me and kisses my head, then rubs my shoulders. "Everything smells delicious, anyway. We can still have a wonderful dinner, just the two of us." He interlaces his fingers with mine.

This fucker really thinks he's that smooth. *Oh honey* and *just the two of us,* like we're some couple in love. He's not that good of an actor. I see it now. He cheated on me with Carla, and it will not end well for him.

My heart is racing. I grab a knife from the counter. A big one. He looks at me with dented eyebrows. *Be very scared, Mr. Fuller.*

"Oops. I thought that was the spoon. I guess I'll get the vegetables started now, and we can eat earlier than planned."

Over dinner, we talk about beach houses, country clubs, our wedding in Hawaii, all things that he'll never get to experience because he's a dead man walking. By dessert, I'm shoving those Lucky Charms cake pops into my face at record speed. In my mind, Lucky Charms equals Matt, and I'm disgusted with myself and my behavior as I inhale the marshmallows and sugary cereal.

Anthony wants to "take a walk" again, but I decline. Let him go alone and meet up with Carla, because now I'm convinced that's what he does whenever he leaves for one of his late-night walks. I wonder if they planned to be in Hawaii together—her and Ron showing up can't be a coincidence. I wonder if every time he claimed to be at the hotel gym or shopping or booking tours, he was having dirty little meetups with her. Ugh, Anthony Fuller and the Real House-wife of Boswell Securities. Doing his boss's wife. I'll have to save the picture of him with his tongue down her throat and her hand on his ass and make sure Ron sees it one day.

Anthony says he'll be back in an hour, so I wash up and crawl into bed and text Matt. *You up? I'm alone. Can you talk?*

He calls immediately.

"Hey," he says, and my heart gets warm and fuzzy. "I told you not to fall in love with him."

I don't even get mad at his passive aggressive *I told you so.* "That was his boss's wife in the picture. How did you even know?"

"No shit?" He laughs. "I've been following him since you left a few weeks ago. I got one of those fancy new Nikon cameras with all the bells and whistles, so I thought I'd use it for something other than my *hobby.* It's the one that can zoom onto the moon's surface. For this asshole, I just had to be across the street. I have a bunch of pictures of places he's gone, but that was the only one where I saw him with a woman, although once he was in a hotel for ninety minutes during the day."

"That could've been a meeting. He does that a lot."

"Are you still defending him?"

"No." It comes out in a whisper.

"Now what?"

Indeed. Now what? Paulina is back. "I'm coming over tomorrow. And I'm bringing the book. It's time to get back on track and also accelerate this plan. How would you feel if he had an unfortunate accident way before the honeymoon?"

"I'd say you're onto something."

"We need to start plotting ASAP. He's talking about us getting a beach house near his mistress in New Jersey. There's no way I'm leaving here for Jersey if—"

"Wait. What do you mean?"

I tell him all about Anthony's plan to join a country club and how he wants us to go to Carla's house on the shore in a couple weeks to check out the area and the club.

"That's great news, Peej. We can use that," Matt says.

"How?"

"You want them both to pay? Get in that house. We kill him and frame Carla."

42
KIM
NOW

"**W**ho are you?" Kim demands again.

The voice on the other end of the line cleared his throat. "You're right. This is Matt. I need to know how you know all this stuff."

Kim was floored. Matt knew PJ, and they planned to kill Tony together. So how did PJ end up dead?

There was a loud sob on the other end of the phone. "PJ was my best friend in the entire world. I don't know what happened. I'm lost without her."

He was probably in love with her. "I think we need to talk in person. You clearly know my address." Kim felt safe. The Stranger, Matt, didn't have it out for her. If anything, they could help each other out. Get to the bottom of what happened to PJ. "Can you come over now?"

"Yeah. I'm not too far from you."

"I'll give you back every cent when you get here." She looked at Murphy, his sweet brown eyes, as if he heard that she was sacrificing him. "I've recently come into some cash that I can repay. But I need the truth about everything. Like why I was targeted to do this."

"I'll tell you everything. I promise."

The call disconnected, and Kim rubbed her temples. She didn't know what she was in for, but she knew genuine grief, and Matt sounded like he had it. If Tony really had anything to do with PJ's murder, Kim wouldn't let him get away with it. Again. Because now she was convinced he should've been the one sitting in that jail cell instead of Jose Sanchez.

A half hour later, there was a soft knock at her door. Not the threatening ones that she'd become used to. She looked through the peephole and—no way.

Tall and fit and chiseled, she knew this guy. He wasn't Matt. What did he want?

She opened the door. "Terry?" It was the new caddie she met last week in the locker room. "What are you doing here?"

He stuck out his hand. "Hi, I'm Matt. Nice to meet you."

Her eyes narrowed. "I don't understand."

"Let me in. I'll explain everything."

She invited him in, and they sat on her couch, where Matt cried over the loss of PJ's life, and Kim even let him lean on her shoulder. Once he collected himself, Matt told her everything from the beginning, starting with him and PJ visiting Jose Sanchez a few years ago, when he told them Tony pulled the trigger.

Kim had always had her suspicions, no matter what happened in the aftermath. His denials, Jose's confession, it was all too easy. Kim knew better. It was that unspoken language they had between them, and she read him like a book. Certain phrases he'd used, certain expressions whenever anyone asked him about it. That was why she begged her parents to leave. Waiting a year to go off to college wouldn't suffice. He'd find a way to make her life hell. She practically left in the middle of the night.

"Are you sure Tony did it?" Kim asked. "Tony killed PJ's mom?"

"I guess we'll never be a hundred percent sure. He said/ he said. Either way, they were both there. One is suffering the consequences, and one is living his best life." The tears never really stopped the entire time he spoke. "If he had that book at his house, then he knew her plan. He killed her, Kim. I'm sure of it."

She nodded. "Why did you get me involved in this?"

"Anthony—Tony, whatever—knew you were working there. PJ found a report on you in his office. She recognized your name from discussions they'd had about past relationships. She knew things didn't end well. Once he suggested joining *this* club, she thought he wanted to reconnect with you. But I heard you crying over your dog in the locker room one day right after I got hired, which honestly was to keep an eye on them and everyone around here and protect PJ. I failed miserably there." He choked back a sob. "I told PJ about your dog. We came up with the idea to get you the money for his surgery, and then some. PJ was The Stranger, and we made a pact not to contact each other for five days after Anthony was killed. We decided I'd check up on you as The Stranger the next day, in case this blew up. We'd keep PJ out of it." He paused. "I didn't know she died until you told me."

Jesus. "I'm so sorry, Matt. I really am. I still don't know why you targeted me."

"You seemed like—like you'd do anything for that dog."

"I—I would. But once I recognized Tony . . ." She let it trail off. "How did you even get hired there? Under a different name?"

"We both have new IDs that we got from a cop buddy back in Texas. He knew a group who hid people in domestic situations, and he vouched for both of us."

"You told them your girlfriend beat you?" Kim couldn't picture it. This guy's chest looked like he played linebacker in college.

"My *boyfriend*. I'm gay. PJ was my best friend in the entire world."

Kim bit her lip, hating herself for making assumptions.

"I don't know how she thought she'd get away with this," Kim said. "Either of you."

"If you would've put that liquid stuff over his dessert, we all would've gotten away with it. It was an antifreeze mixture. Sweet to the taste, blows out of your body shortly after ingestion. It never would've showed up on an autopsy. You'd still have the money to save your dog, and PJ would still be alive. The only one who'd be dead would be that cheating son of a bitch."

What? "How do you know he was cheating on her?"

He let out a breath. "Look, the whole situation was convoluted toward the end, especially the last few months. PJ actually did fall in love with him and abandoned the plan for a while. It never sat well with me that she spent so much time building all that anger and then poof, *well he's so cute and he's nice to me*. So, I followed him and found him in a compromising position. I knew I would. Guys like him are all the same."

"And you told PJ?"

"I showed her the picture. She got over him real fucking fast and back to Plan A once she saw it. Even worse, she said it was him and his boss's wife."

Holy shit. As what he'd just said connected in Kim's brain, Matt shoved his phone toward her. There it was. Tony and Carla, making out like teenagers.

That *was* them at Night Shift. Tony wasn't just slinking around dive bars whispering to her. He was *involved* with Carla. Was that the reason for the divorce? Did Carla have a hand in killing PJ?

"The only thing that still puzzles me," Matt said, "is that she told me she had a failsafe. A backup plan in case you didn't go through with it. You didn't. So why isn't that son of a bitch dead yet?"

43
PJ
THEN

Anthony just brought me to a house that he's in love with. He saw it online and we just had a private showing with a realtor before we head to Ron and Carla's. It's going to be our summer place. Well, it'll be mine and Matt's soon, but let this jerkoff think he's making me happy.

I'm not sure what his end game is with me, but right now he thinks he'll be able to cheat just like every guy with money. The cake and the eating it too thing. The house *is* beautiful and airy, half a block from the beach, and I love it. He tells the realtor that he'll be in touch with an offer next week, that right now we have somewhere to be for dinner. He fails to say it's his mistress's house, naturally.

I'm stunned when we pull into Ron and Carla's long circular driveway, facing the beach. The house looks like their apartment—all glass and windows, except it's at least double the size. The exterior is white, and the windows are all tinted aqua blue, almost mirrorlike. I think of my Ray-Ban polarized lenses and imagine how different the Atlantic Ocean and the scenery looks through them from the inside.

Anthony parks and hurriedly runs to my side of the car to open the door for me. I'm used to it at this point, so I wait. Little gentleman is still doing everything he can to keep me happy for some reason, and he clasps my free hand when the door is open.

"Be careful. The rocks are probably unsteady in those heels."

The part of the driveway where we are parked is made of baby stones, all gray and aqua and white. We're parked next to a Range Rover and a baby-blue convertible Mercedes sports model. The top is down, and it looks like a spaceship inside, with a bunch of knobs and a big flat screen. That has to be Carla's. I can picture her driving around in her bikini top, showing off her fake tits and her fake lips and her fake hair and her fake frozen face.

All things Anthony decided were better than me. I try not to be bothered by it, even though I am a little. I found out two weeks ago, and it still stings. Mostly, because I became such a cliché. I hate myself for abandoning Matt and the original plan.

The original plan. I have to use everything I have in me to be the perfect little fiancée tonight. I have to find a way to get Carla under suspicion when I dose him. Matt and I decided the easiest and most inconspicuous thing to use was arsenic and antifreeze, and we want it done in a public place. We're still working out the details, but if I can do it when Ron and Carla are around, even better. Anthony is lucky I don't have a plan put together yet because I'd do it right now if I could. I hate him and worry I won't be able to contain it—I have the pressure of a seismic fault about to break.

"I love you," I say as I take his hand.

He kisses it. "Love you more," he whispers in my ear.

Of course you do. Except for the cheating part.

Right off the pebbled parking space, there's a paved pathway, which we take to their front door. It's at least ten feet high with a wrought iron handle. Anthony rings the bell, and it sounds like someone in ancient China smacked one of those huge gold symbols, or someone from the Roman empire was calling the ruling families to dinner. So pretentious.

I hear clacking on the other side. I assume Carla is running to greet her lover, and I wonder how she's going to open this huge door. She might be a slut who's screwing my fiancé, but even I know she can't tip the scales at more than a buck ten.

The door cracks and I hear a distinct, low buzz. It's automatically opening. Carla probably pushed a button. We can't see inside through the glass, but I'm sure she sees us standing there clear as day like it's a two-way mirror. When it fully opens, Carla looks like she typically does. Too much makeup, too much hair, and a skintight dress that shows off her tan and her tits.

"Hi, Carla, you look great!" I say it with pep in my step. I know that'll piss her off. She hates that she can't get under my skin.

Her head tilts to one side as she sizes me up, half her age, genetic perfection without all the surgery she has. "Poppy. I have that same dress. That pattern came out last year, so you must've gotten quite the discount."

Yes, it's a bargain basement Prada. Shoot me for liking pink and red no matter what year it came out. I don't wait in line for the newest iPhone either, you old bag.

"Leave it to you to be on the cutting edge of everything." I wink at her.

She tries to hide her half an eye roll, but I catch it as she turns her attention to Anthony and the Cheshire cat smile breaks out. "You look great. Come on in."

Anthony puts his hand on the small of my back and ushers me inside, and I gasp. Her home is a palace. It has a three-story entryway, and a huge crystal chandelier hangs overhead. The floors look marble, and I'm afraid I'll slip in my heels.

"Follow me," she says and walks confidently in front of us.

If I slip and she doesn't, I'll never live it down. I'm mentally saying *left right, left right* as I walk. I swing my head around as we pass through, and much like their apartment, it's decorated tastefully but minimally. Doll furniture. Nothing looks comfortable, from the French-style couches to the Mediterranean-style chairs and trunks. Toward the back of the house is a massive kitchen that overlooks a kidney bean-shaped pool, with one-two-*three* waterfalls, and a slide. There's a hot tub at the edge with water trickling into the pool. It looks like the Andaz in Maui, not a private home.

Ron is opening a bottle of red wine at what can only be called the wine station—there's a hundred-bottle wine fridge and a full wet bar. He's dressed extra casually, which takes me aback. I've never seen him in anything besides those sport coats with suede elbows. Right now, he's in a New York Jets T-shirt and jeans. It's strange, like seeing puppies dressed as ballerinas.

"Hey, glad you could make it." Ron makes his way toward us, bottle of wine in one hand as he shakes Anthony's hand with the other. He then uses that hand on my waist to pull me in for a kiss on my cheek, which I smile and take because even though he's a disgusting creep, I'm a good fiancée who doesn't make waves. "Anthony told me the good news. Let's see the rock."

He grabs my left hand and admires my beautiful engagement ring, and I try to push away the memory of how in love I was with Anthony when he slipped it on my finger.

"It really is perfect, isn't it?" My eyes quirk up at Anthony. Wink. Grin. Ugh.

Carla cranes her neck and glances at it. "You like ovals? I guess everyone has their favorites. To me, it's one step up from a marquis."

I squint. "What's wrong with a marquis?"

She smirks. "Oh, honey." Then she looks at Anthony. "Can I get you a drink?"

By the time we're both handed a glass of red wine, she's lucky it's still in the glass and not all over her *I-just-bought-this* dress. They lead us out into the yard, which of course is complete with a guest house and an outdoor kitchen, and we settle in under the pavilion. A what's sure to be custom made table, seating for ten, is littered with charcuterie boards and bowls of fruit. We all take a seat.

"Don't mind the mess over there," Ron says, motioning toward the far end of the property. "We bought the house next door a few weeks ago, and I'm turning it into a work/live space so I can spend more time out of the city in the summers."

"It was a ghastly bungalow of a thing," Carla says, lips pursed. "A real eyesore. Ron wanted to open up the fencing and keep it on our property, but I insisted on a complete tear-down. If it's going to be an extension of the home, I want it to match. So we'll sacrifice the bathroom and outdoor shower on that side and have a hallway connecting them, eventually. Boswell Securities South."

"That has a nice ring to it," Anthony says. "We've been looking too. We just had a private showing, and I'm going to put in an offer next week. Only a couple miles from here. Make sure there's an extra desk at Boswell South."

"If the architect doesn't bleed me dry, I'm planning on three offices and a conference room. We don't need the space here. I'm doing what I want with that place, no matter what resistance I get." He shoots a glare at Carla, who I'm sure insists that everything goes her way, even her husband's office. "We'll have to get you to the club when you settle in. We wanted you as our guests tonight, but they have some charity event there for one of the senators."

After an hour of small talk, Ron fires up the grill and brings out a platter of porterhouse steaks and lobster tails. I assume it's a good time to excuse myself to use the bathroom. There doesn't seem to be any staff in the place, which is shocking in and of itself, but I'm sure Anthony and Carla would like some time to chat alone while Ron is messing around with the food.

"Inside, to the left, down the hall, third door on the right," Carla says without even meeting my eyes. She can't take them off Anthony, of course.

I close the sliding glass door behind me, grateful it's tinted the same way as the rest of the glass—they can't see inside, and I need to snoop. I take off my heels and run upstairs to their bedroom, which is a cathedral. I beeline right for the corner where I see her makeup station, complete with a desk and a ring light above the mirror. I poke around to see if I can find any jewelry or something distinctively Carla that I can take with me. Matt and I will figure out how to incorporate it all later.

Their bedroom spans from the front of the house to the back, ensuring views of both the ocean and the pool. I sneak a quick glance outside and see Ron is still fiddling with the grill and Anthony and Carla have moved more toward the back of the property. She keeps making a show of her arms, as if she's boasting about the property, but I know better. That's a display for Ron, an *Oh, don't worry I'm just showing him the yard* and less like *I need some privacy with my lover, maybe we'll try to have sex behind both of your backs here, how hot!* I calculate two more minutes before someone will think I got lost and come looking for me.

I open the closet doors, and I'm sad to notice it puts my closet to shame, but I'm not here to compare notes. I move through the hangers and open and close some of the drawers, but it's just clothes upon clothes upon—MY GOD how many outfits does this woman need? Closing the doors behind me, I move to a dresser and go through her things, all bras and thongs. I feel around the bottom of the drawers, but there's nothing of note. For all the jewelry this woman wears, I can't find any of it, which means it's probably all locked away or in another room. I glance out the back again and see Carla and Anthony heading back toward the grill. Shit.

Empty-handed, I race back down the stairs, put my heels on, and head toward the back door when I see Carla approaching. The door opens and she glares at me.

"Find everything okay?"

"Yes. Your home is lovely. I expected nothing less." I may be planning to kill Anthony with poison, but I'll kill her with kindness if . . . well, if it kills me. "Hopefully you can give me some tips if the buyer accepts our offer next week."

"*Our* offer? I hadn't realized your yoga business had taken off so much. You must have a ton of celebrity clientele." Her face is a grimace as she makes fun of the fact that I have no money. Well, she thinks I have no money. *Thanks, Daddy.*

"Me and Anthony are a unit."

"Mm-hmm." She walks to the wine station and grabs a cold bottle of rosé from the fridge. "He loves you *so, so* much."

I swear I hear a chuckle in her voice, and I want to strangle her. She passes me without another word, and I follow her outside, where she opens the rosé and pours herself a glass. She offers some to Anthony, but not to me, or her husband.

Anthony notices Carla's typical chill toward me, so he comes over and wraps his arms around me and kisses my head. "I love you, honey." I feel his hand smooth the back of my hair.

"I love you too." I glare unblinking at Carla as I say it.

And I realize that our little conversation in the kitchen gave me all the ammo I need for my next phase.

44
ANTHONY
THEN

When Paulina Poppy PJ Liar Bitch excused herself to go to the bathroom, Anthony saw his chance to get Carla alone while Ron dealt with the steaks. He made a show of scanning the property, even putting his hand over his eyes like a salute, and squinted, looking far past the pool and the wreck of the bungalow next door.

"Let me show you the back," Carla said, eyes wide, head nodding in the opposite direction of the grill. "You might get some inspiration for your own beach house."

"Excellent."

Carla led Anthony around the pool and to the rock wall they'd had built to house one of the waterfalls. As soon as they got there, she stuck her arm out as if she was offering something on a silver platter.

"Let Ron think I'm showing you this stuff," she said. "I miss you. *Kenneth*." She laughs.

He side-eyed toward the house, then back to Carla. "Sorry we haven't gotten together in a few weeks, *Patricia*. Did you get the stuff in Hawaii?"

"I did. I told Ron I wanted to go to a vodka distillery over by Haleakala. Then I started a fight and ran off to a local market. I found an aunty who—"

"An aunty?"

"Yeah, they're well respected and know everything. Little old ladies who are the busybodies of the village—I did my research. I found one who said if I got the Loganiaceae plant, she'd do the rest with the seeds. Then after I got it and brought it back, she changed her mind, said it was bad juju. Of course, I didn't take it well after hiking over an hour to find it, then over an hour back. I'm not an outdoor person. Someone in the village overheard my . . . disappointment . . . and he followed me. He said he could extract and purify the seeds, for a price, of course. I didn't have enough cash on me, so I gave him a diamond bracelet I was wearing. That thing was worth over five grand. Pissed me off, but whatever."

"We'll get you another bracelet." He smirked. "I can crush the seeds into powder, right?"

"Yeah, but wear gloves. Don't touch them, these things are no joke. I had them wrapped in plastic, then in toilet paper and hidden in my toothbrush holder to get them out of the state. They're in the house, in a small plastic container. I'll make sure you get them before you leave."

"Good."

She fingered his elbow. "Are you going to do it soon?"

He shrank back from her touch. "Careful." He nodded toward the house. Ron was still busy with the grill and paid no attention to them. Why would he? It was his soon to be ex-wife and his employee. Nothing to see there. "Soon, yes. But I still want the bitch to think she's winning this stupid game. I'll have to wait for a perfect time. And you said this stuff is untraceable, right?"

"Yes. Vicious, and untraceable. Unless someone is looking specifically for it, they won't test for it in an autopsy. Who's going to think seeds from a plant in Hawaii killed her? Come on." She looked back at Ron, then swiveled back to Anthony. "Then we can be together whenever we want."

Anthony wasn't so sure about that. It was one afternoon in bed with Carla when she suggested getting rid of PJ after he'd told her PJ was planning to kill him. She wanted PJ to suffer. Anthony remembered the strychnine in that book, and they came up with the whole plan, researching a bad yet plausibly deniable way to go. She found out the poisonous plant could be found in Hawaii and decided to join them on their trip. She said she'd get the stuff, and Anthony just had to feed it to PJ somehow, someway, sometime. Which he didn't mind doing. She always got sinus infections; he'd wait until she needed a reason to take a pill, and he'd replace it with the poison.

Until he saw that little book of hers, he never knew how much of Old Tony was still left in him.

Carla still didn't know that Ron was cheating or planning to divorce her. Or at least if she knew, she didn't talk about it with Anthony. Anthony knew that would turn her world upside down, but he couldn't be the one to let her know. He still had his job to worry about, and if Carla thought he was going to go riding off into the sunset with her once PJ was dead and Ron was her ex, well, she was more delusional than she looked.

He had to appease her somehow. "We should get back. Remember, only use the burner phones."

"I'm not stupid. And I'll make an excuse to go inside. I'm going to put the container with the seeds on top of your driver's side tire. Don't forget to pocket them before you leave. And don't touch them without gloves."

He nodded. They walked back to the pavilion, and Anthony grabbed a handful of cheese squares from one of the charcuterie boards while Carla said she was going to grab a bottle of rosé. She came out with PJ behind her. He still had to play his part, and he grabbed PJ close to him and kissed the back of her head.

"I love you, honey," he said.

Carla looked right at him when he made his hand into a gun, pointed it at PJ's head, and shot.

45

KIM
NOW

"So, Tony's life is still in danger?" Kim asked.

Matt shrugged. "I don't know what she had planned. She didn't tell me. Plausible deniability and all that. She had my back until the very end. And this is how I repaid her—I let this happen to her."

He sobbed again. Rubbed his eyes, wiped his cheeks. Kim stood and retrieved two bottles of water from the kitchen and a box of tissues from the bathroom. She offered him the water and he said, "Got anything stronger?"

Same thought, my new friend. She went back to the kitchen and poured two fingers of vodka each in two separate cups. Then added an extra finger to each for good measure. They clinked glasses and knocked the drinks back in one gulp each. It burned, and she wished she had a lemon or an orange to wash away the heat, but she didn't really care. The whole afternoon had been confusing, and she wanted to erase as much of it as possible.

Kim didn't know how to feel about anything she'd just heard from Matt. His lies about his identity, about PJ's identity, about them conspiring to kill Tony. On the flip side, PJ was the one who was dead, not Tony. He tried to kiss Kim less than a week after PJ died. He was having an affair with Carla fucking Boswell.

Tony wasn't who she'd thought. He never was. He'd always lived a double life. Apparently, so did PJ. Her reasoning made more sense to Kim. PJ did it to avenge her mother.

That deserved Kim's respect.

"What do we do now?" Kim asked. She swallowed heavily before she spoke next. "I have all the money. I don't need it anymore." It had to be given back. Murphy would be fine; she had that asshole Tony's money. She stood and went to her bedroom dresser to retrieve the cash bundles, then back to her kitchen and grabbed a Post-it off the refrigerator, which she used for grocery lists. She wrote down the complicated password, one that she never forgot, for the bank account in the Caymans.

"Here." She handed it to him.

He stared blankly at it. "Blood money." Then he waved it away. "I don't even want it."

She knelt next to him and placed everything in his lap. "If anything, just take it back and do something to honor PJ. I don't want it. I don't want to be involved in this game anymore. I promise I won't say a word to anyone, and I really hope you find out what happened to PJ. And if he really did it . . ." Her words drifted.

If he really did it, she hoped he'd get what was coming to him.

"Before I go, is there anything—anything—you remember about that night?" Matt asked. "About what everyone said? About how she acted? I just want to know what happened. She didn't have allergies. I didn't work past five that day, so I couldn't even say goodbye to her. I don't understand this."

Kim thought back about everything. As much as she'd tried to forget that night, she now forced the memories back into the fore. "PJ was really nice; I remember thinking she was a saint. You had a great best friend. I'm so sorry." She patted his knee. "They all ate and drank. They all shared wine bottles as usual. Tony said she took a pill for a sinus infection. Do you think—do you think that's how he did it?"

Matt shook his head. "No. She really was on antibiotics. She always got sinus infections, ever since high school." He closed his eyes and rubbed his temples, and Kim truly felt his loss. "Maybe it was an effect of the meds with the drinks. I don't know, I'm just spitballing because I've got nothing else. I've done that a million times. Pills and booze."

"What I saw—that wasn't an allergic reaction."

"What do you mean?" He was suddenly alert.

"I mean—it was just what happened to her before she stopped breathing. Like she was dead before she died. I don't want to say *zombie*, but she was all contorted and stiff while still gasping for air. Like—"

"Like rigor mortis set in while she was still alive?" His eyes had a glint of something. Hope. Fear. Recognition.

"Exactly like that."

Matt stood and paced the room, his hand still on his head. "God, I wish I had her book. We had so much stuff in there.

There was one poison that sounded exactly like that. One that she said was too cruel, even for him."

Kim stood and ran to her purse, grabbed her phone, and waved it in the air. "I took pictures. Of every single page."

Matt went to her phone like it was a jug of water in the desert and drank from it just as quick. His fingers furiously swiped until he smiled, but then the light in his eyes was replaced with darkness and more tears. "It was this. Strychnine."

Kim looked at him quizzically. "Where would he even get it?"

"It comes from a Loganiaceae plant. In Hawaii."

Kim's hand flew to her mouth. "He said that's where they got engaged."

Matt nodded. "She also told me that Ron and Carla were there at the same time."

They were? "You should tell someone what you know." Kim's heart raced. It was all coming together. "Blow the case open."

His eyes went wide. "Are you crazy? Tell who what? Tell the cops I know about strychnine because PJ and I were planning to kill him? That neither of us are who we said we were? And then what, that we got *you* involved?"

"Right." Kim shook her head wildly. "You can't say anything."

The silence that followed told them both everything they needed to know about the other. That they were both in it too deep. That Kim's involvement would only serve to get them both in trouble for something they didn't even do.

Until a slow smile broke out over Matt's face. "Wait. I forgot. Anthony doesn't know who I really am."

46
PJ
THEN

The seller accepted our offer on the house, and we closed in under three weeks. It's been great to be out of the city and at the beach most of the time. Anthony said to make the place my own, and *don't you worry*, I will. This place is about to be all mine anyway.

After we left Carla and Ron's beach house, I pouted and cried and said *just how awful* Carla made me feel about not being able to contribute financially to *our* house. I obviously made a bigger deal out of it than it was and told him that maybe he should be with someone *more on his level*. Despite the cheating, Anthony knows where his bread is buttered. He knows how people envy him when we walk into a room and I'm on his arm. He's not giving that up. Within days, we were at a lawyer getting his estate settled with me as the beneficiary for everything, even before we got married. Because he loves me *sooo much*. Cheater.

Matt has since gotten a job as a caddie at the country club we just joined, under his false ID, and we are waiting for the perfect time to do it. Now that everything would be mine, and Matt's by default, I don't have to go through with marrying Anthony at all.

One day, he left a stack of papers for me to sign, and the idiot accidentally had one too many sheets in there. The one on the bottom had information about someone named Kim Valva, and I remembered her name from when we were "discovering" each other and talking about our pasts. He looked up his ex-girlfriend, on top of cheating on me with Carla. This guy was a piece of work.

When I asked Anthony what it was, he inspected the paper and made an *I'm so confused* face, then said it must be something for someone else that his lawyer added to his file by mistake. He placed it aside and said he'd get it back to the guy. Liar. Anyway, she works at the club—probably why we joined—and me and Matt decided to use her to do the dirty work. He heard her talking about needing money for her dog or something.

No one will ever peg her as a suspect. Or us. The plan is foolproof, but if she has access to his food in public, she can get it done way faster than I could ever dream of doing.

That being said, she *does* have a past with him. I told Matt I have a backup plan, but I didn't tell him what it was. I hate myself, but it is what it is.

I've spent the past month shopping and decorating the house, and scheming for my final play. And tonight, we are having dinner at the club, with the Boswells and some other members. Tonight, it all goes down. Anthony will *not* make it home from dinner. Boo fucking hoo.

"Do I look okay?" I ask as I come down the stairs in a tight black Hervé Léger dress. I make sure I look my best, because I know he's going to want to impress people with me as his fiancée. My hair is blown out to bouncy perfection, my lash extensions were done this morning, my face is freshly scrubbed, and my lips are glossed. Looking good is one thing, but one-upping that old bitch is always a plus. Part of me wonders how she's going to react when Anthony drops dead.

"Amazingly gorgeous, as always," he says.

When we get to the club, I'm curious to see what Kim looks like. I looked her up on social, but her accounts were private and the only profile pictures she had were far away, so I couldn't really make out any features. Depending on how many people are there, I'm fairly sure I'll be able to pick her out.

Once we get there, it turns out I don't have to work so hard. I see Carla—that's Carla, right? Her hair is shorter. Must've taken out those ten-pound extensions. She's talking to someone who must be Kim. I know this because the woman scans both of us, and then does a double take. I spot her hesitation because I'm looking for it, and she makes her way over to me.

"Hello, you must be Ms. Walsh. I'm Kim. I'll be taking care of you this evening. Can I start you off with a drink?"

She's pretty. About ten years older than me, but she still has her youth, and seems Botox free, unlike Carla. I decide to go with overly friendly—she knows I'm here with Anthony. No need to make an enemy of the woman. If she does what she's paid to do, I don't want anyone to suspect her over, as Taylor Swift might say, bad blood. I'm not trying to get her in trouble.

"So formal! You know you can call me PJ. I'll have a glass of Merlot." I turn toward Anthony. Thank God his back is to her—he hasn't seen her yet. "He'll have a bourbon. Something small batch."

I'm wet between my thighs waiting to see his reaction when he sees Kim.

"Sure thing, Ms. Walsh."

She heads to the bar without reacting outwardly. Crap. I have to engage her; get her to like me. So I follow her. "Hey, can I ask you something?"

"Sure."

"How long have you worked here?"

"A little over two years."

"What am I in for tonight? With these women? My fiancé works with Ron Boswell, but I haven't met this group of wives yet." I tell her I only know Carla, and that she's *so nice.*

"Everyone here is wonderful."

Her voice is flat and unemotional, so I know instantly that she feels the same way about Carla that I do, but it's her job to be accommodating. I talk to her about myself, the lies I've memorized for a year about graduating from NYU, my yoga, and the time volunteering at an animal shelter, a homeless shelter, and overseeing a website for little old ladies who don't want to leave their houses.

I sip my wine, and finally Anthony turns around.

He sees Kim. I *know* he knows she works here, so his fake-ass reaction is for her. After I introduce him, he squints like he can't believe his eyes.

"Is that really you?" he says. God, I thought *I* was a good actress.

"Oh, wow, Anthony Fuller. It's been a long time." She widens her eyes at him, after she uses his full name. I assume since she knew me as *Ms. Walsh,* Carla must have filled her in that he was *Mr. Fuller.*

"You guys know each other?" I ask, smiling, playing dumb.

"We grew up in the same neighborhood," Kim says. She doesn't give away that they are former lovers. How many people in this room has Anthony slept with?

Kim says that his sister Maria, that bitch, was her best friend growing up and that they all lost touch when she moved. They have small talk, and Anthony turns toward me. "We should sit, Peej. Good to see you, Kimmy," he says.

Kimmy. Yeah, that's intimate. I don't care. Kim knows what she has to do. She just doesn't know she's taking orders from me.

Throughout dinner, Ron unabashedly has his tongue hanging out every time he looks at me. I know that's what Anthony is after. The coveting.

After dinner, Anthony reminds me to take my antibiotic. I struggle with the childproof top again, and he takes the bottle from me and opens it, hands me a pill, and closes it back up. I take it with one of the waters that's left on the table, and I excitedly wait for what's next. The antifreeze-slash-rat poison mixture will be laced in with his dessert. It was the best way to make him not notice the sweet concoction. Showtime.

Anthony revels in his crème brûlée—that's his favorite and I looked up the menu online before we came here, so I knew he'd order it. The poisonous stuff is on top, and once he cracks the sugary coating, he'll never know what's flowing inside as he eats every drop, even scraping the sides. Licking the spoon.

Dead man.

By the time the check comes, nothing has happened. Not even a cough. How long am I going to have to keep him here before it kicks in? They're already paying the bill. It better happen soon, or at the after-dinner bourbon with the guys. I can't go home and have him die there; I'll look too guilty. This has to happen in front of everyone.

And then something happens.

My throat swells and closes completely. I swallow, but it isn't going down, and I start to drool. I clutch my throat, then hit the table twice with my right hand. Hard. Something is wrong.

Oh no. Kim couldn't do it to him. She did it to me instead. Is this the end?

"PJ?" Anthony turns toward me, his brows dented. "Peej? Are you okay?"

I hit the table again. I can't talk. I can't tell him to save me.

"Is she choking?" Ron asks. I see the panic in his face as he jumps up and attempts the Heimlich.

"She can't be choking. There's no food left on the table!" Anthony screams to Ron, ripping me from his arms. "PJ!"

My eyes are open, but I'm frozen. I can't move at all, at least not voluntarily, and my body starts to spasm. The pain is a hundred-plus on the one-to-ten scale, but I can't even scream. I just feel it everywhere, like I'm being stabbed. Like someone is pouring boiling water on me.

Anthony pushes everything off the table and grabs the tablecloth. He lays me down, stroking my head while demanding everyone give me room. "Come on, Peej. Hang on, baby. Hang on."

I hear the noises around me—asking for a doctor, something about 911, as Anthony's tears fall down his face and onto me. He may be a cheater, but he doesn't want me to die. He may be a cheater, but he loves me. He may be a cheater but—

"Come on, Peej. Come on, baby," he says, but I'm limp.

I can't even ask for the help I so desperately need. *Help me, Anthony.* I beckon to him, my fiancé, as my heart stops in his arms. He leans close to my ear and whispers.

"I hope you enjoyed your antibiotic. You're right. Strychnine is a torturous way to go, you fucking bitch."

Oh no.

He knows about everything. He may be a cheater but—he knows. *He* did this to me.

"Come on, Peej. Please. Someone help her, please." Back in action, his cries are desperate as he pounds the ground next to me. "Peej, please, baby."

I was wrong. He *is* a good actor. How long has he been planning this?

Since Hawaii. He had to get the poison there. Fuck, I made the book and gave him the road map for the worst way to kill someone. He, and maybe even Carla, is doing this to me. When we were in Hawaii, and I loved him, and he proposed to me, he was planning to kill me. This whole time.

How the tables have turned.

"Where's the goddamn ambulance?" Anthony shouts, tears staining his cheeks. "Come on, Peej."

Actor, you *fucking* actor. I need to let everyone know it's him. He did this. I try to point, but I know my arms aren't moving. In my head, they are, but in reality, I'm frozen. I try to shout it out, *It's strychnine! It was him!* but only a sound comes out—a gross, muddled sound that's probably as scary as I look. There are medics around me now, but they don't know what's inside me. They don't know it's over.

I do.

Anthony's heart would've exploded, but it would've been quick. He's making me die in pain. Feel every spasm. Every muscle death. I see my mother's face, what I remember it looked like, and her hand is out to me. My father is behind her, shaking his head. He's disappointed in me, that I made this about revenge and that I never got to live my life to my full potential.

But I did it for you. For both of you.

Anthony deserves this. Not me. He murdered my mother and left my father alone.

I'll be reunited with them soon. If my failsafe comes through tonight, hopefully Anthony will drop dead in a few minutes himself. I'll never know.

I think of the picture hanging on Matt's wall, the selfie of me and him after graduation. Don't forget about the picture, Matt. The last conscious thought I have is, *I love you, Matt, my awesomesauce.*

47

RON BOSWELL
THEN

I'm slightly stunned when my secretary—yes, she's a secretary, not an admin, for the love of God—alerts me that I have a call from PJ Walsh.

PJ Walsh? What does she want with me? Hopefully I know the answer. She knows where the money is. The status. The power.

Anthony wants to be me, but I hired him knowing who he was before. Did I care? Not even a little. Money is money, and this man has a penchant for earning it. Caring about what he did in his past was like giving a fuck that Trump had a real estate empire before 2016. All anyone cares about is the here and now.

"Yes, put her through," I say as I wait for the second ring, the special one that tells me my *secretary* put an approved call through.

"Ron Boswell," I answer, even though I know who it is.

"Hi, Ron, It's PJ. Poppy Jade. Walsh. Anthony's fiancée."

She gives me her name four times like I need to know it more than once. I know who she is.

"Yes, Poppy, what can I do for you?"

"Well, this might be a little awkward . . ." she starts.

Awkward how? Is she going to proposition me? I'm sure she saw me and Amy at that party at my apartment in the city. PJ is good people, because she pretended she didn't see it, and Anthony never came to me about it, which means she kept it to herself. Good girl. I can take you places.

"Awkward how?" I ask. Let her get into it. I'm not doing anything wrong, simply reacting to a beautiful young woman.

Fine, I'm a lothario. With this much money, who cares? Clearly Carla doesn't. I told her months ago I was going to divorce her, that I had side pieces, and what does she do? Shops. Botox. She's clearly not sleeping with anyone else because why would she even fuck up her good life?

Meanwhile, I've got this hot piece on the phone. "What's awkward?" I ask again.

"I have a picture you might want to see."

I give her my cell number, and she stays on the line while she sends it. I hope it's a naked picture. When it uploads, I'm a bit in shock. I squint and blow up every inch of it with my fingers, and the heart I don't have nearly stops. Really? Is that—that's—Carla? With—

Whatever, I'm not a saint, but even I know when lines are crossed. No matter what I just thought about doing to PJ.

"I see," I say. Because of the shock thing. Maybe this still hasn't hit me.

"*I see*? It's a picture of your wife Carla kissing my fiancé Anthony, and then entering a hotel. They've been having an affair. He said she's always had a thing for him, and I don't feel safe anymore. What if she tries to hurt me?"

Carla has a vicious tongue, but she wouldn't bother doing anything that would cause her to break a nail. Still, this makes me feel good. Now I'm PJ's protector. "Does he know you know?"

"Nope. I was wondering how you wanted to handle it."

"Me?"

"Yes, you. You're his boss. You're the one with the wife, the marriage. We haven't made it there. Yet."

"Yet? You're going to go through with it after this?" She's just like Carla, isn't she? Turn the other cheek, keep the lifestyle.

"Well, no. I was thinking of another way out. We can both get what we want out of this."

"How do you know what I want?"

Pause. She knows. "I've seen the way you look at me."

Her voice is a purr when she says it. She's teasing me. I like it. I begin to wrap the phone cord around my finger, picturing it being her hair and how it would feel to push her head into my lap.

"You want to get back at them by . . . what? Getting a picture of us in kissing in front of a hotel?" That would be the best way, to be honest. I'd love to get a go at her.

"I was thinking something more permanent."

She goes into detail about spiking his drink with arsenic. She wants *me* to do it when we're all at dinner together at the country club, so there are a bunch of witnesses who never see anything out of the ordinary. All the men usually drink from my private collection I store at the club at the end of the night. And the fact that everyone will have had a few drinks in them by then is even better—no one will be paying attention to me dumping some powder into Anthony's glass, the last bourbon before we leave.

She makes promises if I do it. Promises I've only dreamt about. And man, does she go into detail. She promises me a minimum of two times—before as a down payment, and after for a job well done. I bet I can keep her going after that.

But it's still . . . murder. Even though I want to kick the shit out of Anthony right now, I don't know if I can do it. I'd never get caught, and if I did, I have the best lawyers in the world. I know the DA. I've bribed judges before about insider trading stuff. People know me. I'm kind of untouchable. No one would be able to prove anything.

I'm torn. Then another picture comes through my phone. Flesh.

"Yeah, I'll do it."

48
PJ
THEN

Dear Matt,

I'm sorry for everything I've put you through over the last year. You, undoubtedly, are my favorite person in the world, and I hate myself for questioning that at all. You never should've felt like you were second to anyone. You've done everything for me, and I want you to know that I appreciate you and I love you.

The reason I'm writing this, is I'm getting in a bit over my head. I know what we've been planning. I feel like we played with fire getting his ex involved, and there's a chance she won't do it. So, I came up with a plan to make sure Anthony dies anyway. The only problem is, I've had to put myself into a very compromising position to do it, and I no longer feel safe.

If something happens to me, I'm telling you why.

I never wanted to tell you this, but I slept with Ron Boswell a couple weeks ago. I did it for a good reason, but he's gotten extremely possessive, and he even followed me home from Saks a few days ago. I don't even know how he knew I was there, but it's like he's tracking me and keeps saying he wants "another go at me." He's Mr. Yuck. Anyway, I recorded it. The flash drive with the video is hidden in Saucy Pants. I hope you didn't get rid of Saucy Pants after I moved, but I don't think you ever would. Don't watch the video, it was as sloppy and sweaty as you're probably imagining. Worse. A means to an end.

I did it because . . . if Anthony doesn't die during the dinner we have planned this week, that meant Kim couldn't go through with it, and I needed to make sure he died no matter what, so promises were made. There is a recorded conversation on the flash drive too—one I controlled—between me and Ron. On it, he agrees to spike Anthony's bourbon after dinner, after I showed him the picture of Anthony and Carla. And you still have all those adulterous pictures. I also left a recording of just me, which you can say I left you as a voicemail, if they ever go under investigation. GAME ON.

Hopefully, you never see this letter because if all goes as planned, I'm taking it back from its hiding spot and destroying it. But . . . if something happens to me, I know you'll find it, and promise me you'll still make Anthony pay. Everything I'm giving you is how you get away with it. Ron and/or Carla will look like suspects. And you walk away with the bank account numbers and passwords listed below. Write them down somewhere.

Then burn this letter.
I love you, Awesomesauce.

I fold the letter into three rectangles and hide it in my purse. When Matt tells me he's out with Derek, I go down to my old apartment and let myself in. I hide the letter behind the frame of my favorite selfie of us. In his room, I find Saucy Pants, the bear he won for me at the county fair when we were in high school. I take it to the kitchen and slice open a small hole in its back, one just big enough to slip in the flash drive. Thankfully, Saucy Pants is filled with stuffing and not beads. I push the flash drive in, move the stuffing close to the hole, and place him back on Matt's shelf.

A few more weeks, and this will all be over. Back to the life I should be living, with Matt.

49
MATT
NOW

It's been almost three months since PJ died. I still haven't gotten over it, and I never will. My apartment looks like a shrine to her. I hung all the pictures I had of us on the walls. I had to relocate her favorite one of us, and I got an awesome surprise.

I have PJ's money, because I'm the only one with her passwords. No one even knows where to look to see if she had anything worth taking. Her bank accounts are all in her real name, Paulina Jensen. She has no one to investigate it anyway, because that jerkoff Anthony can't tell anyone he knew her real name. Her parents are gone, she had no siblings. She never had anyone but me. I still have my parents, but she was my person, and the hole in my life will never go away.

I decided that living my best life would be what she wanted, so I motivated myself. With her help, in the form of her money, I put together a professional portfolio of my photographs, spotlighting her favorite one of the people at the bus stop. I contacted galleries all over the city, had meetings everywhere, and finally landed a small gig. It's next month, in October. It's amateur, and I'm still afraid no one will come, but it's a start.

I will do it for you, PJ.

In the meantime, this is my last day of the shaved face and the short, bleached hair, so I can look "clean cut" for my summer job as Terrence Whitman. I miss my long hair and my scruff, but I'll be back to myself soon enough. I couldn't abandon the country club too soon. I didn't want to look suspicious and bolt after PJ died. Instead, I've immersed myself into this world.

They trust me.

They shouldn't.

It's the end of the day for me, a Friday. My last day. I'm emptying out my locker when Kim comes in, getting ready for her waitressing shift.

"Hey, Terry," she says with a wink. "How was your day?"

"I'll never have to come back, so it was great." I nod. "How's Murphy doing?"

She smiles and grabs her phone, then starts swiping through pictures. "Look at this video. He's back to normal."

She presses play, and there's Murphy, batting around a toy, growling at it, making it squeak, and running around like a healthy puppy.

"Awww, that's terrific," I say. "I'm so happy everything worked out."

"Me too."

I let her keep the cash and what was in the Cayman
bank account. I don't need it. I wanted her to be able to pay
Anthony back the money she took from him for Murphy's
surgery. I didn't want her to owe a goddamn thing to that
fucker.

"I can't wait to get to DC," Kim says. "One more month here."

Kim is finishing the season here, which ends on Hal-
loween. Emiko Xiang, a member, knew someone who knew
someone who whatever, we all know how it goes, and Kim
landed a great job at an advertising agency doing graphic
design. She will be renting a townhome in Virginia, just outside of DC. A yard for Murphy. A new start. And at least she's
getting the hell out of here, and the hell away from Anthony.

He already brought some other woman to the club on his
arm, less than two months after PJ died. Jerkoff. I've gotten a
few more shots of him with Carla, though now that her and
Ron are officially separated, I'm not sure it'll matter. But the
ones dated back to April will.

Ron is going down for taking advantage of PJ, and Carla
is going down for helping Anthony kill her. I know they did
it. I just know it.

I look at my watch. "Did you see the drink special on the
menu?"

Kim nods. "I did."

I let out a breath. "One more thing to do before I leave."

She narrows her eyes. I see the slow smile behind her
neutral expression.

Really two things, but first things first. I go up the stairs
and into the bar room. That fucker is sitting in the same
corner where PJ died, having drinks with Ron and two other

guys after his round. He's still in his golf polo and shorts. He'll have one more drink before he goes to the member locker room to shower and change before dinner. Right now, he doesn't have a care in the world.

I approach the table. "Good afternoon, Mr. Fuller, Mr. Boswell, Mr. Payne, Mr. McDonald," I say to them. "Did you see today's drink special? It's amazing."

Anthony looks at the insert on the table. "Sunset of Fire?" he asks.

"Yeah, it's like summer in a glass. Lots of coconut, a few secret ingredients. I'll go grab a few samples for you all to try."

He shrugs. "Sure, why not?"

I tell Lucy to make four half sizes, that the guys in the corner want to try the drink before committing to it. She says she'll bring them over, but I insist on doing it. I have nothing to do—my shift is over. I'm clocked out. I'm not even really here, and Terrence Whitman doesn't exist. Once I'm out of here, I'm *out of here*. She puts them on a tray, and I grab it and hand them out.

"Mmm," Mr. Payne and Mr. MacDonald say. Ron doesn't touch his. How fitting.

"Ooof," Anthony says, making a dissatisfied face. "It's sweet."

"Yes, it really is. The flavors blend better at the bottom. Finish it."

He does. He drains the entire glass and hands it back to me. "Nah. Too sweet for me."

"That's unfortunate." I take the four glasses and put them back on the tray. "I'll get rid of this for you, then."

I bring the glasses into the kitchen and immediately put them on the line, where they all go right into the steamy, soapy water. The tray too. I already wiped my locker down. No fingerprints.

Kim waves to me as I'm on my way out. I give her a salute and a wink.

I get into my car and drive up the hill and then over it, admiring the tranquil end of the day. The sun hasn't started to set, but it's lower in the sky than it was when I first took this gig, to watch over them, to protect PJ.

I'm sorry I failed you, but I promised to make it up to you.

Passing the hut, which checks for membership IDs on incoming cars, I see a line waiting to come in for dinner. The privileged. It doesn't even matter to me. I harbor no jealousy toward them, and I only care about making PJ proud of me. *She'd really love me today,* I think as I look at the small envelope addressed to the local police station with the flash drive. Next stop, post office.

When this blows up in everyone's face, PJ's best friend, Matt Mazzucca, *me,* can play the police the "voicemail he saved." *Awesomesauce, it's PJ. I need your help. I heard Anthony and Carla Boswell planning to hurt me, so I slept with her husband for revenge and now he's stalking me. I don't feel safe. They're all after me. Please call me back.*

PJ was a genius. I waited until it all blew over, PJ was forgotten by everyone, and Anthony was with Ron Boswell. Then it was showtime. They'll all pay for what they did to PJ.

As I take the last turn before the highway, a deer and its baby fawn poke their heads through the pines, walking slowly, sniffing around for dinner. It's peaceful. Golf courses really are beautiful and serene.

The only thing that could ruin it is the sound of the sirens when the ambulance turns in just as I'm turning out.

Man, that club has some bad luck. That sweet drink really must not have agreed with Anthony.

Oops.

THE END

ACKNOWLEDGEMENTS

This has been a particularly terrible year for me, so I'm happy I have some space to acknowledge those that made it better. First, and always, my agent Anne Tibbets, I thank you for always being behind me one-hundred-percent and being my cheerleader along the way. I'm so lucky to have you. My amazing editor, Luisa Smith—to know you s to love you, and I've met so many people in this business at all stages willing to back up that sentiment. I've been with you for every book I've published and I love the way you've helped me grow. Thank you to my publishers Charles Perry and Otto Penzler, my publicist Julia O'Connell, and to Will Luckman and Nadara Merrill for finding glaringly obvious mistakes even though I read this thing a hundred times. Readers, you're up—go find what we missed! Ha.

To the authors who give unconditional support, thank you for being here. Vanessa Lillie, Danielle Girard, Jennifer Pashley, Bonnie Kistler, Linda Hurtado Bond, Mary Keliikoa, Jessica Payne, Elise Hart Kipness, Samantha Bailey, Heather

Levy, Shawn A. Cosby, KT Nguyen, Susan Walter, Greg Wands, May Cobb, Robyn Harding, Christina McDonald, Michele Campbell, Wendy Walker—I know there are a ton more that I'm forgetting, and I love you too. I couldn't do any of this without you.

I also want to thank Kate Czyzewski and Thunder Road Books for being my favorite NJ indie bookstore and welcoming me with open arms whenever I'm back in town, and Dominic Howarth and Andi Pignato at Book + Bottle in St. Pete, FL for hosting my release parties. Thank you to Abby Endler for selecting my last book to be in your crime box for Murder By The Book, and I thank the store for hosting me. I always have love for bookstagrammers-turned-friends Dennis Michel, Kate Hergott, Gare Billings (whose dog Murphy is literally IN this book!), Alicia Rideout, Krista Crone, Kori Pontenzone, Mandy Duncan, and Carey Calvert.

Now for the terrible year part. For those that don't know, I was diagnosed with aggressive breast cancer in January 2024. It's been a challenging time, and I'm writing this while recovering from a mastectomy. But the bookstagram community doesn't just care about our work, they care about us as people too. A wonderful soul, Carrie Shields (@carriereadsthem_all), put together a team to send me a care package once she heard the news about my diagnosis. Carrie, you are a walking angel. Thank you and everyone on the team: Krissy Wallis, Christina (@books_by_the_bottle), Drew Baumgardner, Hailey Fish, Jessica (@thrillerschillersandkillers), Jody Blanchette, Mary (@abookwormwithwine), Nancy Wren, Steph Twist, Beth (@Bookybethw), Jamele Medina, Cindy Jones, Diana (@dianas_books_cars_coffee), Heather Warner, Kate Shelton,

Kelsey (@kelseylitsliftsanddips), Steph (accio_literary_escape), and @thenerdybookwormsblog.

To the doctors who helped save me so far, I thank Dr. Hania Bednarski and Dr. John Myrrh Cox and their staff.

You might recognize a name or two in this book. Thank you to Kim Valva who generously donated to The Arthritis Foundation to be named a character in the book. Good luck finding her! ☺ And to the real life Matthew Mazzucca, your friendship is a treasure.

To all my friends and family, you know who you are, thank you for sticking by me. To my mother, you are everything and I love you always.

And finally, to my husband John, you are tough as nails for sticking by me this year, I know I haven't made it easy. Thank you for all you do, all you've done, and all you will continue to do for me. You're my rock, my sounding board, my friend, my puppy-daddy, and the love of my life. I can't wait to see what the future, whatever it may be, holds for us and our new dog Amber. I love you both. #adoptdontshop

Readers, thank you for reading my word salad, I hope you enjoyed it. If you'd like me to zoom in on book clubs and to answer questions, connect with me on IG: @jaimelynnhendricksauthor